THROW
LIKE
A GIRL

STORIES

JEAN
THOMPSON

SIMON & SCHUSTER PAPERBACKS
NEW YORK LONDON TORONTO SYDNEY

SIMON & SCHUSTER PAPERBACKS
Rockefeller Center
1230 Avenue of the Americas
New York, NY 10020

First Simon & Schuster paperback edition 2007

"The Inside Passage" first appeared in *Another Chicago Magazine*. "Hunger" first appeared in *Mid-American Review,* Spring 2007, Vol. XXVII. "Pie of the Month" first appeared in *Crab Orchard Review,* Summer/Fall 2005, Vol. 10.

SIMON & SCHUSTER and colophon are registered trademarks of Simon & Schuster, Inc.

Book design by Ellen R. Sasahara

For information about special discounts for bulk purchases, please contact Simon & Schuster Special Sales at 1-800-456-6798 or business@simonandschuster.com

Manufactured in the United States of America

10   9   8   7   6   5   4   3   2   1

Library of Congress Cataloging-in-Publication Data
Thompson, Jean.
    Throw like a girl : stories / Jean Thompson. — 1st Simon & Schuster pbk. ed
        p. cm.
    I. Title

PS3570.H625T47 2007
813'6—dc22   2006051259

ISBN-13: 978-1-4165-4182-0
ISBN-10:   1-4165-4182-9

Let us now praise readers and writers.
Thanks to those who helped, by their
encouragement, by their example:
David Sedaris, Bernard Cooper,
Tayari Jones, Pete Rock, Dan Chaon,
Kim Chinquee, and Bob Miener.

CONTENTS

THE
BRAT

She hated her mother and she hated her father too, at least when he was around to be hated. She hated school and all the snotty girls who put their heads together giggling and talking big and showing off their nail polish and their new shoes and new cell phones and whatever else they bought bought bought. She hated her brother but that was easy, it was automatic that they hate each other. She was twelve years old and she wasn't pretty or smart or nicey-nice and she wished everyone she knew would just drop dead. Then she could go somewhere, a city or maybe the ocean, a place like on television where everybody knew everybody else and things were always happening.

Her mother was yelling for her to get downstairs if she wanted a ride to school, honking out her name like she was a car horn: "Iris! Eye-ris! Three minutes, or you're going to walk."

It went without saying that she hated her name.

After she had dawdled enough, and after her mother had screeched some more, so that they both reached a point of absolute contempt for each other, Iris went downstairs. "You can't wear that," her mother said.

"Watch me."

"You look like a drug dealer."

"Yeah, like you really know what drug dealers wear."

Her mother said that there were perfectly nice sweaters in Iris's closet and that her appearance told other people about her attitude and her teachers would pick up on it if she dressed like she didn't even want to be there (ha! she didn't), and at the very least she could stop slouching and for God's sake find a barrette or something to keep the hair out of her eyes. Her mother had coffee breath, bitter and dead-tasting. Iris could smell it from across the room. She studied her mother, the way her forehead bunched together when she was angry, how her chin fat wobbled in an unlovely fashion, how her entire pursy and ridiculous figure proclaimed, Don't ever be like me.

Her mother's voice made an interrogatory pause, a question that Iris was meant to answer, and so she said, "No."

Her mother's jaw tightened. "Fine. Get in the car, then."

In the car Iris did her best to pretend she was something insensate and boneless, some sluglike underwater creature that did nothing but burp plankton. She let her body sag and roll when the car took the turns. Burp. Burp. Her mother gave her a look of loathing. Her mother wanted her to be a lay-dee.

Just when Iris thought they were going to finish the ride in blissful silence, her mother said, "I'm allowed to worry about you. I'm your mother. Oh for heaven's sake, can you for one minute let your face look normal and stop trying to see how grotesque you can make yourself? What happens when you decide you don't want to be a smart aleck and a little brat anymore, what if you want to have friends, I mean normal friends, not that disgusting Rico—"

"Leave the Rico out of this."

"—because sooner or later you have to grow up, sooner

or later certain important, girl-type things are going to happen to you, and everything changes. Am I saying something funny?"

Iris shook her head, no. Her mother meant getting her period. Her mother was completely hung up on it, really looking forward to it, like then she would have won some kind of argument. Iris hadn't bothered to tell her that she'd had her period twice already. Big deal.

Here was school. Iris grabbed her backpack. Her mother put on her blinker to pull up to the curb. How lame was that! God! "Have a nice day, honey," her mother said, and Iris sneered at this new piece of shallowness. Her mother went to hug her and there was a moment when their bodies jostled together like cattle in a chute and that was awful, awful, and Iris said, "Yeah, sure," and escaped onto the sidewalk.

She hated the school building. She hated the steamy cafeteria smell and the echoing halls and the rooms full of faces. She looked around for Rico but she must have been really late, there was hardly anybody in sight. Iris made it into homeroom just as Mr. Poodlebreath was about to call the roll.

"Here," she answered when Poodlebreath got to her name, but she wasn't really there, not entirely. She was still sorting through the waking-up and mother parts of her morning, and two of the snot-girls were sniggering about something, probably her. Iris tried to catch Rico's eye across the room, but he was hunched over his desk, playing his Game Boy. He always thought nobody could see what he was doing if he draped his fat the right way.

When the bell rang for first hour, Iris waited for Rico to shuffle over to her. "Creep," he said.

"Loser."

They fell into step together, which meant Iris had to slow way down, since Rico was marshmallow fat and asthmatic. First hour was social studies. They were doing reports on the fifty states. Iris had chosen Kansas because nobody else would ever want it. Rico had done his report the previous week on Wisconsin, the Badger State.

Rico stopped to get a drink from the water fountain. He had to be careful about bending over because he had so many folds and bulky parts. When he'd wiped his mouth he said, "Saw something really cool yesterday."

"Me too. A dead cat."

"This is better. A tree fell on my neighbor's garage. Well, part of a tree."

"Yeah?" She thought the dead cat was better.

"A really big tree. It was about a hundred feet tall."

Iris considered this. "What kind of tree?"

"I don't know, dumbshit, it's winter."

The social studies teacher was Mrs. Cake and that was her honest-to-God real name. She wore clothes she made herself that looked like tablecloths with buttons, and piled her hair in a bird's nest on top of her head, and you wondered how some people got up in the morning and looked in the mirror and thought they were all right.

Cake was pathetically excited about the fifty states reports. It wasn't fifty because the class wasn't big enough. A lot of states had been left out. Delaware. Oklahoma. Anything that was North or South. Cake stood in front of a big map of the United States that was colored like a checkerboard. She said, "I can hardly wait to hear about all the interesting places we're going to visit today."

Everybody groaned. They knew they weren't going anywhere.

They started with Connecticut, the Constitution State. Then Hawaii, the Aloha State. The reports made all the states sound alike. Cake stood in the back of the room nodding and grinning, like this was first-rate entertainment. Iris wondered if the whole world was boring, if they'd used up all the interesting stuff before she was born.

"Iris?"

It was her turn. She stood at the front of the room. All the snickering, shuffling noise narrowed to a point and beamed down on the top of her head. She wiggled her toes inside her sneakers. One shoelace had come undone and the hems of her jeans had dragged the ground until they were split and dirty. She shuffled her index cards. Index cards were required.

"Kansas, the Sunflower State," she began. "Kansas produces wheat, corn, soybeans, and other important food items. Like sunflower seeds. Duh. The capital of Kansas is Topeka. The state was admitted to the Union in 1861. Amelia Earhart and President Dwight Eisenhower are two of the famous people from Kansas. Also, because Kansas was the Wild West before they discovered the real West, there were people living in Kansas like Billy the Kid whose real name was William Bonney who killed at least twenty-one people before he was shot dead at the age of twenty-one."

A few faces looked up, mildly interested. Iris shuffled her index cards and talked faster.

"At the time of the Civil War, Kansas was known as Bleeding Kansas because of fights about slavery. Slavery was an abomination unto the Lord. It was during this time that Kansas had plagues of locusts, of darkness, of frogs, lice, flies, boils, hail—"

"Mrs. Cake!"

"—and all the cattle died, and all the water of the rivers and water in people's houses turned to blood. That's really gross. Worse than frogs in your hair."

"Mrs. Cake, she's making all this up!"

"I am not. It's in the Bible."

"The Bible didn't happen in America."

Cake said, "Let's finish up, shall we, Iris?"

"Then the firstborn son of every household died mysteriously overnight, and that was when the people of Kansas decided to let the slaves go and be a free state. Then nothing much happened in Kansas until 1959. That's when they had a famous murder that was made into the movie *In Cold Blood*. There was a family named Clutter and all four of them—"

"Thank you, Iris," Cake said.

"I'm not done yet." Iris held up her last two index cards.

"We need time for the other reports." Cake clapped her hands. She called on a boy who had chosen Texas, the Lone Star State.

Iris sat down. Feet kicked the back of her chair. "You are so weird."

"Shut up."

A girl turned around and said, "Are you brain-damaged? Is it something you really can't help?" Iris told her to shut up too. From across the room, Rico mouthed the word, "Excellent."

At lunch she and Rico sat at a table with Barry Hamsohn. Barry was fat, but not as fat as Rico. He had red hair and so many freckles on his nose that he looked cross-eyed. Their table was called the Freak Table.

Lunch was something brown, with mashed potatoes. Iris ate a little of hers and let Rico and Barry finish the rest. She was skinny. Barry and Rico called themselves the Two Tons of Fun. Sometimes she wished she was fat so they could be Three Tons. But then her mother would get all carried away with feeding her carrot sticks and making her enroll in the Chubettes class at the Y. Her mother probably didn't like Rico because he was fat. If there was ever somebody perfect, that's who her mother would be crazy about.

Across the cafeteria, a bunch of boys were doing Freak Table imitations again. One of them was leaning over a garbage can pretending to eat food from it. Another had his cheeks puffed out and was walking in a bowlegged, gut-heavy way. Then he squatted down and pretended to take a giant crap.

All three of them watched this, until one of the teachers broke it up. Barry said, "Those guys suck so bad."

"We should kill them," said Rico. He was wheezing and he pulled out his inhaler.

"How?" Iris asked. There were always a lot of details, the different ways they planned to kill people.

"Guillotine," said Rico. He drew one hand across his throat in a slicing motion. "Gughhh."

Barry and Iris nodded in appreciation. Nobody had thought of a guillotine before. Barry said, "We could put their heads on sticks and carry them around."

"They'd bleed like crazy."

"Buckets and buckets," said Iris. Sometimes she thought she could feel her own blood sloshing around in her, like she was a half-empty milk carton. But talking-blood was different from real blood.

"We should write them death threats," Rico said, and everybody got excited about that. After lunch they all had English together. They spent the hour at the back of the room, passing different versions of the death threats around. By the end of class they had produced four very artistic representations of guillotines, severed heads, and red Magic Marker blood in wavy rivers, blood in shapes like teardrops, blood that spotted and stained the scowling heads on sticks. The death threats read

ATTENTION ALL STUPIDASSES!
THIS MEANS YOU!

Congratulations! You have been chosen to get a free trial of our new Guillotine! It will chop off your head and leave a bloody stump. You have been chosen because you are one of the stupidest people we know and when you are dead everybody will be happy. P.S. You will look a lot better without your head.

Right after English they snuck around to the lockers and waited until nobody was watching. They slipped the notes into the lockers of the four meanest, loudest boys and went off to their next class, feeling pleased. The rest of the day they waited to see if anything would happen, or if anybody knew it was them. But nobody said anything, and by the end of the school day the air had largely gone out of the idea. It was like everything else they tried to do, a big deal that went nowhere. "You wait," Rico said. He wasn't ready to let it go yet. "Tomorrow we sneak up on those guys and make guillotine sounds. *Fff-tt! Fff-tt!* Watch 'em jump."

Iris took the bus home. Nobody was there except her brother Kyle. He was watching television in the den, and when Iris walked in, he threw a Nerf football at her.

"Cut it out," said Iris. She pitched the football at his face. It knocked Kyle's glasses off and he jumped up from the couch and chased her through the downstairs until Iris ran into the bathroom and locked the door behind her. There were other times when Kyle caught her and wrestled her to the ground and she shrieked until she wet her pants and couldn't breathe and it was horrible but thrilling too, and that was when she hated Kyle most of all.

After a while she got bored with being in the bathroom and came out. She loitered in the entrance to the den to see if Kyle was going to start the war again. He was talking on the phone, so she walked in and sat down in front of the television. He was watching COPS. Two policemen were sitting on top of a man and they had his arms all pretzeled behind him.

Kyle held the phone away from his mouth. "Little privacy here."

"It's my house too."

"Nobody," Kyle said into the phone. "Just Coyote Ugly." That was his name for her.

"Who are you talking to, stupid Michelle?" Michelle was his girlfriend. She had big teeth. Kissing Michelle would be like kissing a piano. Plus she laughed at things that weren't funny.

Kyle kept the phone wedged into the couch cushions. He said, "Uh-huh," or, "Yeah." When he got to the end of their love chat, he lowered his voice even further, so all Iris heard was dirty-sounding *heh-heh* noises. When he finally hung up, Iris said, "You and Michelle make a great couple. You're both totally spastic."

Kyle yawned and scratched deeply along the inside of his leg. He was skinny, like Iris, but parts of him were overgrown, his hands and feet and his head, stuck on the end of his neck like an onion on its stem. He said, "So, did you and Fat Rico do it yet?"

"Shut up, asshole."

"Because you two would really make a cool couple. Of course, you'd have to get on top so he wouldn't smother you."

Iris kicked him pretty hard in or near the balls and then she ran upstairs to her room and listened to him rage and curse and rattle the doorknob until he got tired of it and went downstairs again. When she heard her mother come home, she went down to the kitchen to get some orange juice. Her mother asked her what was new at school and Iris said, "Nothing."

They got into trouble for the death threats. Everybody in homeroom seemed to know about it. Poodlebreath walked around looking like a doctor who had to tell somebody they had cancer. All the secret noise of the room, all the whispers and shuffling that went on around and under the teacher talk, lapped around them like a shallow ocean. They came and got Rico, then Barry, then Iris. She sat in the hall outside the guidance office for a long time. She decided she didn't like her hands. They were ordinary. She wished that one of them was a claw, or maybe a robot arm, like Darth Vader's.

The guidance counselor was Mrs. Hopper. She was about ninety years old. "Iris," Mrs. Hopper said. "Goddess of the rainbow."

"Yeah, yeah, yeah," said Iris. It was an old joke with her and the Hopper. They were practically Abbott and Costello by now.

"Why a guillotine?"

Iris thought about this. "For the blood, I guess."

"I'm trying to help you here, Iris. But you have to let me help you."

"Sure."

"We have to take any threat to our students' safety very seriously. Were there other people involved? Do you belong to some kind of group?"

"You mean, like, a band?"

"Do you know what I pray every night, Iris? Dear Lord, please don't let me get shot by some little punk who's mad about his algebra grade."

Iris considered the possibility that the Hopper had finally lost it. Hopper's eyes behind her old-lady glasses had a cracked, marveling look, as if Iris were a dangerous zoo animal.

"This is very serious business, Iris. We may have to call your parents or even the police. You might end up in a juvenile facility."

"Yeah?" Iris wondered if they got to wear jail uniforms and sleep in cells.

"So if I were you, missy, I'd start talking."

"I'll talk so much it'll make your hair curl," said Iris.

Nobody had arrested them by the end of the day. They guessed they were still in trouble but they didn't know how much, because they had all said different things and gotten the story confused. Barry Hamsohn's mother came and picked him up. Iris decided to walk home with Rico. He lived pretty close to school and she didn't feel like going to her house yet, in case the police were already there. She thought that her and Rico could run away someplace if they had to. They could be stowaways on a boat and sneak out at night to get food.

"Fucking little pussies," said Rico. "Hadda go tell their mommies."

Iris agreed, but she was still thinking about boats, and what the best kind would be, and how you found out where they were going. She looked around her at the sidewalks and houses and trundling cars. One advantage of walking with Rico was that you had plenty of time to take in the scenery. Maybe it would be easier to break into somebody's house and hide out in the basement. She said, "What if we disguised ourselves? So when they came looking for us, they wouldn't know it was us."

"Great idea. I'll disguise myself as somebody not fat."

Nobody was home at Rico's house so they fixed themselves

cereal with chocolate milk and played Grand Theft Auto for a while. Iris got bored and said they should steal a real car so they could learn how to drive. She was tired of everything being pretend. She bet her whole stupid life would turn out that way, a bunch of pretend big ideas that never happened.

Rico said he didn't know of any cars anywhere to steal, but they could watch the guy next door cut down his tree, and Iris said OK. There was a saw going; they could hear the racket from inside.

It was a bigass old tree all right, taller than the houses, and half of it had yawned right over onto the neighbor's garage. A man in a blue jacket and a hat with earflaps was up on a ladder, running a power saw that took bites out of the branches. When they fell they made a noise and then an echo, *BOOM* and *boom*.

"That's Mr. Ortiz," said Rico. "It's his tree."

"How's he going to get all the way up there?" The part of the tree that was still standing was really tall. The place where the rest of it had fallen over was like a giant splinter.

"Climbing ropes," said Rico. "See?"

They watched as Mr. Ortiz tossed one end of a rope over a high branch and played it out until it reached the ground. Then he fastened it into a kind of sling and planted his feet on the tree's trunk. He used the rope to walk his way up to the first high branch and swung his leg over it. When he saw Rico and Iris watching, he waved at them.

"That is so cool," said Iris. Cutting down a tree was a real thing. You could stand right there and watch it happen. It went from Tree to No Tree. "You think he'd let us help?"

"Like I could get my fat ass up that high."

"We could carry the branches away or something," suggested Iris, but Rico didn't seem excited about that, so they just watched some more. Mr. Ortiz tied ropes around one of the big limbs, and when he cut it off, he hitched the rope up and seesawed the limb back and forth until he had it where he wanted it to land. Then he let it drop. He had already cut all the small branches from the part of the tree that had landed on the garage. It looked like a cactus, with its bare, chopped-off arms. It was cold outside and Rico wanted to go back in, but Iris said they should stay at least until the next big piece of tree came down. Rico said they could see just as good from inside, and the cold was bad for his asthma.

"Dude, everything's bad for your asthma. Except eating."

"Suck my dick, bitch."

"Suck my dick, bitch," Iris said right back. It didn't mean anything, it was just what kids said. But there was a little curdled thought in her head now because of stupid Kyle and his stupid ugly talk. Sometimes she got into a state of mind where she couldn't look at people without imagining them naked. Once she'd seen Rico with his shirt off because he'd spilled hot soup on his stomach. It was kind of awful. Rico had boobs that hung down like something melted.

Iris was about to tell Rico she was going home, if he was such a candyass that he couldn't stand a little cold, when she saw somebody walking toward them from a couple blocks away.

"Isn't that Jovanovich and his brother?"

"Oh shit," Rico said. Jerry Jovanovich was one of the guys they sent the death threats to. His brother's nickname was Goombah. Nobody knew his real name.

"Maybe they're just out walking," Iris said, unconvinced.

Rico said he wasn't sticking around to find out. He ran up the front steps and inside, and Iris ran too. They locked the door and watched out the windows as Jovanovich and his brother came into view. The brothers stood on the sidewalk outside Rico's house and yelled something, but Mr. Ortiz's saw was running and when they opened their mouths only saw noise came out.

"They know we're in here," said Rico. He was wheezing because of the cold and the running. His voice squeaked and jumped. "We could call the police."

"Oh sure. Like the police won't arrest us first." Iris lifted a corner of the curtain. Jovanovich picked up a stick and thrashed at the shrubbery with it. Goombah had his hands in his coat pockets and was chewing on something that he spit out. He was one of those guys who shaved his head. "When does your mom get home?"

"Not till late." Rico was still puffing and choking, so Iris ran and got his inhaler from his backpack. Rico jammed it into his mouth and slobbered a little, trying to get it going. Iris knew about asthma. It was when you couldn't breathe because your airways closed up. It would have made a good plague back in Kansas.

"Dude, you want me to call nine-one-one?" She didn't like the goldfish way that Rico's eyes were bulging. But Rico put the inhaler down, hacked a little more, and shook his head.

"Sometimes it takes—," he began, but right then the house shook, *BOOM BOOM BOOM*, like a tree crashing right on top of them. It was Jovanovich and Goombah, trying to break down the front door, and Rico and Iris both screamed in high voices like little girls which even in the middle of being scared embarrassed them.

"Those guys are crazy!" Iris yelled. She ran to the front hallway. The door was the kind with wavy glass panels on each side. Jerry Jovanovich's face was flattened against the glass. His lips were turned inside out like some weird pink corsage.

"Get outta here!" she shouted. She couldn't see Goombah.

"Back door! Go lock the back door!" She listened to Rico groan and hoist himself up and lumber off toward the kitchen. "Today, man!" She crept up to the door and put her fingers against the glass. Something hard, a rock or a stick, hit the door and she jumped back and shrieked.

"We're gonna call the cops!"

"Go ahead. See how fast they don't get here." Jovanovich's voice sounded close but hollow, like he was underground. "What are you two pervs doing in there anyway, playing with each other?"

"Fuck off, Jovanobitch." Iris listened for Rico in the kitchen. If Goombah broke down the back door, he'd kill Rico. All he'd have to do was punch him and he'd stop breathing. She'd have to run in there, find a knife or something. She wondered how hard you'd have to stab somebody to get a knife all the way through their clothes.

Rico trotted in from the kitchen. His legs rubbed together when he tried to move fast, and he was still wheezing. "I put the—huh—chain and the deadbolt on."

Iris felt like she'd swallowed electricity. Her heart was spazzing out. When she tried to look at things they jumped around. Mr. Ortiz's saw started up again, a high, whining racket. "What if we call the cops and pretend we're somebody else?"

"They can tell who you are from your phone."

"Shit." She'd forgotten about that.

"Come on out, skank face! Bring your lardass boyfriend with you. We got something for you."

"Bite me."

There was the sound of something heavy being dragged across the porch. Dark shapes passed back and forth in the wavy glass. They were doing something with Rico's mother's flower planters.

Rico's mouth hung open a little, like a drawer that wouldn't shut.

"Maybe one of your neighbors will call somebody," Iris said. Though she already knew that Rico's neighbors weren't the kind who got excited about kids acting rowdy. It was one more thing that Iris's mother didn't like about Rico. Iris thought about calling her mother or even Kyle and telling them she needed a ride home, having the car scare Jovanovich away. But she wasn't ready for this to be over yet. What if nothing like it ever happened to her again?

She said, "We could go upstairs and drop stuff on them from the window."

"We could shoot them," Rico said.

"Oh yeah, right."

"If you had a gun, would you shoot them?"

"Sure," Iris said. She thought about Billy the Kid. "I'd probably have to practice some first."

"My mom has a gun."

"She so much does not."

"Does too. It was my grandfather's."

"Then it's old and it's no good."

"It still has bullets, OK?"

The front door shook and rattled in its frame. Iris and Rico jumped. Rico put his mouth to the crack. "Hey Jovanobitch. You wear rubbers for hats."

"Come outside and say that, you fat shit."

"Uh-uh. You come in here."

The door shook again, and then one of them was at the back door kicking, and Iris and Rico ran up the stairs. Iris ran. Rico was behind her somewhere. Once Rico told Iris that sometimes he slept on the living room couch so he wouldn't have to climb the stairs.

Iris reached the top. She didn't hear any more kicking noise, so she guessed the lock held. She'd only been up here a couple of times. There was striped wallpaper with something wet soaking through part of it. Light came down from a high window at one end, white and smeared. The upstairs had a smell like boiled vegetables. "Hurry up," Iris hissed. She could hear Rico stumping along and blowing like a horse. "Hurry," she said again, uselessly.

When Rico finally reached the top stair he said, "Whew." They went into his mother's room. It was smaller than Rico's and almost all the space was taken up by the bed. It had a pink bedspread and some fancy pillows with fringe. There was a closet with a chest of drawers inside it. Rico pushed the clothes on hangers to one side and then the other.

Iris went to the window. She could see the street in front of the house, and some of the yard, but not Jovanovich or Goombah. She guessed they were on the porch. Mr. Ortiz was still up in his tree. He looked a lot closer from here, almost like you could have a conversation with him. He was sitting on a big limb, riding it like it was a horse, and pulling his ropes up from the ground. It looked lonesome up there with nothing but the sky and the bare branches.

Rico was scraping around in the closet. "She must of moved it. The gun."

"Uh-huh," said Iris. She watched Mr. Ortiz take his gloves off and blow on his fingers. It was probably real cold up there. She wished she was him. She wished she was a hundred miles up in the sky, away from everybody else in the world, and that all along she had been somebody else.

Iris opened the window. It was stuck shut, and she had to bang on the frame and push on it one side at a time. She unhooked the screen, knelt on the bed and stuck her head out. She could hear

Jovanovich and Goombah walking around on the porch. She looked for something to throw to get their attention, but all she saw was pillows.

"Hey." Rico was on the bed, trying to squeeze in at the window. "Quit hogging."

"There's nothing to see."

"Well let me see it."

Iris let him take a turn. With his knees up on the windowsill, he looked like something the window couldn't swallow. He backed out again, carefully, and unrolled his shirt to show her something he had tucked away in his stomach folds. "What'd I tell you?"

The gun didn't look real to her because after all it was just Rico holding it. But once she held its dense, heavy weight, heavy like it was made out of some metal that came from deep inside the earth's core, once she rubbed her finger along its oiled, dull shine, it was the realest thing in the world.

"Is it loaded?"

"Course it is."

"How can you tell?"

"Give it back here."

She didn't want to let it go. Her hand liked the feel of it. But she allowed Rico to show her how to pull apart the barrel and see where the bullets were, nine of them, each one in its little slot, like seeds. "It's a revolver," Rico said. "A twenty-two. You could play Russian roulette with it because you can spin the bullets around."

Iris said she wanted it back. She stuck her head out the window and looked around for something to shoot. "How are you supposed to aim it?"

"Just squint along that little bump thing at the end."

Iris pointed the gun at a car parked across the street, and then at an ugly fancy lamp in somebody's picture window. She swung it toward Mr. Ortiz but she decided she liked him and wasn't even going to pretend to shoot him. She backed away from the window. "So have you shot stuff before?"

"Sure," Rico said. "Lots of times."

"Liar. You lie like a rug."

"You don't know shit," Rico said, but Iris knew she was right. Rico never did anything he said he did. It wasn't exactly lying. It was only things he wished he could do.

Jovanovich and Goombah started making their racket again, banging things around on the porch. Iris leaned out the window. "Hey!" She wanted to get them out where she could see them. "Hey donkey dicks!"

The racket stopped. They were probably surprised to hear her from upstairs. Jovanovich's head popped up at the edge of the porch. Iris couldn't see the rest of him. It was like his head really was on a stick.

"Guess what I got," Iris said.

"A face like a bucket of worms."

"Ha. Ha. Ha." Iris brought the gun up to the windowsill but kept it close in so Jovanovich couldn't see it.

Rico was making his asthma sounds again. "I left my inhaler downstairs."

"We can go back down in a little."

"I seriously need it, dude."

Rico wheezed and choked some more. Maybe he really couldn't breathe, or maybe he was just scared of what she was going to do with the gun. Jovanovich was still grinning up at her. He had a pushed-in, piggy kind of face. He would never be anything other than ugly. If she shot him, nobody would ever have to look at him again. That would definitely be something real. Or she could take the gun home and shoot her mother or Kyle.

Rico was making snoring sounds. Something squeezed inside of her. She bet she had her dumb period again. Rico's hands were paddling, one on each side of his face. His eyes had that goldfish look. "Oh all right," Iris sighed.

She spun the barrel of the gun Russian roulette–style. She shook the bullets out into her hand and showed them to Rico. "See? It's no big deal." She threw one bullet down at Jovanovich and it hit the gutter and bounced off. "Bang!" she said. At least the bullets were real. "Bang!"

In the corner of her eye she saw Mr. Ortiz struggle briefly to keep his balance, then topple over and fall with his arms outstretched and the ropes curling and snapping around him like banners.

THE
FIVE
SENSES

Having exiled herself forever from her old life, she looked into this new one and found nothing to recognize.

Here was the ocean. It wasn't what she expected. Instead of the frill of blue you saw on postcards, it was this enormous swollen rolling mass, gray, like some shaggy wild animal. Jessie—that was her name—had not realized that the ocean was always trying to climb out of itself, out of its space, a brimming cup. And it was huge. She remembered, from school or somewhere, that most of the earth was covered in ocean. Yes, and it wanted the rest of it too.

It was cold, she hadn't imagined Florida being cold, that was another thing. She'd left her winter coat back in the room, thinking she didn't need it, so she walked along with her fingers curled up in the sleeves of her sweatshirt. The sky had no depth or shape to it. Cloud or fog, she couldn't tell which, or maybe its gray was just the color of cold. Nobody else was out walking as far as she could see. It was just a strip of less desirable, gravelly beach across the highway from the motel. In one direction, far off, were fishing piers and restaurants and the fancy hotels that had their own beaches. At the other end, a scrubby tangle of trees blocked your way. Jessie felt stupid out there alone. She wished she had a dog or something. With a dog you could at least throw sticks.

She looked for seashells, but the only shells she found were flattened, ordinary, and when she picked up one that was two halves still joined together, she could see something dead inside. Something dim, webbed, and sticky. "Oh God," she said aloud. "R.B.?"

But of course he wasn't there, and if he knew she was getting weird again, something she had promised to quit doing . . . Well it wasn't just an act, she was weird, she couldn't help it, you might as well try to stop yourself from vomiting as try to keep the weirdness from coming out. Her hands felt soiled. She rinsed them in the gray water and dried them on her pants.

R.B. was still asleep back in the room. He didn't like getting up early or walking just for walking's sake. He was full of such things, little prickly dislikes. People who went around acting like theirs didn't stink. Certain movies, the stupid ones where they didn't do anything but talk. Certain kinds of foods. It was all Jessie could do to get him to drink orange juice instead of orange soda. He only ate when he was hungry, didn't make a big deal out of it. He didn't care about a lot of things other people thought were so important.

He was proud. He didn't like her paying for things, even when it was her own money; she had to slip it to him beneath the table in restaurants. It was as if all the ordinary hungers he didn't have or couldn't be bothered with went into being proud. She understood that about him, she had reached out with her heart and soul and touched that hard, hungry part of him.

Jessie turned her back on the ocean and crossed the road, wondering if he'd want something to eat once he woke up. There was a doughnut shop a couple of blocks down, she didn't mind going into places like that where nobody noticed what you looked like or who you were. Jessie stood patiently in line, flicking her eyes over her reflection in the mirrored panels. An average-to-plain girl with long straight hair falling in her eyes, no one you'd remember, and for the first time in her life she was glad for that because nobody was supposed to know where they were. She bought six doughnuts and a large iced tea which she balanced carefully on her way back to the room. She couldn't believe they were staying in a real motel.

R.B. was still asleep. He slept like he was a puppet dropped from some great height. Arms and legs flopped everywhere. His head was flung back and his mouth was open. Watching him sleep was still new to her, so she just sat there for a while. How amazing that when he was asleep, not talking, moving, watching things and working them around, he wasn't really R.B. at all. He was this long, blue-pale, skinned-looking creature, like a shell, but she had to stop thinking about those.

Jessie drank her iced tea and ate one of the doughnuts and then because she was getting bored she made some small, experimental noises to see if he might wake up. Scooched around in her chair. Ran water in the bathroom. She had already learned that if she wanted him to get up she should go about it in this roundabout way.

Finally his eyes fluttered and he regarded the ceiling. Then he rolled over. "Hey," Jessie said.

"What are you doing?"

He meant the doughnuts. Jessie held the bag out to him and he rummaged around in it. "Chocolate. All right."

And she was happy, because the doughnuts made him happy. R.B. got up to go to the bathroom with half a doughnut still clamped in his mouth and that was both funny and awful, to think of him doing both those things at once. Well, this was her new life, she should get accustomed to all manner of strangeness.

When he got back into bed he patted the space next to him, meaning she should lie down with him which also felt strange, since she was dressed and he wasn't wearing anything. She rested her head on his chest and R.B. ran one hand down her back and underneath the top of her pants while his other hand worked at getting a cigarette going. Once she heard the snap of the lighter and smelled smoke, Jessie said, "So what do you want to do today?"

"Here I just woke up and you're already after me to make plans."

"I was just asking. Come on."

There was a little while when the smoke drew in and out, then he said, "I think I'll go get me a new girlfriend."

"Oh sure. Funny."

"Hot car, long blond hair, killer bod. Plenty of money."

"How are you going to work that, hypnotize her?"

R.B.'s hand administered a little slap. "One that's not so damned sassy."

"Oh, I'll show you sassy. Wait and see," she said, knowing that he liked it when she pretended to talk back. She kept her ear on his chest, listening to the muddy bumping of his heart as he put his cigarette down and used both hands to pull at her pants. Jessie wriggled out of one leg, then kicked the other loose. She understood what he wanted, which was for her to get him hard with her mouth and then climb on top. It was different for guys, the things they liked.

When he was done, he said, "You're sweet, you know?"

"Do you like me that way? Sweet?"

"You know that I do."

Then that was what she would be. In a new life you could start over, change your nature. R.B. was her new life. It was that simple.

He clicked the television on and Jessie figured this would be another day like yesterday where they stayed inside doing nothing and they could have done that anywhere, there was no need to come such a long way.

But R.B. got up to take a shower and when he was dressed and had his hair dried he said she should get ready, they were going out.

"Out where?"

"Outside, Miss Worry Wart."

He was in that kind of mood, pleased with making secrets out of nothing. So Jessie put her clothes on and got herself outside. The sun was shining now, and just like that it was instantly warm and the glimpse of ocean she caught was blue, changed all of a sudden like a magic trick. R.B. was walking fast, she had to trot to keep up with him. The sun made the inside of the car hot and kicked up all its scruffy smells, vinyl and cigarettes and whatever R.B. had tracked into it. The car was the first thing her parents had not liked about him, before they even met him. Of course he hadn't bought it new, so there was another layer of grit, smells, stains that didn't belong to anyone they knew, only more of the lurking filth of the world, stupid dirty vomit-making horrible stop that. She pinched her nostrils shut and breathed through her mouth.

They followed the main road into town. With the sun out, things looked a lot more like Florida. There were palm trees and hibiscus and houses painted pink or blue or mint green in little square yards of crimped grass. Once they reached the business district, R.B. found a place to park. He led her down a sidewalk as if he knew exactly where he was going, although when they'd come here they'd driven straight through town. He was like that, confident.

He steered them into a House of Pancakes. R.B. got pecan waffles and a Coke and Jessie ordered a salad because she couldn't remember the last time she ate anything that qualified as a vegetable. She poked around in the mass of watery lettuce. They didn't talk much. R.B. didn't like talking at meals. He said it wasn't the way he was raised up. Jessie was trying to figure out a good time to ask him some of the important things like where they were going and what they were supposed to do from now on.

"So don't you trust me? Don't say yes just because you think it's what I want to hear. I can tell."

Which confused her, because if he knew that much, wouldn't he know if she trusted him? She lowered her eyes. She didn't want to look at him and have him see something she hadn't really meant.

"Yes or no. I'm not gonna get mad at you."

"Yes. I trust you."

"You better be sure about what you're saying because this is absolute, this is no halfway, half-assed contract between you and me, this means you trust me with your life and I trust you with mine and there's no going back. The bastard world hasn't done right by either of us but that's about to change. Come here. Don't be scared. Don't you know we're one person now?"

R.B. finished his waffles and shoved his plate away and got another cigarette going, his eyes shut against the sunlight. It was strange sometimes, here they were so close and yet she could examine him as if he was someone she'd never seen before. It felt disloyal to be doing so, but she couldn't help it, couldn't always stay in the zone of closeness, be half of one person with him. It was the weak, untrusting part of her. She loved his face but it was not at all a good-looking face, once you took it apart feature by feature. His skin was patchy and his eyes were too close together and his hair never sat right. But even his looks were something he could work around to his advantage. People underestimated him, dismissed him as common, underbred, some dumb hick with his head full of wrestling and beer. She'd seen them do it, stare right past him, and then be as surprised as hell when they wound up losing out to him.

R.B. was for Ronald Boone. She'd known him most of a month before he told her what the initials stood for, that's how much he hated being Ronald Boone. Ronald Boone was a slow learner, a discipline problem, a bad influence, a mug shot, a loser. It was a name with a permanent bad record. R.B. was somebody he could make up as he went along.

R.B. put his cigarette out and said, "You get enough to eat? That didn't hardly look like a mouthful."

"It was fine."

"I don't want anybody saying I can't take care of you. I don't want you thinking I can't take care of you."

"You know I never would. Come on."

"Because if it's a matter of money, that's the next thing on the list. I know you're used to better."

"Come on," Jessie said again, embarrassed when he brought up money and the house she'd grown up in and all the things in that house, so different from the way he'd lived, and why couldn't he believe that none of it mattered or had ever made her happy? She was afraid her old life would turn out to be something he always held against her.

R.B. put the cigarette out and dug for his wallet, fished out a twenty-dollar bill. "This is for if you want more to eat. I gotta go do something."

The worry in her started up again like a clock. "Where are you going?" she asked, knowing that he wouldn't say. The more she asked, the more he wouldn't tell.

"No place you need to fret about."

"When—"

"I'll be back when I'm back. My job today is taking care of business, yours is to wait right here and eat pancakes. Now who has the tougher job? Nope, not that face. I don't want to see you getting into a mood. Try looking like you're on the vacation you always wanted to take. That's my girl."

Then he was gone. God she hated this. He'd go off somewhere she wasn't allowed to be and she'd sit for hours, maybe, never knowing when he'd take it into his head to come back.

The waitress stopped at the table and asked Jessie if she wanted anything else and Jessie said she'd have coffee, not looking up. They wouldn't kick you out if you were drinking coffee.

But what if they did make her leave before R.B. came back and she went looking for the car and it wasn't there? Even if she found a ride back to the motel, she didn't have the room key. Even if she was brave enough to show her face at the office and talk them into giving her the key, what was there in that room to make a life of? What if she never saw R.B. again? She had nothing to go back to and no way of going forward.

"Honey? I know you don't want to believe me, but he is really not a nice boy. I don't just mean that he comes from a different kind of home. I'm not even talking about manners, although those are

28

important also and from what I've seen he doesn't have any. He
doesn't know how to behave around a nice girl. You know that if
someone doesn't respect themselves, they can't respect other people.
Maybe it's not even his fault, since he hasn't had the advantages you
take for granted. Now you think that because he's hanging around
and paying attention to you, you have to pay him attention back,
but sweetheart, I promise you there will be other boys, you are a
wonderful, beautiful, intelligent, special girl—"

Jessie stared down at the placemat. The placemat had pictures
of mermaids and anchors and seashells, the kinds of shells she
had wanted to find: starfish, speckled cowries, sand dollars,
conchs with their openings polished to the color of a rosy sunrise. She thought about asking the waitress if people ever actually came across the really gorgeous ones on the beach, or if
maybe there was a factory that turned them out for tourists.
Pretty things that weren't real. What was real was the inside,
the horrible stuff.

Coffee coffee coffee, she didn't even like the taste and it
made her brain itch, but she kept drinking it down. From time
to time she picked up the menu and frowned at it, as if con-
templating another order, trying to make it look like she had
some reason for staying. Not that anyone seemed to mind her
sitting there. The place was dead, acres of empty tables and the
waitresses off in the back somewhere, what time was it anyway? She hadn't wanted to keep track of how long he'd been
gone but it had been lunch and now it was not and if it got to
be dinner what was she supposed to do? Maybe he was with
some girl. He made jokes about it but what was stopping him?
She knew he'd had other girlfriends, slept with them, sure.

Who was she anyway, nobody special. What if he stopped being in love with her, what if he already had? She knew he didn't spend every second worrying about her the way she did about him. He'd get bored with her, shrug her off. It was a lot easier to imagine this than to believe in some perfect happy life. She wasn't meant to be happy. R.B. was only the particular way she had chosen to be unhappy, the sign that announced to the world that she was a truly fucked-up person. She almost hated him, him and his big plans and the blood trouble between them.

Calm down. It was the coffee ripping through her and getting her so weird, oh sure, like coffee was the only thing wrong with her. She kept having to pee but she held it until it hurt every time because she was afraid R.B. would return while she was in the bathroom, see the empty table and walk out again.

And wouldn't you know it, she was on her way back, hurrying, and here was R.B. coming through the front door. He spotted her and waved, and when he got closer he said, "Hey Kathy, I want you to meet some friends of mine."

There were two people, a guy and a girl, man and woman really, crowding in behind him, but Jessie didn't focus on them right away, wondering what he was up to. He'd told her that there would be times when they'd go by these different, traveling names. She was Kathy and if anybody asked, she was eighteen. He was Steve. Everything else she should leave up to him. So she said, "Hi, nice to meet you" to the two of them, the big husky burnt-pink blond guy, and the woman with her hair fixed in stiff curls on the top of her head and a lot of gold bracelets and a navy blue blazer with gold buttons that was supposed to remind you of sailors. Jerry and Pat. She thought he was Jerry and she was Pat, although it could have been the other way around.

R.B. said, "Jerry here's got this boat. I'm gonna help him figure out what's wrong with the engine."

Jerry said, "Yeah, we're dead in the water." He laughed, like this was the funniest thing in the world.

Pat shook her head. Her hair didn't move, as if it was made out of icing. "It's the oil pressure. The big doofus didn't check the oil."

"You're not supposed to have to on a brand-new boat. Cherist."

"All the way from Mobile I said, what's that light doing on, that red one, and he'd say, oh, it's a new boat, don't worry. Then when he finally goes to check it he can't find the thing, the oil thing."

"Hey, it's a design flaw."

"Yeah, your head's not supposed to be up your ass either. More bad design."

They all laughed like crazy at this. Jessie figured they'd been at some bar.

R.B. said to her, "So, if you're ready to shake a leg . . ."

R.B. paid the bill at the register. Then they were out on the sidewalk, Jerry and R.B. up ahead, she and Pat behind. The sun was low and the air had turned hot and heavy, so that sweat started up under her arms and slid along the insides of her jeans, and she found herself walking slowly as if wading through water. "So," Pat said. "Steve tells me you're from Ohio."

They weren't, but Jessie nodded, wondering what else R.B. had said, what else she'd have to go along with. She hoped Pat wasn't a nosy type. What if she asked where in Ohio?

But Pat was still going on about Jerry and his boat. "I just love to give him shit about his little toy, all the money he spends on it. He tries to sneak the checks past me. Fat chance."

"I guess boats are real expensive," said Jessie, just to keep up her end of the conversation. It was so hot. They must have moved the heat in like furniture while she was inside the restaurant. Her head felt cottony. She didn't want to think about what R.B. might be planning. She guessed that Jerry and Pat had a lot of money, although they didn't act like it. They were too drunk.

R.B. and Jerry were now instant best friends, pounding each other on the biceps and yukking it up. Jessie hoped they weren't walking much farther. No one but her seemed to mind the heat. Pat was walking and talking and trying to get a cigarette out of her purse, all at the same time. She had long, silver-polished fingernails and big knuckles with sparkly rings perched on them. The rings looked cheap. Flashy, Jessie's mother would have said, but they were probably real diamonds and real gold.

Pat said, "So is Steve a good mechanic? I mean, we can always have somebody from the boatyard look at it."

"He's good with cars," said Jessie truthfully. "I guess a boat engine's not that different."

Pat got her cigarette going and blew smoke. She had a narrow face and deep, gouged wrinkles around her eyes and mouth. "Oh, Jerry's probably hoping there's some quick easy fix. He's putting off having the engine pulled and finding out he wrecked it. He thinks he can sort of ease into the bad news that way. Then maybe I won't get on his fat ass about it." Pat cocked her head and smiled at Jessie, like they were girlfriends sharing secrets. "Men. Little boys, every blessed one of them."

Jessie smiled back. She tried to imagine talking that way about R.B., like he was somebody you could be fond and jokey about.

"He's a little old for you, your Steve."

"I'm eighteen," Jessie said and watched Pat not believe it.

"Wish I was your age again. Young love, nothing like it.

'Course how would you know that, what do you have to compare it to. You plan on getting married?"

Jessie said yes, probably, just not right away. Making that up along with everything else. Pat nodded and blew smoke through her nostrils. "Well, don't feel like you have to rush it. Marriage. It's like a damn bathtub. Once you're in it and you're used to it, it's not so hot."

The sunlight was so thick, she had trouble focusing on Pat's voice, which was melting into a sloppy buzz. Where was this boat anyway? She didn't see a harbor or anything like that, just streets and parking lots and the heat deep down in the pavement where you couldn't get away from it.

"Jer and I been married eight years. I was married before and he was married before. So we're experts at it. Sex doesn't stay the same after a while. I'm only telling you because I wish somebody would have told me."

Was there any way to get her to quit talking? She couldn't believe it, this woman she only met two seconds ago. Jessie said, "Thank you."

"Oh, now you're upset, don't pay attention to me, you get as old as I am, you lose all shame."

"It's OK," Jessie said. "Really." Pat probably thought she was embarrassed. She was just tired of everybody who thought all the sex stuff was so important.

She felt Pat's hand brush against her hair, graze her shoulder. She held herself rigid. "You ever think about wearing your hair up? You have such a pretty little face but you can't see it." The hand dropped away. "Now what does that fool want?"

Jerry was waving at them to catch up. "How about a grocery run? Something to throw on the grill."

They were right in front of a grocery store. The rest of them seemed to think this was a good idea. Jessie could tell the kind of evening this was going to be, starting off in one direction, then getting distracted and heading off in another. At least the store was air-conditioned. She left Pat and Jerry at the shopping carts, fussing over what they should buy. R.B. was standing in front of the ice-cream freezer.

"Lookit that." He indicated the freezer shelves. "Butter brickle. You can't hardly find it anymore."

"Who are these guys, why are we hanging around with them?"

"Relax. I'm gonna do them a favor. Then they're gonna do us one."

"That lady's kind of strange. How old are they anyway? I don't think we should be going around with people as old as them."

R.B. opened the freezer and picked up the ice cream one-handed. "I said relax. Nobody's going to get bad hurt."

She stared up at him, trying to tell if he was joking. "What are you going to—"

"You ever been on a fancy boat like they got? Mommy and Daddy have one of those?"

"Please, R.B."

"I'm just messing with you, Worry Wart. We're gonna drink their beer and get their boat fixed so they can go on their merry way."

"Promise we won't have to stay real late. Promise—"

R.B. made a sign to her to be quiet, because Pat and Jerry were coming up behind them with the cart. They'd already picked up different bottles of steak sauce and barbecue sauce and two jars of fancy olives. "Mesquite chips," Jerry said. "Help me remember that. Mesquite chips, mesquite chips, mesquite chips." R.B. put the ice cream in the cart and they wandered up and down the aisles, adding anything that caught their eye, a platter of cocktail shrimp, big red trays of steaks, tomatoes, garlic bread, tubs of bean salad and macaroni salad, a frozen coconut cream pie. Then Pat and Jerry got into another stupid argument about how were they going to get it all back to the boat because they hadn't even gotten to the liquor aisle yet and didn't they need ice too?

R.B. said it was no problem, he'd go back for the car and drive them to the harbor. Pat and Jerry acted like nobody in the history of time ever had such a good idea. Jessie wondered if it wasn't something R.B. had planned all along. And anyway, now he wouldn't have to help pay for the groceries.

So here she was, trailing after the two of them, Pat and Jerry, like she was their kid or something. Now that would be strange. If they did have a kid, it would be totally screwed up. It seemed that the longer they were in the store, the more reckless Pat and Jerry got about piling things in the cart, frozen waffles, cashews, onion dip, rice, nothing that made sense in terms of a meal. She couldn't imagine eating any of it. Something had come in between her and hunger lately. Jessie figured Pat and Jerry were just warming up for the liquor aisle. Sure enough, once they reached it they started hefting the bottles like pros. Jessie wandered off.

She was bored. One of the odd things about this new life was that she didn't have to *do* anything, school or chores or homework or anything else. It took some getting used to. She and R.B. just ended up in one place or another, doing the next thing that happened. It hadn't even been that long. A bunch of days. But already it felt like she'd never lived any other way. R.B. said it was better like that. They had made a clean break. They were born again, just like people sang about in church except it was better than church, it was their own invention, nobody but them could live like this, brand-new every minute. And Jessie believed him, except there were still those weird times when the gray and floating part of her mind got in the way.

"Now I know you are an intelligent person, so I am going to discuss things with you in professional terms. I'd like us to work on self-esteem issues. Unfortunately, our culture doesn't always do a very good job at making young women feel positively about themselves and their achievements and their futures. There are books about it, I can loan them to you if you'd like to read them. I'm offering to do this because, as I said, I know you are intelligent enough to understand them. And I'm sure you understand why your parents are so worried about you. They feel that Ron is not the sort of person who will help you reach your full potential. That even if he cares about you, even if he has the best intentions, you would be making choices that you'll—"

"No."

"I beg your pardon?"

Jessie had been staring at the totally uninteresting carpet. Nubby beige. The whole office was designed to give you nothing you could really look at. "That's not why they don't like him."

A small silence while the woman rearranged her voice to be especially patient, neutral, and flat, a voice like a beige carpet. "Why not, then?"

"They're afraid people will see the two of us together, me and him, and I won't look like anyone they'd want to be their daughter, I'll look like I belong with him."

She drifted back to Pat and Jerry when they reached the checkout. Pat couldn't find Camel hard packs and didn't want to settle for soft and wouldn't quit going on about it. Jerry was puffing out his cheeks and poking his tongue around like he had food stuck between his teeth, a serious expression on his face. They were idiots, she didn't care what happened to them. But what if this was her punishment, that they would be her parents now? R.B. would disappear forever and leave her with these horrible braying fools making her follow them around.

Then she saw her father sitting on a bench at the front of the store. Even as she knew this was impossible, even as she recognized that it was just another thick-faced old man wearing a cowboy hat, something her father would never do, Jessie couldn't work free of the shock of it. The way the man in the cowboy hat kept his mouth set so nothing could get in or out of it unless he gave permission. He was alone on the bench, no one anywhere near him. He had a fierce expression, meant to let people know he preferred it this way and nobody had to feel sorry for him, nor would he acknowledge that he was old now, that he was slack and puffy and angry about everything and he was wearing a ridiculous hat that someone must have put on his head without his noticing, just to make a fool of him, *Oh Daddy*.

"Want some gum?"

Jerry was holding out the pack to her. He already had a big wad of the stuff working; hot sugary breath wafted from him. For a moment she couldn't remember where she was or who she was supposed to be. "No thanks."

"You sure? Double your pleasure."

She shook her head. Pat was still in the checkout line, yanking the cart around and pawing through the fifty-seven grocery bags, looking for something. Jessie couldn't decide which one of them was worse to be stuck talking to. When she looked over at the bench where the man in the cowboy hat had been, he was gone.

"This your spring break?" Jerry asked her. "Fun in the sun?"

"No, it's just . . . a trip. I'm not in school anymore."

"I went to UAB for a year," Jerry offered. "But I was a dummy."

"Ha ha," said Jessie, politely.

"You're a quiet type, aren't you. Still waters."

"I guess." It was as good an excuse as any not to talk to him. He kept working the gum around, showing all the wet mechanics of his tongue and teeth. Why were there always things you didn't want to see?

"*Bali Ha'i*. That's the name of my boat. Like from the movie. What's its name. You know the one I mean?"

She stared out the windows, willing R.B. to appear.

"*South Pacific*. That's it. Bali Ha'i is this beautiful beautiful island, people go there to get the hell away from it all. Isn't that a great name for a boat?"

He seemed to want her to answer. She figured he was one of those guys who needed somebody saying yes or uh-huh to him every two seconds. The underside of his tongue had a pulpy look. "Yeah, it's great."

"Because a boat's sort of like an island. Once you get in the middle of nowhere. Nobody watching you. Total privacy."

It was harder not to hear than not to see, because you couldn't close your ears. *See hear taste smell touch.* You ought to be able to shut them down when you didn't need them.

The car pulled up and R.B. honked the horn. Jessie wound up in the back seat, squished in with Pat and the groceries. She could tell R.B. had cleaned the car some, thrown out the worst of the junk. Like it wasn't still the same old wreck. Was he trying to impress them, fool them? Steve and Kathy, that nice young couple from Ohio, whose old but clean car didn't have Ohio plates although there was an explanation for that. In the front seat Jerry was telling R.B. about Bali Ha'i. There was a song too, which Jerry tried to sing in his bellowing voice, "Bali Hi-iy may call you," until Pat told him he just sucked. Jessie caught R.B.'s eye in the rearview mirror and he winked.

She decided she would just go along with things but not really be there in any feeling sense. Maybe you couldn't help seeing and hearing and all the rest, but you didn't have to think about it. She would be an island, all to herself. They parked in the harbor lot and walked past rows and rows of boats until they came to the *Bali Ha'i*. Jessie thought it was kind of small, though she didn't say so. It had a cabin over the wheelhouse, and some padded benches around the edges of the deck, and a ladder leading down to whatever else there was. Right away Jerry made a big deal about filling the beer cooler and getting a pitcher of margaritas started, even before he and R.B. went to look at the engine. These guys were total alcoholics.

"Come on, we'll get the groceries squared away," Pat said to her. Jessie lowered herself step by step down the ladder. Even tied up like this, the boat had a wobble to it. The kitchen was just a corner space that was instantly too small with both of them standing in it. "Home away from home," Pat said breezily. Behind them a door was half open on a room almost entirely filled with a double bed. It was rumpled and unmade. Jessie turned away from it, not wanting to see where they slept and did things to each other.

Pat handed her a plastic bowl. "There's crackers or pretzels or something you can put in here. I should get that grill started. So what do you think of Jerry?"

"Oh, he's—" She stopped. Did she have to think anything about him? "What do you mean?"

"I think we can get by with paper plates, don't you? Oh, nothing. Just asking. How about a shrimp?" Pat balanced the platter and stabbed at it with a plastic toothpick in the shape of a sword. The shrimp looked like a skinned knuckle.

"No thanks."

"We just have to get you into more of a partying mood. How about a drink? Well, suit yourself."

Then her and her big hair went back up the ladder. Jessie found the pretzels and put them in the bowl. Her stomach rocked back and forth with the boat's motion. She thought she would just stay down there until someone made her do something else. She was supposed to say she liked Jerry, the same way she was supposed to like shrimp and margaritas. Was this part of her new life? Was she going crazy, or was it just that crazy things were happening? She kept trying not to look at that bedroom, that half-open door and the wreckage of the sheets.

She must have spaced out, floated away, stopped feeling things right there as she stood. Here was R.B., his hands and arms all oiled and grimed from the engine, saying, "Babe? What are you doing?"

"Nothing."

"You're not getting weird on me, are you? We got no time for that shit."

"No, I'm just . . . Where did they go?"

"Who, Popeye and Olive Oyl? No place. They're up there burning the ass off those steaks. Come on, we're gonna go for a little cruise."

"I thought the boat didn't work." She kept talking so as to smooth over the muffled panic in her head. She was imagining the vastness of the world, skies and oceans and the shapes of the continents as seen from space, and herself, very small, down in a hole on this boat in a place she'd never been before.

"It works fine now. What are you worried about?"

She shook her head. Nothing.

R.B. put his mouth right up against her ear so she couldn't not hear him. "You think I can't handle these guys? You think I can't take care of you? How'd we get all this way here? You remember all I done for you? Oh yes, it was for you. Anything you're too scared to do for yourself, here I am to do it for you. Now can you be sweet for me like you promised? Can you put a smile on your face and come up and eat these people's food? I want to hear you say it."

"Yes."

"Like you mean it."

"Yes. I can."

"What's my name?"

"Steve."

He gave her a nudge and she started up the ladder ahead of him. By the time she came up the stairs she was smiling, she had his arm wrapped around her waist, dirt and all, so it appeared as if they'd been down there carrying on and were just a little bashful about it. Pat and Jerry looked drunker. Funny how that was the first thing you noticed about someone. Jerry's mouth was sloppy with barbecue sauce he hadn't wiped away. Pat's hair seemed lopsided. Whatever held that stack of stiff curls on top of her head had tilted. "Lookit the lovebirds," Jerry said. He swatted Pat on her bony rear. "Were you ever that young and cute?"

"I was but you weren't. Fix yourself a plate." Her hand with its silver dagger nails and fistful of rings indicated the food spread out on the benches and deck chairs, a mess of wrappings and opened jars. One of the steaks was still on the grill. It was dry and gnarled. Jessie filled a plate with other stuff instead. It was easy to smile and tell them how nice everything was because she wasn't really inside herself anymore. She'd crawled out and left only the shell behind. It was cooler now, the sun was down and a breeze ruffled the water. R.B. was in the wheelhouse. He must have figured out how the boat worked. Jerry kept calling him Skipper.

Then the boat was moving. The engine vibrated. The dock slipped away from them. "Hey Skipper, slow down for Christ's sake." It took a while to get out past the other boats. Behind them, a V-shaped trail of water churned up white. She was no longer on land but on the enormous, greedy ocean. The shore was outlined in lights. It kept getting smaller and smaller and the ocean darker until there was just a line of light marking the edge of the world and if you took that away you could turn the earth end over end and wind up nowhere.

The boat's engine stopped. There was a light in the wheelhouse where R.B. and Jerry stood. Pat was sitting next to her now, saying was she tired, did she want to take a little nap downstairs? Jessie said she was just fine. "Oh come on," said Pat. "I want to show you something. Jerry needs you to help him with something downstairs."

"No," she said. That bed and those disordered sheets were the insides of everything, the last place she wanted to be. Pat lit a cigarette. She snapped her lighter shut and took little mad puffs. Then she went away. Jerry was standing in front of her now, saying, "What'sa matter, huh? What'sa matter with the party girl?"

R.B. was gone. Pat was gone. She'd spaced out again, missed something. There was only Jerry. He was too close to her. He was blocking the light and she could smell him more than see him. He held out a drink. "Here you go. Jump in."

She took the glass but didn't drink. Although she had not moved, her skin began a slow, shrinking retreat. "Where's R.B.?"

"Where's what?"

"Where's Steve?"

"Around somewhere. He's a nut, you know? Regular hell on wheels."

"Go away."

"Why're you so sad? You always sad like this?"

"I'm not sad."

"Or scared. Don't be scared. This is *Bali Ha'i*."

He kissed her. It wasn't like she would have expected. His mouth tasted sweet, from the barbecue sauce.

Somebody screamed but it wasn't her. Jerry staggered and his weight and heat landed on top of her. The boat caught a wave and the deck heaved up. Jerry tried to get himself on his feet. ". . . the fucking . . ."

Pat's head appeared in the hatch of the staircase except there was something wrong, her hair was gone, the tower of curls. Her hair underneath was short and slick, wet-looking, and her nose was bleeding. She opened her mouth and you could see blood there too, dark and glossy, and then before she could scream again, something pulled her back under.

Jerry cursed and struggled to get himself upright. Finally he was gone and she closed her eyes and ears and lay face down on the bench, seeing hearing feeling nothing nothing nothing

"You don't have to do nothing, just get me in the house. Get me in, then stand aside or go on back to the car. This is no chickening out, you know it's the right thing to do because they're never gonna let us be together, never gonna let up on you, you'll never be good enough for them and their big-shot life. Don't you trust me?"

Because there was no chickening out, she unlocked the door from

the garage and led him in through the kitchen with its ticking clock and the refrigerator that even in the darkness was busy with its humming work. The house slept, the shadows breathed. At the foot of the stairs she stopped and let him go ahead. She couldn't go any farther. She saw R.B.'s face turn back to her as he climbed the first step, couldn't read its expression, just its paleness, although she thought he raised his eyebrows, a question. She nodded her head, yes. But she didn't want to watch him climb those stairs. She fled the house and its shadows and went back to the car to wait. How could she see without eyes, hear without ears, but she did, as R.B. approached that dim room at the top of the stairs where her parents slept, their shapes curving toward and away from each other, the sheets like veils breathing in and out. R.B. aimed the gun and made the sheets jump and scream and bleed. After a little while he came back out to the car and said that was it, everything was over.

The boat was moving again. Or else the ocean itself was moving and carrying the boat along with it. R.B. was calling her. She raised her head and the shoreline was close enough to tell one light from another.

"Come on over here," he said. He was in the wheelhouse. "I need you to watch and tell me if you see another boat coming. You can do that, right? Am I asking you to do something hard?" R.B. cut the engine and swung down the ladder and stayed out of sight for a long time.

She had left her old life behind her and this new one was like the ocean. It took you places without your knowing. When they got back to the dock R.B. said, "If you see anybody, don't look at them." He was wearing a leather jacket she hadn't seen before, and carrying a duffel bag. She wondered if Pat's hair was in it.

They got in the car and drove. R.B. said they weren't going back to the motel, in case somebody saw them. They drove and drove. Jessie felt sleepy. She curled up in the front seat with her head resting on the leather coat.

"R.B.?"

"What, baby."

"Didn't you like them?"

He wouldn't answer right away. Then he said, "I don't think of it that way. I just think, they're somebody who isn't you or me."

The car was a boat, the night was the ocean. She would fall asleep in one place and wake up in another. The only thing that stayed the same was R.B., the only one she would know by sight or skin or anything else was him.

IT WOULD NOT MAKE
ME TREMBLE TO SEE
TEN THOUSAND FALL

Jack Pardee signed his enlistment papers in May, right after graduation. The Army recruiter had been working on him for most of a year. His report date to Fort Sill wasn't until mid-September. In June he and Kelly Ann got married in the Methodist church, with the reception at the Laborers' Hall the next town over. They had already been living as man and wife in the upstairs apartment of Jack's parents' house. Their daughter, Tara, had been born that February. In Leota and places like it, people paired off young and got their lives settled quickly.

Kelly Ann hadn't wanted Jack to go to the Army, not when there was a shooting war. But Jack said he was going to put in for transportation and get trained as a mechanic. He'd be safe as houses. He probably wouldn't get any closer to the war than a base in Kuwait, he'd probably sleep in air conditioning and eat at a Pizza Hut. Secretly they both looked forward to his first trip home when he'd be wearing his uniform and have his new shaved haircut. A soldier was someone to be taken seriously.

At first it seemed like a long time until September, like any other summer. Jack did sit-ups and push-ups and ran to get ready for his PFT. He picked up some shifts at American Dowel. The afternoons he was at work Kelly Ann lay out in the back yard on a blanket while the baby napped in her stroller in the shade. The suntan oil made Kelly Ann's wedding and engagement rings slide around on her knuckle. So far, being married didn't feel all that different to her.

Most nights they left the baby with Jack's mother and went driving, usually to somebody's house out in the country where there was a perpetual low-grade party, beer and cards and music. Kelly Ann fell asleep on the couch until Jack was ready to leave. On the way home he drove too fast, like he always had, like everybody did, the fine old tradition of getting liquored up and roaring up and down the county roads. Sometimes there were crashes, and stupid deaths of the sort that everyone vowed wouldn't happen again, until the next time when they did. More often the cars banged around in the ditch, and then the etiquette was to stop your own car and holler down, "Are you kilt yet?" and the answer would come back, "Naw, just messed up."

When Kelly Ann asked Jack to slow down because didn't they have the baby to think about, he said she had to quit worrying about every blessed thing.

Some weekends they dressed the baby up and took her to see Kelly Ann's parents at their big house on Bayles Lake. Even with a baby to fuss over, the visits didn't go that well. Kelly Ann's father never had anything good to say about Jack and thought she'd made a bad bargain with the marriage, gone down in the world. The Army didn't impress him because he'd been a Marine. The four of them sat around in lawn chairs drinking Cokes in foam holders, waiting for the baby to do something remarkable so they could talk about it. After enough time had passed to count as a polite effort, they headed home. Kelly Ann wished they could just quit being her parents, if they thought she did everything wrong.

Sometimes they drove out past the consolidated high school, sitting like a prison complex in a cleared space among the cornfields. They found it hard to believe they were no longer students and no longer had any purpose there. Because of the baby, Kelly Ann was making up coursework at home; she'd get her diploma in the mail in August. Jack said he'd seen old Jonesy, the English teacher, filling up her car at the Clark station. "I told her I enlisted and she started in with some poem. One of the patriot ones."

"She is so out of it," Kelly Ann agreed.

"She said to tell you hi."

"I thought she was mad at me because I dropped out."

"You didn't drop all the way out."

"You know what I mean," Kelly Ann said. She'd always gotten good grades, teachers liked her. She probably would have been voted Least Likely to Get Knocked Up.

Then, like any other summer, it was over. There was a series of rowdy parties for Jack. His mother exhausted herself with cooking for him, and Jack and Kelly Ann did their best to wear the bed out. On the morning that Jack's father drove him to Saint Louis, so he could catch his bus, there was a lot of crying and carrying on, especially from the mother. It was almost a relief to Kelly Ann to have that part over with, even if her chest felt hollow, her heart like a drum banged over and over, beating out the word "gone."

Jack could only phone once a week during basic. He always said he was fine, things were going fine, but it was hard to tell because the phone got in the way, and he mostly talked about the crazy guys in the barracks and the stunts they pulled. He said to send more pictures of her and of Tara, all the guys thought Tara was a cutie and that Kelly Ann was hot. "I love you," Kelly Ann said when it was time to go, and Jack said, "Love you too," and then he hung up.

Most of her girlfriends were still single and they called Kelly Ann to try and get her to go out. Jack's mother was always happy to take the baby. She said it was a good idea for Kelly Ann not to coop herself up. The town was so small that everybody knew everybody else's business, which meant she couldn't get into any real trouble even if she had a mind to. She didn't, but she didn't like the feeling of being left behind either. Her life had started off in one direction and then switched course, as if she'd traded Jack for a baby, her parents for his, and she hadn't seen any of it coming.

So she went out with her girlfriends on weekends, four or five of them together in one car, driving forty miles down the highway to the state university. They headed for the campus strip, debating which places were hottest and which were the easiest to get into. Once they settled on a bar, they ordered Long Island Iced Teas and flirted with the college boys. They always pretended they were in school too. It was a big game to see how many drinks they could get the boys to buy them, how long they could keep the joke up. Kelly Ann sat with her left hand in her lap so nobody could see her rings. She thought it was all kind of a dumb stunt but she went along with it for the others' sake.

One night a dark-haired boy in a pink polo shirt sat down next to her, singling her out. "My name's Matt," he bawled. The bar was full of thundering noise.

"I'm Kelly Ann."

"Yeah? That's pretty." He bobbed his head and grinned, as if he'd said something winning. One of Kelly Ann's girlfriends raised her eyebrows, meaning, *He's hot.* They thought it was hilarious when guys came on to her. She decided he was good-looking in an unexceptional way, that is, when you surveyed his face there was nothing wrong with any particular part of it. She never trusted the really gorgeous guys who were so totally full of themselves. She always thought that Jack was just good-looking enough, without giving you cause for concern.

"So, Kelly Ann, you having a good time tonight?"

He leaned in a little, as if to hear her better, but mostly so he could look down her shirt. She said sure, she was. She recognized this as a kind of trick, like a salesman asking questions you had to say yes to. Matt said it looked like her friends were having an even better time. They were drinking a round of shots that some-body'd bought for them and collapsing with laughter, laughing at nothing with their loose smeared mouths.

Matt asked if she wanted to do shots too and Kelly Ann said, "No, not really." She wasn't that into drinking since the baby. There was no chance now to sleep in and enjoy the fuzzy edges of the next day. "That's cool," Matt said, and then he turned to look out over the room, as if he might be missing something. Kelly Ann studied him. She didn't know one guy back home who would wear a pink shirt.

He turned back to her again, stretching his smile wider. She felt a little sorry for him, since she knew how things would end up, and he wasn't going to get what he wanted. "Are you guys freshmen?"

She said that they were. She wished they hadn't decided to do this stupid pretending thing. It had something to do with looking down on the college kids because they were rich and spoiled and deserved to be treated like the assholes they were. But of course here they were, trying to look and act just like them.

Kelly Ann asked Matt if he was a freshman and he said, "Sophomore. I'm in Finance. But you have to have junior standing to take Finance courses, so right now I'm just doing intros and some gen ed requirements. I've got Triple E, Anthro, and an Afro-Am survey that doesn't suck too bad."

Kelly Ann nodded. Like she knew what any of that was. She hoped he wasn't going to ask her about her courses but he raised his hand and made a fluttering arc, like a bird flying away. "School," he said dismissively.

She could have gone on to college if she hadn't had the baby. Maybe not the state university, but somewhere. She didn't think she was any dumber than this Matt guy, who'd probably had everything handed to him all along.

He said, "Yeah, you need a break from it now and then. Some of those profs are such jerks, like their stupid class is supposed to be so important."

"Then you probably shouldn't bother taking it, if it's not important to you."

He decided she was being funny. "Right. You should see the Anthro guy, he is classic. Wears his pants practically up to his armpits."

Kelly Ann didn't say anything. The noise in the room was tremendous. It blotted out hearing and replaced it with white, roaring space. She thought about Jack, about making love to him, the memory so sharp and immediate and unbidden, she wondered if he was thinking about her that very moment, lying on his bunk in the barracks, surrounded by the soldiers' unquiet sleep.

"Hey." Matt again, working up his smile. "You want to go to a party?"

She shook her head. "I have a boyfriend."

He made a big show of shading his eyes with his hand, looking around. "So where is he?"

"Oklahoma."

"That's pretty far away."

"Uh-huh." He smelled of whatever cologne he'd put on at the start of the evening, baked in by body heat, and she could tell he was a little drunk, but nothing that was going to cause real trouble.

"Your friends could come too."

"I don't think so."

"What if I asked really really nice?"

"I don't even know you," she said patiently.

"Well I don't know you either, so that makes us even."

"No."

"Oh come on." He stuck his lower lip out in an exaggerated, babyish way, except he really was pissed off because she wasn't going along with things, she could tell, and mad at wasting his time being nice to her. "Why even bother coming out, if you don't want to have any fun?"

"Maybe my idea of fun's different than yours."

"Yeah, cause yours kind of sucks."

"Thanks for the opinion," she said, hoping he'd just go away now, attach himself to one of the sorority girls at the next table. They looked as alike as purebred puppies. But he was just drunk enough to feel his pride deserved a little more mouth directed her way.

"So maybe you should just get yourself to oh-oh-Oklahoma, who is he anyway, this guy, some Okie?"

He was just a boy who knew that life wasn't going to get serious for him for a long time, and who only used his manners when he thought they could do him some good, and she shouldn't let him get to her but he did. She put her left hand on the table, stretching it out so the diamond in her ring flashed. "He's not my boyfriend. We're married. He's in Oklahoma because he's in the Army, doing a man's work. We have a little girl, she's almost seven months old. I don't go to school here, none of us do. The last thing I'd want is to be around the likes of you full-time. I'm from Leota. I bet you never heard of it. I bet there's lots of things you never heard of."

She waited until he took himself off, then she asked her friend for the keys and sat behind the wheel of the car until they were done for the night.

Jack came home after basic, just in time for Thanksgiving. They all went down to Saint Louis to meet him, Kelly Ann and the father and the mother, who didn't like long trips in the car but didn't want to stay home fretting. They sat in the bus station waiting room until his bus was called, and then they stood up against the windows to catch sight of him, an unfamiliar silhouette in his uniform cap, shouldering through the crowd. He'd lost some weight, you could see it in his face and the loose way his neck moved around inside his shirt collar. But he made a good figure in his Army blues, everything about him signifying solidity and purpose. He kissed the baby and Kelly Ann and his mother and shook hands with his father and said, "Man, I could sleep for a week. That's what the Army does, makes you fall in love with sleep."

Jack sat in the back seat with Kelly Ann and the baby. Kelly Ann leaned up close to him and he draped his arm around her. It felt like he'd been gone a long long time. The father and the mother asked him questions, how was the food, and had he learned to salute and stand at attention and all the other Army things. Jack said, Oh yeah, he was a regular saluting fool by now.

He talked about the sergeant who turned on the barracks lights every morning at 4:30, the explosion of light like the end of the world crashing down on you, how they made you run everywhere, run to chow, run to the head, run to formation, how they were always in your face, screaming at you, you were worthless, scum, lower than a cockroach, and they didn't spare the cuss words. But that was all right. It was meant to break you down and then build you back up again, into a warrior.

He finished talking and they were all quiet. The word "warrior" seemed to hang in the air, like an echo without an answer. The car's heater was on high to keep the baby from getting chilled. It made them all drowsy. It was Thanksgiving weather, gray and cold, with a low, bulging sky and a scouring wind. The farm fields had been harvested down to trash, bleached-out corn and bean stalks. Kelly Ann inhaled the wool smell of Jack's uniform. When his arm slackened and his breathing turned slow and even, she knew he was asleep. She had not wanted everyone to go along to pick him up, but now she saw the wisdom of it, this time in the car when they wouldn't need to talk and could get used to the idea of each other again.

Jack had ten days before he was to report to Fort Benning, in Georgia, for his AIT. He slept a lot and played with the baby and ate heroic amounts of his mother's Thanksgiving dinner. He wasn't as mouthy now, as if the Army had shouted him down, and he even drove a little slower, which she was happy about. One night he wore his uniform over to the VFW and everybody there bought him drinks and told Kelly Ann how proud she must be of him. She could see how excited the older men were to have him, a real serviceman, among them, how it kindled something in them, got them to telling their own war stories. Kelly Ann wondered if that was just the way men were, always trying to tell you about exciting things that had already happened. Or maybe it had something to do with living in Leota, a farm town where so many of the farms had been sold off, a railroad town that the railroads had given up on a long time ago. It was home, but it wasn't a place that made for many new stories.

Kelly Ann and Jack had the baby on the bed with them and were watching her try to scoot herself up, bottom first. She'd push on her forearms and grunt and labor until the weight of her head pulled her back down. Jack's mother said it wouldn't be long until she'd be able to grab on to things and stand. Jack said, "She won't even remember who I am."

"That's not so."

"I guess kids get by all right. If they never know you, they can't miss you."

"Come on, she knows you. Tara, where's Daddy? Daddy Daddy Daddy."

Jack said, "I guess you could show her pictures. That would be something. If I wind up getting killed."

"That's no way to talk," Kelly Ann said. Even though there was a part of her that thought knowing somebody killed in the war would be romantic, the heartbreak and all. Just the idea of it, which didn't mean you wanted it to happen.

"I'd rather be plain dead than come back without any legs or half my brain, like some of those guys."

"Stop it, OK?" There were things she didn't want to think about. Pictures you saw, guys and sometimes girls too, pieces broken off of them like they were gingerbread people. It wasn't even that great of a war. But the country had called, and Jack and all the others had answered.

She said, "Maybe me and Tara could come with you and live on the base. They have that, don't they? Family housing."

"No, you're better off here. I don't want to have to worry about you once they ship me out."

"We could have our own place."

"We already got this place."

"I mean a start-from-scratch place."

Jack rolled away from her so he was on his back, staring up at the ceiling. "You act like we're not lucky to have it and we are. We don't even pay rent." They'd put Jack's signing bonus in the bank and weren't going to touch it. It was a future they weren't allowed to have yet.

"I know we're lucky. I just wish—"

But she didn't finish her sentence. It made her feel guilty to want more of anything, when Jack was going to a foreign land and putting himself in harm's way. Even though she did wish lots of things were different, a million large and small wishes, and here she used to think that if she had Jack, that was the whole world.

Jack left for Fort Benning, one more good-bye, and Christmas and New Year's passed without him. Kelly Ann got used to having him gone, as she guessed he got used to doing without her. She missed him, she tried to keep missing him as hard as she could, but the edge had worn off. For the baby's first birthday there was a party with a cake and both sets of grandparents and they made a video and sent it to Jack. On it they got the baby to say da-da, which was a big success, although she made a lot of sounds now and you couldn't always tell if she meant anything by them.

In March Jack called and said he was going to be "sent overseas and into a hazardous situation." That was all they were supposed to say, like anybody would be thrown off by it. Mechanic's school hadn't come through and he was regular infantry. He wanted Kelly Ann and the baby to come down for a visit before he left, and so she bought a plane ticket and made the arrangements. But at the last minute the baby came down with a fever and a cough and the doctor said to keep her home. So it was Kelly Ann alone who went, a friend driving her through squalls of thin sleet to the Indianapolis airport. It was the first time she'd ever flown.

She landed in Atlanta, then changed planes for Columbus. Jack was there to meet her when she came out of security, not wearing his uniform, as she'd imagined him, but his regular old denim jacket. His hair was a little longer now and he'd gained his weight back. He looked older to her, a layer of heaviness in his face, and she wondered if she looked different to him as well. He had a bouquet of carnations wrapped in stiff plastic for her and Kelly Ann carried them in her free hand so as not to crush them. She couldn't decide if it was better or worse that the baby hadn't come along. Worse because now Jack might not see her for a long time. Better because it could be just the two of them again, the way it was before everything got so complicated.

They stayed in a motel in Columbus, and the next day he took her to the base and got her a visitor's pass so she could see it for herself. Or not all of it, since she couldn't go into the barracks or the rifle range or any of the other actual training areas. But there was plenty more. The base was a whole city, with streets and street signs and its own hospital and stores and gas pumps. It was already spring this far south. Where there was grass it was green and perfect, as if each blade had been given its own military haircut. The streets were swept and the curbs freshly painted. When Kelly Ann remarked on how clean everything was, Jack said it didn't get that way by itself, and there were three ways of doing anything, the right way, the wrong way, and the Army way.

They went to a recreation center with pool tables and a bowling alley and a bar that served soft drinks, since enlisted men couldn't drink on base. There were other soldiers there with other visitors, moms and dads, but mostly wives or girlfriends and children running in shrieking circles. And since there were women soldiers too, there were husbands and boyfriends.

Jack saw a guy from his company who was there with his wife, so the four of them sat down together in the snack bar and ordered hamburgers and fries. His name was Peterson, and Jack introduced him as Pete, even though his name was really Wayne. In the Army, they hung nicknames on everybody. Jack's nickname was Party.

Pete's wife's name was Lucy, and they were from Texas. Lucy had a beauty parlor hairdo and a red manicure. She was dressed up too, in a skirt and heels and a plaid jacket, and a handbag that matched the plaid. Kelly Ann wondered if she should have worn something other than jeans, since she could tell that at least part of the visit was about showing her off.

But Jack didn't seem to notice or care what she had on, just shoved their chairs close together so he could put a hand on her leg. Pete Peterson said, "So how's it goin, huh, you two finding enough to talk about?" Kelly Ann knew that what he meant was sex. He had one of those Texas accents that made everything sound fake.

Jack said, "Don't you worry about us, buddy. How about you guys, you enjoying the hospitality of the U.S. Army?"

"Lucy here wishes it had more of a resort feel to it. She wanted waterskiing and maybe a casino."

Lucy gave him a drop-dead look. She wasn't doing anything besides sitting there all dressed up and prissy. There was a silence that stretched on and on, then Kelly Ann said, "I was supposed to bring our little girl, but she got sick."

Pete said, "You don't hardly look big enough to have a baby. A shrimp like you."

"Well I did have her. Didn't I, Jack. He was right there."

"Oh yuck."

"They don't have kids yet," Jack told Kelly Ann.

"Nor never will, if I have to watch."

Lucy gave him another nasty look, this one suggesting he wasn't going to get the chance to even start any kids.

Kelly Ann would have liked for Jack to say something about what a wonderful experience it had been, watching his daughter come into the world, because it *had*. But Jack just started in on his fries, as if none of this had anything to do with him. Kelly Ann was beginning to wish she hadn't brought up the subject in the first place. So far she wasn't too impressed with the class of people the Army attracted.

"Now that is one thing I could never do, be in some delivery room," Pete said, twisting his face into a comical expression. "All that blood and gunk coming out of her."

"That's funny talk for a soldier," said Kelly Ann, when no one else would say anything.

"Think I'd rather get shot at."

"I wouldn't want you there anyway," said Lucy, then she closed her mouth for good.

Kelly Ann looked out the windows, where ranks of soldiers in camouflage uniforms were marching right down the middle of the road, like a parade. A sergeant ran alongside, counting cadence. She wished the rest of them would just drop it.

They began talking about the war, about getting to the hot zone. Because after all, that was the main event, the whole reason for the base and the uniforms and the manual of arms and the flags flying and all the rest. She understood that for Jack and the other soldiers, everything else was only talk and waiting around, and nothing else up to now had ever been so important. Not her, not even the baby. Jack said, "Man, I do not want to be in that stinkin place. But if I got to go, I say let's get it over with."

"It's messed up," agreed Pete. "They can't do one thing for themselves. Here we're supposed to be what, the evil empire? And they're the ones blowing everything up."

There wasn't anything more to say to that, since everyone was in agreement. When they were through eating, Jack and Kelly Ann got up to go, and they all said, Nice to meet you, to each other.

When they were outside, Jack said, "Texas," and shook his head.

"I'm glad we're not from there."

They went back to the motel and took off their clothes and lay on top of the covers with the air conditioning turned on high. It was muggy for so early in the year and it felt good to be out of the sun and back in this place that was as much theirs as anywhere else, now that they'd made love in it. Jack said, "Two nights and three days. That's all we got."

"I don't want to be counting," Kelly Ann said.

Once Jack had left the country, there was an anxious time before they heard from him again. Kelly Ann knew that word would reach them if anything truly bad happened, so that no news was good news, of a sort. But it kept her from sleeping, trying to imagine it all: heat and sandstorms and women wrapped up in robes like in the Bible, and the dark, angry men you saw on the television, gathered into furious crowds. She watched for Jack on television too, every time there was any footage of GIs. Now that was silly, but she couldn't help it. Whenever they showed soldiers out on patrol, swinging their rifles from side to side, or speeding along in a Humvee, she tried to see the faces beneath the helmets. After a while she knew she wasn't going to see Jack, but she still paid close attention. She wanted to be able to follow along when he told his stories.

Finally he called, although he called his parents instead of her, and Jack's father had to come upstairs and get her. That upset her but there wasn't an opportunity to say so in the excitement and hurry-up of talking. Jack's voice sounded tinny and flattened, squeezed through a long series of relays until all the feeling was beaten out of it. The parents went into the next room to let her talk, although there wasn't any such thing as privacy. She said that she was fine, the baby was fine. "What are you doing over there, what is it like?"

Because of the long long distance there was a lag or hitch in between saying a thing and getting an answer, so that conversation had an outer space quality. "Ah, it's OK, I guess. Parts of it are really wasted. Blowed-up cars. Blowed-up buildings. What kind of people trash their own country? Makes you wonder. Other parts are nice. Base is pretty nice."

"Do you have to . . ." She wanted to ask if he had to shoot people, but that was probably something he wasn't allowed to talk about, and she didn't want to get him in trouble in case the Army was listening in. "I hope you don't have to do anything real terrible. Or see it either." She didn't want him coming home all crazy and dangerous, like some of them did, because the war had turned them mean.

"Chow's pretty good, for the Army."

Maybe he hadn't understood her. She wasn't going to ask him again. The mother wanted another turn to speak, and Jack was running out of time on the phone, so she told him to please be careful and call again real soon, and he said he didn't know when he could do that but he could probably e-mail.

Hey there,

   I'm kicking back with a cold one just like Friday nights at home the difference is its no bullshit one hundred and five degrees at ten o'clock at night. I have a pretty good adjustment to the heat but its not a natural way to live. Maybe if your born here. Don't worry too much, the guys in my unit are the best there is and everybody watches out for everybody else. Just about every day is something you wish hadn't happened but it is a job like any other, you put your head down and do it. I wish you could send me some sexy pictures of you but I guess not. Tell Tara Daddy misses her lots, you too.

xxxxx Jack

Kelly's father, who had been a Marine, said that even the Army—he always made clear he held it in low regard—would be good for Jack. The service would make a man out of him. It toughened you up and taught you discipline. The bond you made with the men you served with was a blood bond that would last a lifetime. Kelly Ann thought about Pete Peterson and wondered if she was in for a bonded lifetime of him.

She heard something wistful in her father's words, and in the spaces between the words. It was the same for the men down at the VFW. Whatever they'd done in the service, they'd polished it up like a medal. It had been the best part of them, their real and secret life. It was a brotherhood of secrets. And when he came home, Jack would be in on it.

One morning she left the baby downstairs with Jack's mother—Tara had her own crib there by now—and drove to the next county to see Jack's recruiting sergeant. It was summer again, with a red-winged blackbird shrilling from every fence post, and big cotton clouds in a hot blue sky. This time last year, the Army hadn't yet turned into anything personal.

The recruiting office was in a little mall next to a larger mall. There was a manicure place and a phone store and a Chinese take-out and then the recruiter's, like it was just one more thing to buy. Kelly Ann parked and walked in the front door. No one was visible in the front section of the office, which was just a couple of desks with chairs. A movable partition screened off the rest of it, the coffee room and the room where they showed movies of Army life. Posters illustrated different kinds of military missions: the grubby camaraderie of the unit gathered around a tank, the helicopter pilot with his hands steady on the controls, the honor guard standing at attention. In all this there were two women soldiers and three black ones, a proportion that Kelly Ann guessed had something to do with who the Army wanted to attract and who they didn't want to scare away.

She waited, and after a minute Sergeant Crissy came out from behind the partition. "Hi, can I help you?"

She'd been there any number of times, sat there with Jack while he and the sergeant went over all the things the Army would require of him and all the things the Army would shower on him in return. Kelly Ann spoke her name, and Jack's, and watched the sergeant's face register her. "Well sure," Sergeant Crissy said. "If you'd have come in with Jack, I would have known you in a minute. What do you hear from him, everything going good?"

He told her to sit down and he asked about the baby too. The sergeant was tall and well put together. Here in the office he wore green fatigues and combat boots, but when he'd come to the high school he'd worn a dress blue uniform and his service medals. He was the cleanest man any of them had ever seen, clean down to his shoelaces, polished up to his buttons, and all that powerful barbering. They'd all fallen a little bit in love with him on the spot, boys as well as girls.

When they'd finished the small talk, Sergeant Crissy said, "So what brings you down here? Anything I can help you with, anything at all?" The military was one big family, she'd been told, and while she didn't much believe it, she didn't mind making him go through the drill.

"I need some information. About enlisting."

He didn't get it at first, and even when he did he pretended she was joking. "Now why would you want to go and do that?"

"Same reasons as anybody else."

"You're thinking of enlisting."

"That's what I'm saying."

"Well that's something." He was giving himself time to think. "What made you come up with that idea?"

"It's a good opportunity. It's worked out pretty well for Jack, and we could decide if either one of us wanted to make a career of it. We could be stationed together. Not right away, but somewhere down the line."

"What does Jack think about all this?"

"He's open to the idea." She had not yet told him.

"And your little girl?"

"She's good with Jack's folks. One or the other of us could come back on leave from time to time. And once we got stationed together, we could have her with us."

He was too smooth to make fun of her outright. He was going to be patient and reasonable. He hiked his chair so that it was a scant inch closer to hers. He must have become a recruiter because he liked to convince people of things, persuading them with his big handsome head and body. He said, "It's hard on the spouses. Always is. And here you are with a baby. Of course you miss Jack and you want to be with him and this seems like a good way to go about it. But the Army's a lot more than that. A good four years more, if nothing else."

"I remember the terms all right."

"No offense, Kelly Ann, but can you do even one push-up?"

"I can manage." She'd tried and she'd wound up with her face in the carpet more than a few times. But she was getting better. "I can train, just like Jack did."

"Run two miles? Carry a full pack?"

"If you think I can't do anything at all, just say so."

"That's not it."

"What it sounds like."

"Say you go through basic and your AIT, there's still no guarantee you'd be posted anywhere near each other."

"I thought your job was to sign people up."

"Kelly Ann, there's no pleasure or anything else in it for me if you take your oath and then show up right back here after three days."

"How about you just walk me through it."

She made him lay it all out for her, the enlistment bonus, the commitment, the training, the family policies. He displayed the list of lying, glamorous careers open to her: public relations specialist, animal handler, meteorologist, flight medic, intelligence analyst. "What am I most likely to get?" she asked him.

"Troop support. Clerical, maybe. You could end up driving a truck. Or in food service."

"I guess somebody has to do it." She wasn't going to let him scare her off with his dismal talk.

When she left, she had a plastic bag full of applications and brochures, all the slick colored paper the Army printed up to sell you on itself. That evening she dug out her old running shoes and a pair of shorts and drove over to the high school. There was nobody else around. She set her water bottle on one of the bleachers and started a slow jog around the rubber track that circled the football field. In one corner near the fence, a killdeer had built a nest. It ran ahead of her for a little ways, pealing and dragging its wing, to lead her away from the eggs. After the third lap it decided she wasn't a threat and left her alone. Kelly Ann got a stitch in her side after half a mile but she thought that wasn't bad for a start. Nobody was going to expect much of her, and that would be some advantage.

When she e-mailed Jack about enlisting, the answer came back almost right away: "ARE YOU CRAZY????" She knew if she kept at it, she could talk him into it. Of course he'd be worried about Tara, he'd say that a child needed its mother even more than its father. But most of the time Tara seemed to belong to Jack's parents as much or more than to her. It was almost as if she'd had the baby for them and wasn't going to get her back for a while anyway.

Crazy was pretty much what everybody thought, including her father, who was old school about women in the military. Her girlfriends acted like they thought it was a great idea but she could tell it was the last thing on earth they'd do themselves. Their lives were boyfriends and the drama that went along with the boyfriends, and watching the same television shows so they could talk about them, and wishing the world was more like television. They weren't anxious to try any other way of life. Jack's parents went along with it, as they went along with everything, even when it bewildered them. "We sure would miss you, Kelly girl, but you do what you feel is best."

Jack said, "If you end up getting shot or something, everybody's gonna say it was my fault for not making you stay home."

"Unless you shoot me yourself, I wouldn't worry about it." She listened to the click and hum of the long-distance line.

"Since when did you get so willful? I never knew you to have such a hard head."

"I guess it's come on by degrees."

At the end of August, Sergeant Crissy came out to the high school and watched her do the two miles around the track. Then she stretched out her stomach muscles and started in on sit-ups. She did the push-ups last, and by then it was like walking through a wall of fire. Sweat ran into her eyes and blinded her. Her legs were cramping and she was afraid she would throw up. When she finished she rolled over on her side and tried to get breath back in her ragged lungs. Sparks of red light exploded behind her closed eyes.

"All right," the sergeant said. "All right, you proved your point. Welcome to the Armed Forces."

She was set to report on October first, the week after her nineteenth birthday. The summer heat stayed all through September without letup, a yellow furnace that scorched the crops and turned even the shadows hot. One afternoon Kelly Ann drove the small grid of Leota's streets, the baby strapped into her carrier in the back seat. She was trying to imagine missing anything here: the IGA and its window banners advertising lettuce and store-brand cola, the post office, the Farm Service, the beauty parlor where they still did wash and sets, the tavern that opened at 5 a.m. to serve coffee and sweet rolls.

She drove a little distance down the highway to the Sonic, where she could order from the car and not have to carry the sleeping baby inside. She was waiting for them to bring her food out when someone in the next parking space tapped the horn.

Kelly Ann looked over and saw it was Mrs. Jones, Jonesy, her old English teacher, waving away to beat the band.

Jonesy looked like she wasn't going to quit on her own, so Kelly Ann turned the air conditioner on for Tara and got out to stand next to Jonesy's open window. "Kelly Ann, I declare, I was just thinking of you the other day."

"How are you, Mrs. Jones?" Kelly Ann asked politely. Jonesy had been teaching English at the high school for a hundred years. She dyed her hair black and teased it into a puff, and she wore a lot of peasant-style wooden jewelry. She had made them memorize "The Man Without a Country," and "In Flanders Fields." There were so many people, Kelly Ann thought, that she never wanted to be like.

Jonesy was dressed up for school, and she had a large-sized paper cup of something. "I can't believe this heat. I drove straight over here for a root beer float, I had a taste for one. Is that your little girl? Oh, she's just beautiful."

"Thank you. She's mine and Jack's. Her name's Tara."

Jonesy asked how Jack was, and Kelly Ann said he was pretty good so far, and you just had to hope for the best. Jonesy took a pull at her root beer float and the straw rattled in the bottom of the cup. She'd heard about Kelly Ann going into the Army; everyone had heard of it. She said, "I hope it works out for you, dear. I hope it's not too hard on you."

"It's an opportunity to help my country."

"Well sure it is. And to be near Jack. I understand that. You're young, and youth must be served. Did we ever do that ballad in class, the one about the girl who disguises herself as a soldier to go look for her true love on the field of battle?" Jonesy raised her eyes and drew herself up in her seat, the stance she assumed when reciting:

Your waist is light and slender
Your fingers neat and small
Your cheeks too red and rosy
To face the cannon ball.

Although my waist is slender
My fingers neat and small
It would not make me tremble
To see ten thousand fall.

"That's how it goes. There's a lot more, but I can't recall it."

"I don't think we got to that one." Out of the corner of her eye, Kelly Ann saw the carhop coming out with her food. "It was real nice seeing you, Mrs. Jones."

"You were such a good student. You were one of those that made me look forward to class."

"Thank you," Kelly Ann said. Jonesy backed her car away from the curb in another fit of waving. Kelly Ann paid for her food and decided to take it home with her. She was surprised to find a blur of tears in her eyes. Jonesy might be ridiculous, with her rattling beads and her old-fashioned poems, but it was also true that she'd been a good student and that Jonesy was fond of her, and it made Kelly Ann feel bad to be deceiving her along with everybody else.

Because she was like the killdeer, dragging her wing to lead intruders away from her real reasons. Joining the Army didn't have all that much to do with Jack. Her feelings toward him had settled over time. She figured they could pick up where they left off on the other side of the Army, or maybe they wouldn't. Either way, she was going to be a warrior. She was going to have a life worth remembering. The baby stirred in the back seat, waking up, and Kelly Ann spoke to her in the coaxing voice she used to keep her from fussing. There was a moment when her heart misgave her, but she made herself imagine the way they'd stencil her name on her uniform: K. PARDEE. A name she hadn't had before, but now it was out there waiting for her.

THE
FAMILY
BARCUS

For a time when I was growing up, my father liked to see his family dressed in matching outfits. There were five of us kids. Ruth Ann was the oldest, then my brother Roy, then me in the middle, then Wayne, then Louise, the baby. Our mother sewed. She did heaps of mending and alterations—this was long before Wal-Mart or anything like it, long before cheap, nearly disposable clothing—but the fancy sewing was her pride. We had a variety of dresses and blazers in stair-step sizes. There were seersuckers and printed cottons for summer, and a nautical ensemble with sailor collars, and olive drab twills, and snowflake-patterned pullovers for cold weather. At Christmas we were photographed in red tartan pinafores and waistcoats. My mother worked up a skirt for herself of the same material, and a red plaid bow tie for my father. "Season's Greetings from the Family Barcus," our card proclaimed, and the grandness of that inversion spoke of my father's vision for us.

This was back in the late fifties and early sixties, when you could do such things to children without it seeming remarkable. People gave us looks of fond approval as we trooped past in our homemade finery, on our way to church or some other outing. "Step lively there, Barcuses," my father said encouragingly. "Eyes forward, shoulders back. Pick up the pace." He complained that we resembled a straggling parade of ducklings. What he had in mind for us was always more purposeful and robust. I think he would have liked a larger family, six or maybe seven kids. It wasn't so unusual back then, even if you weren't Catholic. But my mother held the line. She had her own powers, of resistance, silence, and obstruction, even as my father issued orders and proclamations.

Ruth Ann was in charge of us during our public appearances, a responsibility she took seriously. Roy challenged her with his strutting and insolence, while Louise whined and dawdled, and Wayne and I plodded on, undistinguished foot soldiers. Ruth Ann was one more person giving me orders, and I resented her for it. She was two years older than Roy and five years older than me. The clothes were hardest on her. Adolescence hit her first, and she suffered public shame. She looked gawky and wrong in my mother's ruffled confections. Girls her age wore madras blouses, narrow skirts, loafers, charm bracelets, circle pins. This was the look she had on schooldays, only to succumb, on Sundays and special occasions, to my father's version of the Von Trapp Family Singers. She wasn't an especially pretty girl; none of us, except baby Louise, gave any promise of beauty. Ruth Ann had long, coarse dark hair that never took to bouffants, small, intent brown eyes, and a lumpy figure. She needed every particle of style she could get. In the family photographs, Ruth Ann is the one looking out from behind her hair, hating the camera.

My father was an only child. His father, my grandfather Barcus, was a carpenter and odd-jobber who picked up what work he could. When my father was seven, eight, or nine years old, there were times when Grandpa would come home and tell him, "Get in the truck, you're coming with me." They'd drive out to a construction site and my father would be sent up a ladder with a pouch of roofing nails and a hammer. Darkness came on while he was still up there. The roof was high, the wind treacherous, the ladder unsteady. Grandpa wasn't forgiving about mistakes. We heard this story from my father often enough, so it must have been a formative, if miserable, experience. "Get in the truck, you're coming with me" turned into one of those catchphrases we kids used when we were horsing around. Grandma was still alive when I was little, although she exists only as a dim, disapproving memory and a smell of Vicks VapoRub. She had come from Finland when she was a girl. The cold glooms of that place clung to her. She was closemouthed and thrifty and her cooking was meager. It wasn't surprising that my father grew up wanting more of everything.

"Your grandparents were fine people," he used to tell us. "But they didn't have much family feeling."

The church we went to was Presbyterian. I'm not sure why. The Presbyterians didn't have any particular denominational flavor to them, at least none that anyone was able to make clear to me. I grew up thinking there wasn't that much difference between the various Protestants, as if they too wore matching outfits. On Sundays we rode to church in a '57 Chevy, sea green, festooned with chrome, pneumatically cushioned, not quite big enough for the four oldest children to sit in comfort in the back.

Ruth Ann tried to hold herself steady on the edge of the seat. She was squeamish about touching thighs with the rest of us, especially Roy, who at twelve was already showing goatish male tendencies. Wayne bounced and squirmed. I was usually capsized into a crack in the seat, my legs stuck straight out in front of me, my feet in their turned-down anklets and patent leather shoes. I hated those shoes. They pulled my socks down at the heels and left me with scabby and bleeding feet.

The back of the front seat was equipped with two plush ropes, attached at either end to accommodate folded coats. Wayne liked to tug and snap at these. "Stop that," my mother said without turning around.

"I'm not doing nothing."

"Anything."

"I'm not doing that too."

"Sit back and be quiet."

"Cindy keeps kicking me."

"I didn't hardly touch him," I said. I was preoccupied by a violent itch within my underpants and trying to rub it against the seat cushion. "It was about a millionth of a real kick. Where did I kick you, huh?"

Roy said, "Hey Wayne, what does *a-s-s* spell?"

"Shut up, poop-head."

"Make me."

Ruth Ann said, "I smell socks. Who didn't change their stinky socks?"

"Naw, that's your perfume," said Roy, to general applause.

"That's about enough," said my father. "Don't make me pull this car over."

This caused us to subside, since the threat of the car pulling over was somehow connected to the wrath of an angry God we heard about in Sunday school. Floods might be loosed, or fire and pestilence. Louise, the baby, sang one of her songs, about the itsy-bitsy spider. It was winter. We wore black-and-white houndstooth-check woolens. Buttoned, buckled, and zipped into our fancy clothes, we gazed out the windows with dull eyes.

But Wayne wasn't through yet. "Why do we have to go to church anyway? It's the boringest thing in the world."

"Most boring," my mother corrected, automatically.

"How about because I say so, and I'm your father."

"Big deal," said Wayne.

My father pulled the car over and shut the engine off. It made small ticking noises as it cooled. Our hearts went quiet waiting.

My father threw his arm across the back of the front seat and hiked himself around. His eyebrows were heavy and dark and at such times they carried on an angry life of their own. "We go to church to honor God and his creation. And because Jesus loved you so much he died on the cross, and how do you think he'd feel if you didn't love him back?"

"Well nobody asked him to," said Wayne in his piping, smart aleck's voice.

There was an awful moment when my father's face went red-gray, like old meat, and anything could have happened, but my mother put a cautionary hand on his arm and he turned around and restarted the car. My mother murmured that Wayne was, after all, only seven. "Yes," my father said. "Traditionally the age of reason, when children were held accountable for their actions, and could be executed for crimes."

We had Spike Jones and Topper on the television, as well as Hopalong Cassidy and Roy Rogers, Zorro, Robin Hood, and Sky King. We sang along to the jingles for Poll Parrot shoes and Ipana toothpaste. I thought Dinah Shore and Loretta Young were prissy and uninteresting, a separate, alien race of unfathomable adult women. But I didn't have much use for Dale Evans either, who never seemed like a real cowgirl, only a kind of dressed-up cheerleader for Roy. The Lennon Sisters, as you might imagine, were objects of special hatred. Sky King's niece Penny wasn't so bad, although she usually needed rescuing and had a pert blond ponytail that my limp-haired, towheaded self could never aspire to. And I was pretty sure I didn't want to grow up to be my mother.

The year I turned eleven, my father changed jobs. For as long as I could remember, he'd worked for Mr. J. G. "Jack" Spratt, who manufactured and sold a line of wood-veneer products. The things you grow up with become articles of faith, pillars of the universe, and so we children all believed in the thrifty, practical virtues of top-of-the-line, superior quality veneer products. Our house was furnished almost entirely with veneer credenzas, bureaus, coffee tables, nightstands, and so on. Our father worked in the front office, doing mysterious office things. He wore a white shirt and tie to work and for special meetings kept a sports coat in a cleaner's bag hanging in the office closet. There was also a showroom, filled with product samples and arranged in room-like groupings resembling a giant dollhouse. We used to love going to the office with our father on weekends and being loosed to run and dodge among the pretend rooms where nobody lived.

Then the air around us changed. Children have antennae that are fine-tuned to the whispered conversation, the low-pitched argument behind closed doors, the rising or falling barometric pressure between parents. "I just don't know," my mother said, and said again, while my father's tone was wheedling or impatient. ". . . always holding me back," we heard him say. "A man could make something of himself, if he wasn't so tied down." My mother replied that he had five mouths to feed and she was all for any plan which included that. Then my father would reappear among us in the TV room and regard us with silent displeasure, while we tried our best to look unhungry.

We began finding brochures lying on the kitchen table, as if by accident, although we knew this was not the case. They had full-color drawings of golden landscapes, soft valleys with orderly rows of crops and fruit trees. Purple mountains, shining rivers. This was the backdrop for tableaux of happy cartoon people. A family picnicked in a green velvet park. An older lady watered her lollipop flowers. A group of men in overalls were building a house out of colored blocks. Above it all, in bold letters, were the words "VITA-JUICE! FOR HEALTH AND WELL-BEING."

Roy caught me standing in the front hall, teasing one of the brochures out of our father's briefcase. I snatched my hand away, waiting for him to send up the cry that I was snooping in Dad's things. But he only snorted. "Vita-Crap. I bet it tastes just like turd juice."

Roy always did have a mouth on him. He usually got away with it, since allowances were made for boys and their imperatives. "What," I said. "What's Vita-Stuff?"

"Dad gave them all our money so he can be a Vita-Juice distributor. It's like Geritol," he added, since I was still confused.

"It's supposed to be good for you?"

"You better hope somebody thinks so," said Roy cryptically. He stalked off and I put the brochure back.

The next week a hand-lettered sign was taped to the refrigerator door, one of my father's executive communiqués:

FAMILY MEETING 7 P.M.
ATTENDANCE REQUIRED

Family meetings were always held in the living room. Like most people, we didn't spend any normal, relaxed time there. My mother had made her most severe efforts at decorating in that room, with matching lamps and swagged draperies and a bowl of sticky wax fruit. My father shooed us all in and surveyed us from where he stood in the clear space between the sofa and the skirted easy chair. He looked to be in a good, if nervous, mood, one hand fingering the coins and keys in his front pocket. "Settle down here, Barcuses. I need your complete attention."

How much of anyone's childhood is spent in miserable sitting, on the receiving end of someone else's wisdom?

My father began by recounting his history with Spratt's, how just after the war Mr. Spratt had begun his enterprise, sensing a burgeoning market, a mighty swell, the growing demand for houses and everything that houses contained. And thanks to this shrewd and accurate judgment, Mr. Spratt had prospered. One had only to look at his spacious and well-appointed home in the fortunate suburbs, his powerful automobiles, the self-assurance that came from the knowledge that his family was well provided for. When a man could seize the tide of human affairs and was unafraid to take his destiny into his own hands and risk all, great rewards awaited.

I was aware of my mother sitting next to me on the couch, her hands folded in her lap, a heap of worn fingers. She had lost another battle.

My father said, "For the last few months I've been in negotiations with the Vita-Juice Company of Rutherford, New Jersey. And I've reached an agreement in principle to become one of their distributors in the Midwest region."

My father paused, as if expecting some response, applause, perhaps, or excited questions. Nobody spoke. The older children knew better, and the youngest were uncomprehending.

My father shifted gears. He began to speak of the benefits of good health, something that we were too young and thoughtless to appreciate. Sure, we had the occasional tummyache or toothache, brought on in most cases by overindulgence. But all in all we were a rudely sturdy bunch, blessed by an abundant diet and first-rate, expensive medical care. It was only when we grew older that we would understand what he meant: the nagging little aches and pains, the unpleasant familiarity with certain of our internal organs. Oh yes, we'd see.

Maybe he didn't use those exact words. It's hard to remember. But the import was, we had benefited from privileges and largesse, and only when they were withdrawn would we cease to take them for granted.

"Vita-Juice is a patented, scientific formula. It was developed to meet the body's nutritional needs and is manufactured under the strictest health and safety standards, made in small batches to preserve freshness. It's invigorating. Appetizing. And available only from your authorized Vita-Juice distributor."

This was the sales pitch. We were to hear it many times as my father practiced his delivery before the bathroom mirror. There was more. Test results that showed dramatic, beneficial increases in memory, digestion, circulation, restful sleep, and energy. (Energy was a big selling point, repeated again and again. It wasn't until years later that I realized Vita-Juice was in part being hawked as a kind of sexual tonic, meant to revive legions of pooped moms and dads.) My father rolled on. He was a good and forceful speaker. It was only his audience that was wrong. With Vita-Juice, one could translate continued good health and mental acuity into the expectation of a longer working career, and a corresponding increase in lifetime earnings. There were other, less tangible benefits, such as serenity, confidence, good will, etc., and though he stopped short of offering the keys to the kingdom of heaven, they were at least implied.

My father reached full stop. Again we were too bewildered and sullen to respond. It was Wayne, finally, who asked, "So where's the juice store?"

"Vita-Juice. There isn't any store. Each distributor sets up his own operation. Inventory, sales, ordering, the works. It's all going to be happening right here at home. Each of you is going to be part of the Vita-Juice team."

"Not me," said Ruth Ann. "I have band practice."

"Track and field," said Roy.

I was pretty sure I didn't want to be on the Vita-Juice team, but I couldn't come up with any good excuses, and so I remained silent. "That's just great," my father said. "That's just the kind of negative thinking and bad attitude that gets you nowhere in this world."

"Dad, I'm first-chair flute," Ruth Ann protested, but my father was already stalking out the door.

Later I sought out my mother in her sewing room. No one has sewing rooms anymore. It was only a windowless cubbyhole, crowded with the heavy-duty Necchi machine, the cupboard filled with jewel-toned spools of thread, pieced-together garments on hangers, the box of patterns, and another for notions and zippers and cards of buttons. She was letting out the hem on one of my school dresses. There was always a worn line where the old hem had been, a dingy equator around my knees. "Why is Dad so excited about this juice thing?" I asked, and she looked at me over a mouthful of pins, trying to tell if I was being a smart aleck.

She considered her answer as she skewered pins one by one into the navy blue serge, then held up a length of rickrack trim around the bruised old hem. I shook my head violently, and she sighed. "Men always need a challenge. They get bored and impatient with things the way they are. It's just their nature. Your father wants to be his own boss. He sees other men running businesses and he thinks he's just as smart and hardworking as they are."

"Well is he?"

"Cindy," she scolded. "Of course he is. He's your father."

We both looked at the neatly pinned hem and its telltale scuff marks. I thought about my father being bored and impatient with us. I thought of him as a boy, sitting at an oilcloth-covered kitchen table, eating his mother's thrifty soup during a silent mealtime. He must have warmed himself with the hope of having a family of his own, and presiding as Head Barcus. There would be high spirits and cheerfulness and good-natured kidding among his attractive, well-mannered children. Somehow he'd gotten us instead. My mother said, "How about if I cut out some felt appliqués and stitch them around the bottom? I could do flowers, different cute flower shapes."

I burst into tears. "Oh honey," my mother said, gathering me to her. "Never mind. I can save it for Louise and make you something brand-new. I could do pleats, maybe, or a little kilt, would you like that?"

But I couldn't stop crying. The sadness had gotten too deep inside of me. That first sadness, which comes from family, and never entirely goes away.

The shipments of Vita-Juice began arriving. In spite of anyone's misgivings, it was a time of great excitement. The products arrived by special freight, and a delivery truck had to back up the driveway, assisted by shouted instructions from my father and Roy. It unloaded a wooden pallet packed with cardboard boxes. Each box was divided with a honeycomb cardboard inset to hold two dozen plastic bottles, like small-sized milk jugs. My father used his pocketknife to slit the cardboard and extract a single bottle, which he carried inside to the kitchen. We all wanted to see it. He shielded it in his hands as if it was a light-producing object, then put it down on the table.

The plastic was cloudy-clear so that you could see the contents. Vita-Juice was a hectic green color, like artificial Easter grass. Darker particles floated in it. Although the bottle wasn't moving, constellations of these darker spots eddied and circled in slow orbits. "What's in this stuff?" I asked.

"Vitamins," my father said. "Vegetable essences." He fetched a number of juice glasses from the cupboard, opened the bottle, and decanted an inch or so of the substance into each. "Go ahead, try it."

Although technically a liquid, Vita-Juice had an uneven, clotted texture. We lifted the glasses and sniffed them and let the stuff approach our lips before it slid back down again. Roy mouthed something behind my father's back that I'm pretty sure was "turd juice." "Oh come on," my father said. "Quit playing around and drink it."

I tried a tiny sip. It tasted grassy, with an undertone of something stronger, spinach or perhaps seaweed. I could see from everyone else's faces what my own must look like: quizzical, puckered, recoiling. "For crying out loud, it's medicine, not soda pop." My father poured himself a full-sized glass and drank it down in one long gulp.

Fearful, we watched his Adam's apple wiggling. He tilted the glass to get the last drops, then set it smartly on the table top. Sweat beaded on his upper lip, but his expression was triumphant.

As always, just when we were ready to doubt and dismiss him, he revealed his powers.

The car was moved out of the garage to accommodate the new

enterprise. My father set up a desk in one corner amid the Vita-Juice boxes. Each day he dressed up just as he had to work at Spratt's, in his white shirt and tie. The bathroom was fragrant with steam and his aftershave. He went out on sales calls, days and often evenings too, anytime he thought he might find a potential customer. He wangled invitations to lodge meetings and firehouses, book clubs and trade shows. Sometimes he took Louise with him, dressed up in her fanciest Sunday outfit, all sashes and lace.

In spite of what he said about us all being part of the Vita-Juice team, the rest of us weren't asked to do anything. Perhaps this was intended as a punishment for our lack of faith. In any case, once the new routine was established, it was almost as if nothing had changed. My father kept busy with work, which as always involved knowledge and decisions of a gravity and complexity that was beyond our understanding. We got used to the cartons of Vita-Juice arriving as deliveries and leaving in the trunk of the car. As always, my mother put meals on the table and kept her peace. Christmas would be on us before we knew; already she was cutting ominous patterns out of green felt. But all of this was overshadowed by a momentous development. Ruth Ann had acquired a boyfriend.

She was sixteen now, and we routinely teased her about the time she spent primping in mirrors and her goopy, giggly friends who tied up the phone talking about who was their favorite Beatle. An actual boyfriend was a gleeful shock. We could hardly believe our good luck in having such a target. At the same time it disturbed us in obscure but powerful ways.

His name was Arthur Kelly and he was in the high school band along with Ruth Ann. He played tenor sax, which wasn't as bad as clarinet or trombone, but not as virile as drums or trumpet.

There once was a couple named Kelly
Who went around belly to belly
And in their haste they used toothpaste
Instead of petroleum jelly.

This was Roy's contribution. I didn't understand it, but I appreciated that it was something dirty. Arthur was a tall, dark-haired boy with white white skin and spreading brown freckles. When he smiled, his gums showed. We thought he was a dork and made fun of the way his cheeks puffed out when he made the saxophone squawk and of the truly icky gesture common to all reed players, mouthing and tonguing the reed as if it was a baby bottle.

It was excruciating for Ruth Ann. We spied on her and mocked her any time she got one of Arthur's phone calls or came home from band practice with her collar looking lopsided and pawed. Arthur didn't have his driver's license yet, so they couldn't go out on real dates. Once that fall the band was playing at a football game across town, a night game, and it was arranged that Arthur's mother would pick Ruth Ann up and drive the two of them there.

It was a big deal, a boy coming to the house for my sister and riding in the back seat of a car with her, even if she was dressed up in her marching band uniform with the ridiculous gold trim and scratchy wool pants. Wayne and Roy and I were beside ourselves. Roy said, "I bet old Arthur's excited. I bet he's trimming his nose hair right now."

Wayne said, "I bet he's practicing his kissing. I bet he's running all over the house, kissing stuff."

"Shut up! Mom! Make them shut up!" Ruth Ann was near tears. My mother had given her a permanent the day before and it hadn't cooked right. Her hair was lopsided and frizzy, and her nose had broken out in pimples. "Mom, I'm not going! I look like a freak!"

My mother soothed her and led her into the bathroom. I snuck in and sat on the edge of the tub to watch. My mother worked brilliantine through Ruth Ann's hair so that it resolved itself into separate, if greasy, curls. She dabbed some dark pink foundation over the pimples and stood back to gauge the effect. "There. Don't you think that helps?"

"She looks shiny," I volunteered from my seat on the tub, and Ruth Ann shrieked and my mother shooed me out.

I rejoined my brothers. Just then my father came in from the garage, where he'd been doing his Vita-Juice work. He looked tired and irritable, as he often did after a long day of Vita-Juice. "What's going on?" he asked, sensing the peculiar energy of the moment.

Wayne said, "Ruth Ann has a date." We heard the bathroom door open. Ruth Ann walked in, her hair flattened and kinked, her face patchy with dabs of makeup. She looked so fiercely grotesque that even Roy and Wayne fell silent.

My father spoke first. "What's this about a date?"

My mother came in, rubbing cold cream on her hands. "She's getting a ride to the game from Arthur and his mother, that's all."

"Who's Arthur?"

We couldn't help it. "He's Ruth Ann's *boyfriend!*" we chorused. Ruth Ann's mottled face turned raging red.

I don't know what we expected my father to do or say, maybe join us in our hilarity, but we instantly saw our mistake. His jaw locked in the fury position. "Since when does she have a boyfriend?"

My mother began to say something patient. My father cut her off. "Where does she know him from?"

"Oh for heaven's sake, Walter, they're in the band together."
My mother produced a comb and attempted to smooth Ruth
Ann's tragic hair.

"He plays sexophone," Wayne offered. It was a joke we'd been
making, although not in our parents' hearing.

My father kicked at a plastic truck and sent it crashing into the
wall. We gaped at him. "How can you have company when this
place looks like a pigsty?" There was a pile of small phonograph
records on the floor, the kind Louise played on her kiddie phonograph, "March of the Wooden Soldiers" and "Lonely Little Petu-
nia in an Onion Patch." He brought his heel down on them and
they splintered. "I want things cleaned up around here, pronto!"

The doorbell rang. We froze, waiting to see what would happen next. Ruth Ann shook herself loose from my mother's min-
istering hand and went to answer the door. But first she stopped
and surveyed us calmly. "I hate each and every one of you," she
said.

Later that night, after Ruth Ann had gone out and returned
without speaking to anyone, I heard my parents talking. The
laundry chute in the basement was next to their closet, and I'd
learned that if I crept downstairs quietly, I could eavesdrop. My
father's rumbling was harder to make out than my mother's
softer tones. "Well if you didn't spend all your time in that
garage, you might have noticed." I didn't hear my father's reply,
but I knew he was saying that he had to work hard, that he only
did it for us and he got no appreciation. "And they'd appreciate
you more if you didn't charge around screaming at them."

My father got up and padded down the hall to use the toilet. I
endured the sound of his falling urine, and the flush, and then he
came back to bed. I heard him say clearly, "Do you remember
how great it was when they were all babies? Each one of them was

like a little ray of sunshine." I couldn't make out what my mother said.

Sunday came around, and I was the first one downstairs. My mother had set out our clothes the night before, so I was wearing an autumn-hued shadow-plaid shirtwaist. It was from last year and my chest pulled at the buttons, leaving gaps. The elastic of the puffy sleeves chafed my arms.

Ruth Ann came down next. She had on a white sweater and a denim skirt. "Aren't you going to church?" I asked.

"Uh-uh."

"Well you better get dressed."

"I am dressed."

"Oh boy," I said.

Ruth Ann went into the kitchen and poured herself a glass of orange juice. I trailed after her. "Dad's going to have a fit."

Ruth Ann pushed the refrigerator door shut. She'd done something bright blue to her eyes. The sweater made her boobs stick out. "I don't care. I'm sick of pretending we're some high-wire act or something, the Flying Barcuses. When I get married I won't even be a Barcus anymore. Neither will you, and neither will Louise."

I hadn't considered that before. "So who would I be instead?"

"That depends on who you marry, dope."

My mother came downstairs then. "Oh Ruth Ann" was all she said.

"Mom, relax, OK?"

The boys appeared next, both in their shadow-plaid blazers. The sight of Ruth Ann transfixed them. "Wow," said Roy, quietly. Wayne said, "Mom, can I wear something different too?" My mother told him to hush.

My father descended the stairs whistling. We waited for the

thunderclap, but he barely glanced at Ruth Ann. "All right, Bar-cuses, let's saddle up." To my mother he said, "Louise needs help with her shoes."

"Dad," Wayne began, in an aggrieved tone, but Louise came clumping down the stairs then in her untied shoes, and my father swept her up and perched her on his hip. "Who's my little pony," he said, flapping his hands and making faces until she squealed with pleasure. "Who's my pony pony pony girl?"

I sat in my Sunday school class, listening to Mrs. Fugate tell us about Jesus speaking with the elders in the temple, amazing them with his wisdom, when he was no older than you are, boys and girls. We slumped in our chairs. We were used to being exhorted to measure up to the overachievers. Brian Billings was playing with himself behind a propped-up copy of *Bible Stories for Young People*. He always did it and everybody else pretended not to notice.

I was thinking about how somewhere out there in the world right now was a boy I was going to have to marry, and a perfectly strange name that I'd have to call myself. At school there was a boy named Zitt and one named Thulstrup, and while I wasn't going to marry either one of them if I could help it, I was left with an unpleasant sense of the possibilities.

I thought about my father too, and if he would ever be happy with us again. Maybe we could get Ruth Ann to go back to dress-ing like the rest of us. We could try harder to get along with each other, stop the fighting and sniping and name-calling, be more helpful and pleasant. Because as much as we might all roll our eyes at our father's generalship of our lives, his rules, his enthusi-asms, his angry disappointments, we could not help wishing to be enfolded in the greater entity of Barcus, stamped with approval and belonging and rightness.

Ruth Ann broke up with Arthur Kelly. She said he was "juvenile," and if there was some new boy she made out with in the practice rooms after school, she kept it to herself. She continued to wear her ordinary school clothes on Sundays and she and my father continued to ignore each other whenever possible. The rest of us maneuvered around them, heading for an exit whenever we were in danger of being in a room with the two of them. All of us wondered what would happen at Christmas, if she'd still refuse to cooperate. There might be no Barcus Christmas card, no wreath of happy faces dressed in holiday colors.

Then, just after Thanksgiving, my father came up with an idea that cheered him. He would construct plywood letters to spell out MERRY CHRISTMAS and display them on the front lawn. It was the kind of hands-on project he enjoyed, and for a week he hauled materials into the garage and filled the air with industrious sawing and hammering. Then he emerged with a flock of enormous letters, three-and-a-half-foot high Rs and Ms and Ss. His intention had been to paint them Christmas red, but the paint turned out orange, and with a peculiar fluorescent cast. Still he was pleased with the results and busied himself with setting things up in the yard, measuring spaces and anchoring each letter with its own built-in stakes and supports. There were floodlights too, so that at night the letters were illuminated, and their giant tilting shadows fell across us as we walked from room to room.

My mother was not happy. She complained that it looked like something a Polish bakery would come up with. My father smiled and treated it as a great joke. The signage seemed to restore his hopeful spirits, bruised as they'd been by Ruth Ann's defection. He took to hanging around outside and waving to the neighbors, who often stopped to chat with him and admire his creation. We children were morbidly sensitive to ridicule, and we suspected that many of these same neighbors went home and laughed themselves silly.

MERRY CHRISTMAS had been up perhaps three or four days, and my father was delighted to realize that only a few more letters would allow him to spell out HAPPY NEW YEAR, and then he would be set for HAPPY EASTER, and so on. We didn't need much foresight to imagine the Fourth of July, and Hallowe'en, and Thanksgiving, and perhaps Veteran's Day and Labor Day thrown in there also. There would be articles in the hometown newspaper. We would never live it down.

But one night as we were just starting our dinner, there was a knock on the door, and a policeman asked my father to step outside with him.

"Sit," my mother told us when we tried to get up and follow him.

"Is Daddy getting arrested?" Louise asked.

"Of course not. Drink your milk."

"I bet it's illegal to have stuff like that in your yard," said Roy, but my mother told him not to be silly.

My father came back inside and sat down. His face was grim, and when we clamored to hear what had happened, he wouldn't say. I looked past him to the front room. The curtains were dark; the floodlights had been turned off. My father filled his plate with salmon patties and creamed corn. We stared at him, stricken.

"Somebody rearranged the letters."

What, what? we all asked.

He didn't want to tell us. "MERRY S-H-I-T," he muttered finally.

I was sitting across from Roy and I watched his face process disbelief, then evil joy, then caution, as my father picked up his fork and began to eat in silence. The plywood letters took up residence in the back of the garage and weren't mentioned again. We never found out which of the neighborhood bad boys had done the deed. But the wicked and subversive among us began exchanging discreet "Merry Shits."

Years later I went to one of those restaurants that revolved on the top of a skyscraper. The gear that made everything turn sent out a rubbing, vibrating noise, faint and nervous-making, that forced you to imagine the mechanism revving into overdrive and sending the whole restaurant—diners, waiters, tables set with white linen, shining glassware, coffeepots—spinning away like a Frisbee. The rotation itself was very gradual. You knew it was happening, you tried to see it, but only when you closed your eyes and reopened them was the movement perceptible. So it was with the world I grew up in, and my father's pride, his buoyant vision, and the inexorable process of change.

But sometimes the world spun hard enough to make you dizzy. We knew that my father's business was not prospering. We could tell from his weighty silences, and the increasing amounts of time he spent away from home, even the occasional overnight trip. He kept having to range farther and farther to sell his product. The problem, I understood from more basement eavesdropping, was that while my father was a persuasive and successful salesman, few people, once they had tried Vita-Juice, were moved to keep on drinking it. Even the weather was glum. The cold settled in early that year. There were mornings of heavy, icinglike frost that made the grass snap underfoot. The old Chevy was still parked out on the driveway. If the temperature was below freezing, it balked and wouldn't start, and my father would have to wait until the day warmed up, or else ask Mr. Schwartz across the alley to come over with his truck and jumper cables.

"What a stupid car," Wayne said, watching my father labor under the hood. "We should drive it to the junkyard and leave it there. Then buy a new one."

"Cars cost money, mister," my mother told him. "Now eat your oatmeal."

"I don't like oatmeal. I want Sugar Frosted Flakes."

"Packaged cereal costs money too."

"Then let's get some more money," said Wayne, nine years old and single-minded.

"We are. I'm going to start working at Nancy's Fabrics."

Wayne and I were the only ones in the kitchen. There was no one else to look at but each other. "Mo-om," I protested.

"It's only part-time. You won't even notice I'm gone. Now that Louise is in school, I need something to keep me busy."

The idea was ludicrous. She was never not busy. "Does Dad know about this?" I asked.

"Of course he does, honey. It's just a little pin money. Your father's the one who holds down the real job. That's what fathers do."

The Chevy's engine turned over. My father waved to us as he backed down the driveway.

My mother worked at Nancy's Fabrics from nine in the morning until three in the afternoon, when Louise's school let out. She said it was a pleasure; the other ladies who worked there were so nice, and of course there was nothing she liked better than sewing, talking about sewing and helping the customers with their projects. But more often than not she came home tired and went into her bedroom to lie down.

The house echoed without her. My brothers held silent, vicious wrestling contests in the living room. Louise trailed me around the house, fretting, and I fed her chocolate milk and graham crackers to keep her quiet. Ruth Ann had band practice and whatever she got into after band practice.

Then one afternoon she came home lugging a guitar case. She refused to say where it came from. She wasn't going to be in the band next semester, she announced. She was going to play guitar instead.

"Rock and roll!" Wayne said.

"Folk songs," Ruth Ann corrected. "Protest music."

"You can't play a lick," Roy scoffed.

"Says you. There's a guy who's teaching me. For free." Ruth Ann slung the guitar strap around her neck and tuned up. She was letting her hair hang long and straight these days. With the guitar on her knee and her hair falling in her eyes and her sullen, intense expression she looked, for the first time in her life, nearly glamorous.

"What about the flute?" I asked.

"You can't sing while you play the flute." She strummed a careful chord and cleared her throat.

In Scarlet Town where I was born
There was a fair maid dwellin'
Made every lad cry "welladay"
Her name was Barbara Allen

She stretched out "maid" so it was "may-ayd." Her voice wasn't terrible, a little scratchy on the high notes, but it was weird hearing her, like watching her get undressed. And not one line of the song made sense to us. Roy said, "I'd stick to the flute if I were you," and Ruth Ann told him to shut up.

Not long after that came a night when I got out of bed in the room I shared with Louise and went down to the kitchen to gorge on leftover tuna noodle casserole. Such secret eating was becoming my refuge and my solace. I had thought that everyone else was asleep, but once I was gobbling out of the casserole dish by the light of the open refrigerator, my father appeared in the doorway, dressed in his bathrobe and pajamas. "Cindy? What are you doing?"

My mouth was full of the cold tuna paste and I couldn't answer. He crossed the room and turned on the small light over the sink. "You know your mother was saving that for lunch tomorrow."

I was too miserable and guilty to meet his eye. I'd reached that pubescent stage where baby fat solidifies, and my father had already made a number of critical remarks about my increasing size. I heard him rattling in the cupboards, then he scooped a helping of the dangling noodles out of the casserole and onto a plate. "Here," he said, handing me another plate. "Don't eat straight out of the dish."

We ate for a time in silence. I have to emphasize how relatively rare it was for any two of the Barcuses to be alone together. My father encouraged as much togetherness as possible. Even if it hadn't been encouraged, the house was small and we were always climbing over each other like a bucket of crabs. We experienced each other mostly as obstacles to be negotiated, or as mouths saying, Me me me. This could not have been the first or only private moment I'd shared with my father. But it's the only one I remember.

When we'd pretty much cleaned out the casserole, I expected him to tell me to scoot on off to bed. But he seemed to be in a meditative mood. The refrigerator motor hummed, then shut off with a thud as he stared into the solid black of the kitchen window. He said, "You kids are lucky that you have each other. You don't appreciate that now but you will. You'll all grow up and get married and have your own families, and everybody will have a ton of cousins and nieces and nephews and aunts and uncles."

"I'm not going to get married," I said. It wasn't anything I'd decided until then. It wasn't anything I knew I was going to say until it was already out of my mouth.

My father gave me a startled, appraising look. "Don't be silly. The right guy will come along, and bells are going to go off, and pretty soon your old dad's going to be paying for a wedding."

"I don't like weddings." I was imagining myself in a big white dress, a church full of people looking me up and down. "I don't want any family. I want everybody to leave me alone."

He was quiet a moment. "You don't mean that. Family is everything. It's our sword and shield against the world. Wait until you really are alone sometime. Then you'll see. You'll want all the family you can get."

But I was tired of being told what I should want and not want. "I'm going to live in a big house all by myself except for a lot of cats and dogs. And I'm going to paint the furniture all different colors. Red and blue and green and white."

My father sighed but his mood seemed to lighten, I suppose because he didn't believe me. He stacked our dishes in the sink and ran hot water over them to soak. "You just make sure you do your homework and mind your mother and be a good girl."

I wanted to be Roy Rogers and Zorro and Sky King. But there wasn't any point in telling him that.

A few days later, he was gone. There was a note on the refrigerator saying he was very excited about exploring new, untapped markets for Vita-Juice and that he would be away for a little while. We'd better mind our p's and q's while he was away. He'd find out if we didn't, make no mistake about that.

It took us a while to realize that he wasn't coming back. After an interval of sorrowing guilt and confusion, we adjusted. My mother got on full-time at the fabric store. Ruth Ann took a job after school and weekends, waiting tables. Roy also found work, bagging groceries at the A&P. Wayne and I did most of the household chores and ganged up to boss Louise around. My father had taken the Chevy but left the cartons of Vita-Juice behind. They stayed in the garage until they began to leak an evil-smelling fluid, and then we threw them out. The matching outfits hung in the back of our closets until we had safely outgrown them.

We got by. There was a way in which we missed our father, but there was also a way in which we could not allow ourselves to miss him. Our lives moved on without him, closed over his absence like water over a stone. He'd given up on us, or given up on himself, and this great sadness and failure was something we had to pretend did not concern us, did not exist.

Wayne drew a Christmas card that year and put it on the refrigerator door. It showed a deep blue night with an incongruous rayed sun in the center, and off to the side, a slim crescent moon and five little lopsided stars. Even when he was not among us, my father took up all the space in the sky.

LOST

I was twenty years old and about as pretty as I was ever going to be, although I didn't know that yet. I had long long hair, all the girls did. Mine was nearly down to my waist. It swung across my back like a bell. I had nice legs. There was always some boy I was crazy for, always trouble with some boy. There was never any useful purpose to it. I could never figure out what to do with them, besides wanting them to distraction. I was working as a counter girl in a photo studio and going to school part-time. I went to school mostly so I wouldn't have to say I was just a counter girl. But school wasn't that important and neither was work. They were only the background for the main business of my life, which was to have exciting things happen. That was me back then.

A black-haired boy on a motorcycle turned around to stare at me as he rode past. He kept his head swiveled around for most of a block. It was almost comical, like a cartoon where someone smacks into a lightpost with a lot of exclamation points. Of course he didn't crash, just kept going until he was out of sight. I'd never seen him before. He looked like a pirate, with that head of black hair and his black mustache and beard. The way he stared burned through me. You think it has to mean something, a moment like that, and sometimes it does.

I met him two or three weeks later. I'd asked around, I knew a few things about him by then. He'd been in my mind, the way that something not yet real occupies space in your head and takes on different, agreeable shapes. I'd been thinking about him and the next minute there he was, like a magic trick.

I was sitting in the school's Commons, the big hangout spot in the basement. There were people who never seemed to do anything else besides sit there. They'd hold court at their favorite tables, little groups of them engaged in lounging and spite and the other minor vices. Outside it was September, still hot, with a polished sky and color in the trees. But down in that basement it was always lurid midnight on some seasonless planet. Unhealthy yellow fluorescent lights turned the air intense and artificial. You have to realize how much people smoked back then. Curtains of smoke wavered and reformed, like the currents of talk and gossip, everybody watching everybody else, eyes like smoke, wandering everywhere.

The black-haired boy was tall, he had that tall kind of walk, all long legs. He came across the room to sit down across from me. I forget just how we started talking. He was older than I'd thought, a few years past me. He had blue eyes with a black rim around the iris. I'd never seen eyes like that before and I haven't since.

After a while he said, "You should come for a ride on the bike with me."

"Maybe sometime." I was pretending not to be that interested. I had a paper cup of something melted down to watery sweetness, and I tipped the cup so the liquid touched my mouth, though I didn't drink.

"How about now? Come on."

Around his neck he wore a bullet with a hole drilled through it, threaded on a rawhide lace. I'd never seen anything like that either. Oh my heart was a monster. It roared and showed its teeth. Back then I wanted what I wanted when I wanted it. I still do, I guess, but now I've learned that I can't necessarily have it. And so I stood up and walked out with him.

Everybody watched us go. I knew he had a girlfriend, or an old girlfriend who wasn't quite gone yet. I knew who she was, a blonde with one of those naturally expressionless faces, like a cat's. They had some long, messed-up history. I had a boyfriend, sort of, one who came and went. And now here we were, giving people a whole new story.

I tucked my hair into my shirt collar so it wouldn't blow around wild. I climbed on the back of the bike like I'd been doing it all my life. That big loud engine started up beneath us. He drove fast, showing off. I held on to him hard. And even though holding on was one purpose of a ride like this, I wasn't doing it for show. I felt dizzy-sick. The realness of what I was doing caught up with me. I had to remind myself that the road flying away beneath my feet wasn't moving at all. And the sky was the sky. And this boy whose face I couldn't see was only going to be a stranger for a little while longer.

We rode out past the straggling ends of town, where there were little shops for auto parts and furniture repair. A grain elevator. A cemetery looking lonesome. Here and there were islands of trees, and maybe a few houses, some half-built subdivision rearing up through the flatness. But mostly it was farm fields and ditches full of zigzag weeds. A rail line ran parallel to the road, banked high above us on its gravel bed. A tractor churned through the fields, knocking over cornstalks and stripping the land down to its hard skin. I leaned into that boy and felt him lean into me. I squeezed my eyes shut against the wind and looked out through my eyelashes. Although it was a fine bright day that showed everything in its best light, the only thing beautiful out there was us.

We turned around and headed back into town, as if we'd proved some point about there being nothing we wanted in that direction. The boy—or was he a man, and how did you tell the difference, one more thing that thrilled and scared me—asked me where I lived, and I told him. Boy or man, they were all so dumb, in some ways. I already knew very well where he lived.

I had a place of my own on the third floor of what had once been a stately home. A turret grew out of the roof. There was a big sagging front porch and bits of frail, lovely stained glass above the transoms. The landlord had crammed a lot of cheap plumbing and fixtures into every available corner and chopped it up into rental units. You could lift the linoleum of my kitchen floor and see the lights shining in the apartment beneath. There was a bathtub that felt like getting into a coffin. The stove gave off a smell of gas. The rent was fifty-five dollars a month. It was my first real place. I loved that it was shabby and odd and had walls painted crazy bright colors and was more like a treehouse or a sailing ship than a normal house.

I led that boy up my stairs. I wanted what was going to happen so bad, I couldn't stand the waiting. In some sense I wanted it to be already over and done with. I closed the door behind us and we kissed standing up, and then we were on the bed. We lay side by side, touching each other through and under our clothes. There wasn't time to think about anything, no voice that comes in and reminds you, Pay attention, this is your life happening.

Next there was the awkwardness of getting out of our clothes. It's funny how being naked is almost less embarrassing.

His skin was both white and ruddy and I tried to see as much of him as I could before he got himself on top and inside of me.

That's how we began and that's how we finished, though for a while in between he rolled me up to kneel over him so he could watch me work. And then we were done with that and later I went down on him and he said, "That was the best one of those I ever had." And I know there's a difference between fucking and love, a good fuck and true love, at least, I know you're meant to think there is. I know all the serious, cautionary things you're supposed to say. I know you can have one without the other. But even so. They're both about wanting and finding, wanting and finding.

Then we lay in bed and talked. It was our first normal conversation. He told me he was twenty-three. He'd been in the army, enlisted for the reasons young men usually do, that is, to measure themselves against something big, and to get their growing-up accomplished. He'd been to the war and come back, one of the lucky ones. (This was the ugly, misbegotten war of our time. It was every bit as bad as you've heard.) Now he was in school again, trying to be serious about it this time. There was a sunken place along his arm about the length and width of a pencil, a war wound. If I wasn't a goner already, that would have done it for me right there.

I told him about myself, or whatever version of myself I was laying out at the time. It wasn't dishonesty. I just wasn't sure of anything beyond the kind of facts you could put on a driver's license. Was I smart or dumb? Pretty or plain? Brave, or just crazy? The different pieces of me skittered around too much for me to get a fix on them. It got to where I didn't much like to try. So I just said, "Oh, I guess I'm like everybody else. Your average basket case."

"You don't really believe that."

I looked at him, propped up against the pillows, the arm with the bullet scar stretched out behind his head, and the bullet around his neck. This time yesterday we hadn't yet spoken one word, and here he was with opinions. But I thought he was probably right. I didn't think I was like anybody else.

When it was time for him to go we kissed some more and grinned at each other. It was all too nice to mess up with saying too much. I watched from my window as he walked out to the street and got back on the bike and rode away. I know he knew I was watching. I made the bed and put on some music. I forget what song it was, it didn't much matter. It was one of those times when music pulls the heart out of you and takes it on a sweet ride, and maybe you sing along and think you sound great.

A couple of days later my boyfriend, not that he ever wanted to be called that, came by. I didn't like it when he just showed up and hung around waiting for me to guess his various wants and needs and then do something about them. He was a silent, gloomy boy. Over time we'd stopped having fun and were down to irritable sex. This day wasn't any different. We got smoked up and then we went to bed. It was no big deal anymore. Afterward I was in a hurry to dress and start doing something, put dishes away or straighten books, because I didn't want to lie next to him in bed.

He got up too, and dressed, and said, "So what's going on?"

"What do you mean?" Although I knew exactly what he meant.

"With that biker guy."

"He's not a *biker*. Not like that."

"Well what's the deal?"

I said, "I don't know." And I didn't. I wasn't planning anything out, including what I said next. "Look, maybe we shouldn't do this anymore." I'd just fucked him good-bye, though I hadn't known it at the time.

"Fine. Great." He was pissed off, he said some things about sneaking around behind his back and I said no, it had all been pretty much right out in the open. And since when did he act like he cared about what I did or thought or wanted? Did we ever talk about anything, even the basics, like Let's let's not fuck other people? Hell no, because he didn't want to embarrass himself, didn't want to pretend we were anything important, didn't want to be bound by anything resembling a rule.

I'd saved all this up to tell him. I laid it on him and he didn't have much to say back and finally he slunk away. Even though I was through with him, I thought he should have tried harder to talk me out of it. Then again, trying harder was the part he could never bring himself to do.

This was what I knew about the blonde girlfriend with the face like a bored cat's: they went to high school together, right there in that same town. There was some high school stuff between them. Then when he got out of the army they'd started up again, moved in together. Her parents were religious, Baptist I think, and they'd squalled and threatened and made for a lot of drama. Then she wanted to go to California, and so they did, and while they were out there she broke up with him, reason unknown. And (this was the part he told me later) he crawled into some kind of black hole. Depressed, broke, lonesome. Days he never got out of bed. Drinking. Suicide thoughts.

I admit, I had so much crude and awful vanity, I wished it was me, that I could make someone suffer like that.

And then I guess the blonde changed her mind, about California, about him, and they came back here, and broke up, and renegotiated, and broke up again, but never entirely. It was a Situation. He told me the next time I saw him. Full Disclosure. Truth in Screwing.

"Just so you know," he said. We were in bed again and we'd torn the place up. Literally. One of my old bedsheets had given out in the middle of us carrying on, and we'd put our feet through it and torn a big hole. We thought that was so funny. We laughed and howled and kept at it until the sheet was only ragged ribbons.

But now we had to quit being funny. I said, "What am I supposed to know, exactly? And what's she supposed to know?"

"I didn't tell her about ..."

"No. I guess you wouldn't."

He said, "I don't know what I want anymore. I used to think I did."

"You just mean you want more than one thing."

He looked unhappy. I knew this much about him by then: that he had a store of tender feelings, that he didn't like to think of himself as dishonorable. I said, "All right, now I know. Cheer up. You look all tragic."

"I don't want to do this to you."

I made a joke out of that, how I was pretty sure he wanted to do it to me, but I knew what he meant. We were already stuck in some trouble, like a fly in the last gluey inch of a honey jar. I decided I didn't want to make a scene. Scenes were not acceptable. None of us back then liked to think of ourselves as hung up on jealousy and possessiveness, which were equated with materialism and bourgeois values and all things bad about the old order. It was an attitude my sad-sack now-ex-boyfriend had taken to extremes. The ideal was to be free and honest and open and careless. It worked about as well as you'd expect.

I reached for the bedsheet and tore a big strip off the end and made another joke about how he was going to have to buy me a new one and all the while another voice in me said, Murder murder murder.

He said, "It's not like her and me get along that great. We fight a lot."

"About what?"

"Stupid stuff."

"Like what?" I could tell he didn't want to talk about it, but I wasn't going to let him off the hook. If I was going to have the blonde crammed down my throat, I wanted the goods on her.

"Like spending money or being on time or being late or who didn't clean up their mess."

"Oh, wife stuff."

"I don't have a wife."

"You might as well."

He was getting mad. I didn't care. Mad was probably what I wanted right about then. I said, "Yeah, I guess that's what happens when you're together a long time. You turn into Ma and Pa. Not that it's such a bad thing."

"Cut it out."

"The wife, now, I bet when you talk about sheets, it's a conversation about fabric softener."

"Not funny."

"So, life between the sheets. Tell me about the ups and downs. The ins and outs. Ins and outs, that's funny, isn't it? Where's your sense of—"

"Shut up."

"Make me."

He was on me that quick. He pinned me so hard I had trouble drawing breath. "Wife," I got out in a choked kind of voice, just to taunt him, and he wrestled me down and lord he was strong, I might have been created for the express purpose of being a weak thing he could use his strength against. He eased up and let me breathe again. He wasn't trying to hurt me. But I was trying to hurt him in any way I could, and I'd already used up words so I was left with fucking, with opening my legs around him and taking him in and punishing him with how good I could make it, how hard and fast he'd have to want me.

And when we were done it was as if we'd been through some ordeal that had ended happily, rescued at sea after days adrift, or plucked out of an avalanche. My God, we said, and kept saying, and there was a lot of kissing and we both got a little weepy-eyed. When he had to go he told me not to get up, that he wanted to keep looking at me just as I was. And so I stayed right like that, naked in the middle of the ruined sheets. This was who I was turning into, the girl you came to when you wanted to wreck things.

I know for a fact that I went to school, went to work, wrote papers, talked with friends, did normal life things. But all I can really remember of that year is the time we spent in bed. The weather turned cold. We had more clothes to climb out of now, and I piled quilts on the bed. I said, "I'm never really warm unless you're right here with me." The sky was gray and bulging and a steady cold rain rattled the panes of glass above our heads. I made us tea with hot milk and it was nice being there together, and not worrying about anything outside. He said that school was going all right for him, he wasn't quite as dumb as everybody said, and I told him who was everybody, what did they know.

I touched the scar on his arm. The tip of my finger slid into the groove of puckered flesh. "Did it hurt?"

"Not right away. That's shock. You have to figure out what happened first, then it hurts like sin."

"Tell me."

He started talking in the careful way of a story you've told before, following the trail of words you've laid: "We were on base. People don't get shot on base. There's a secure perimeter, and razor wire, and sandbags, and all the ammo in the world. You get so you think nothing bad's allowed to happen. You forget, the whole point of the damn war is anything can happen. One second I'm standing there drinking coffee, the next I'm in the dirt. Timber. And everybody's shouting and kneeling over me and I still don't get it and I turn my head—"

I watched his head on the pillow incline toward the arm with the scar. His blue-black eyes had the memory in them. I thought if I watched his eyes long enough, I might get inside the memory too.

"—and here's this piece of my arm not there, and guys calling for the medic. It was some kind of weird good luck the bullet knocked me down. The bastard was aiming for me. If he'd had another shot, he might have finished me off. No, we never caught him. You never saw who was shooting at you. Sometimes you'd see guys get hit and you could tell, they didn't know they were dead yet. It all happened that fast."

We both lay quiet for a while, thinking how strange life was, the bullet that hit him and the bullet that missed, all so he could end up a world away, in my bed on a rainy afternoon. I put my head against his chest and listened to his heart speak its one word over and over again, alive alive alive. I said, "I bet you were a good soldier."

"Now how would you know that."

"I guess I can just tell things about you."

He was quiet for a moment and I knew I was right. Whatever he set out to do, he wanted to be purely good at it. In one sense, he was a soldier all his life. He said, "It was a really stupid way to get shot."

"I don't think there's any smart way." Neither of us was a big talker, but there were times we could say things and have them land in the right place.

We didn't do any more talking about the blonde girl. Sometimes he was with me and sometimes her. It wasn't much of a secret anymore. On occasions I'd see them together down in the Commons or on the street. I hated that girl, but even then I knew there was something formal and technical about certain kinds of hating. Sometimes I wonder how her life turned out, if she kept finding people to love her. That's how it is for some girls. They never set foot beyond a certain boundary, an idea of themselves as precious commodities, and everything follows from that.

It was past Christmas but still winter, a time of year that has no excuses for itself. The weather of the world matched the weather down in the Commons, and I spent a lot of days in that stale, used-up air, studying or not studying. Everyone I knew was holed up in there, smoking and waiting for life to land on them. Come spring a lot of them were going to graduate in spite of themselves. The boys were worried about the draft. Nobody had any such thing as a job offer, or any intentions of finding a real, grown-up job. My friends were English majors, history majors, poets. They prided themselves on not being useful. They had plans to go to Europe or California or maybe Japan. Or they were going to buy farmland and live in stoned harmony with nature, or do something beautiful and artistic and not care about money. But I think we knew without wanting to admit it that a lot of things were coming to an end, including that kind of aimlessness.

If I walked into the Commons and the black-haired boy was already sitting there with the other girl, I ignored them and took a seat on the opposite side of the room. They'd pretend not to notice me. It never worked in reverse, me with him, and the blonde walking in to encounter us. I don't remember ever seeing that girl out anywhere on her own, as if she was a doll that had to be taken down from a shelf.

But on this particular day I was feeling mean and resentful from another session of work, where the boss gave me a hard time just because he could, and school, where I was made to feel unimportant in other ways. I was tired of chapped skin and of the lumpy winter coat I'd worn every day for weeks—it was beginning to look like some unclean animal—and of picking my way across icy crudded sidewalks to get to places I didn't really want to go anyway. I walked into the Commons and there they were, him reading a newspaper with his long legs stretched out, her tearing crumbs off a roll, making a mess of her food until it wasn't anything you'd want to eat.

It wasn't any different from any other time I'd seen them together, but it was one more time. And on top of everything, or maybe it was at the bottom, I guess I was mad at him, the way you build a mad out of all your unworthy grievances. A friend of mine was sitting at the far end of the same long table, and my friend waved and said, "Hey, come on over, grab a chair," and so I did.

I didn't say hello or even look at them. I launched into an unnaturally natural, vivacious conversation with my friend. Right away the blonde girl got up and walked over to the women's bathroom. She stayed in there a long, long time. I know that mercy and charity and forgiveness and all those soft virtues have value, and the world is a better place for them. But there's nothing like the rush of pure righteous triumph you get when a rival won't stand their ground.

By the time she finally came back and sat at the far end of the table on my side, there were a couple of people who'd filled in the space between us. The black-haired boy asked her if she was all right, and she said yes, in a whiny little voice, and I hated him for asking it like he cared and I hated myself for going along with this messed-up deal in the first place.

It was the end of playing fair, or maybe there had never been any fairness in it. I wanted to do something horrible. I looked over the heads of the people between me and the blonde. I said, "You know who I am, right?"

She didn't turn my way. She still had that plate of picked-apart food before her and she stared into it like it was a face staring back. I said, "This is so stupid. Really. I quit. He's all yours."

There was enough noise at the table, three or four different conversations going, that no one else had paid attention to me at first. Then they got a whiff of what was happening and they all quieted down. Now I had to keep going. "You can tie him to the front porch so he doesn't stray. Whatever."

She got out of there fast. Scooped up her coat and flew. I waited for him to go tearing after her so they could have one of those big reconciliations they were so good at. I didn't care what happened anymore. Everybody was watching us. Waves of watching spread out from our table across the room. I guess I'd had to say things in front of other people so it would be for real.

He took his time getting up and he didn't say anything, which I guess disappointed the crowd but didn't surprise me, none of this having much to do with words in the first place. But he gave me a look and the look said, *Is this how you want it?* And my eyes said, *Yes. No. Yes,* and he walked out but through another door, and I left a little while later, all three of us going off in different directions.

I wish I could say that was the end of it. The big scene, the clean (or jagged) break, the gradual return of clearheadedness and self-respect, the lurking regrets and shames and then life moving on to the next absorbing challenge. It wasn't that way. The very next day I went to his place, where I'd only been once before—the fear being that the blonde girl might stop by—and that's why I went there now, to kick all that caution in the face. I told him if it was finished he had to tell me now, right here. And I'd meant everything I'd said, and nothing could be the same. He only had one room, a little space for a bed and all the rest, and he paced it from one end to the other and said I wanted him to say things he didn't mean, and I said no, feel free, tell me she was prettier, sweeter, whatever more than me, I could handle that. He said it wasn't like that but he owed her something after all those years, he had to be loyal, and I had myself a laugh over his idea of loyal. It was one of those fights that are about everything all at once, with no rules or boundaries, and you end up fucking just to put an end to argument.

And in spite of everything he might have promised or I might have threatened, eventually we went right back to the way things had been. Sometimes I could feel almost philosophical. It was nobody's fault that there were two of us and only one of him. Weren't there places in the world, times in history, where this was how people arranged things and everyone was happy about it? Or was it only the way men wanted it and the women were bullied into going along? I guess you'd have to be a cow not to care, some big calm slow-moving animal who didn't much notice what was going on back there. Sometimes when we were in bed I'd try to lift myself out of my body and be that animal, reduce everything to matters of sweating and friction. But it was nothing you could pretend your way out of.

The weather turned warm in a hurry that year, and in my

memory it's as if we went from ice storms one week to bees and white clouds and new grass the next. I know that's not true, but I know why I see it that way, because the end was coming up fast even as it seemed like a beginning. He and the blonde girl had one more enormous, pointless fight and finally wore each other out. It seemed I'd won through arbitration, or by process of elimination, but I was too happy and greedy to care. If there's ever been a time in your life when everything was perfect, you know you can't really do it justice, can't get inside it. It's like looking at someone else's vacation pictures. But I will say I stood in front of a grove of flowering trees, although I don't remember where, and the trees were an explosion of pink and white blossom, although I never knew what they were called, and it's true my mind was probably bent around some drug at the time, but I thought if I died right there and then, it would be all right.

And that would be a good place to end a story or a life, except nothing ends that pretty. When someone says, We have to talk, it's nothing you want to hear. He told me the blonde girl was pregnant. I asked was she sure, and was he sure, meaning, sure it was his. He said yes and yes. He wouldn't sit down, as if standing was some kind of penance, and he looked sick and shaken but I had no sympathy for him.

"How could you let this happen?"

"Nobody let it. It just did."

"She did it on purpose."

"You don't know that."

"I know I'd never do this to you. Make you be with me because of a baby."

Because I knew he was going to do the upright thing, take her on as an obligation if nothing else. I was crying by then. "You should have met me first."

He didn't speak. We both knew there was no point in wishing or unwishing things, but I said, "It should be me you can't leave."

"Yes. It should be you."

He walked back down my stairs and I covered my ears so I wouldn't have to hear the exact moment when he wasn't there anymore.

I had to get to work only a little while later and so I wrung out a cold washcloth for my eyes and put on my counter girl clothes and walked downtown. When I opened the door the owner put on his annoyed face, ready to start in on me. The owner was a middle-aged man who limped from childhood polio. He was short and rat-nosed and bald except for a slick of rat-colored hair, and when he was angry about something, which was most of the time, his upper lip would draw back and twitch in a way that could scare you. He said, "Let's check that attitude at the door."

"What attitude?"

"None of your backtalk, missy. How about you quit the princess act and get to work now."

"Don't call me missy."

He stopped shuffling his way toward the back room and turned around. "What's that?"

"Don't call me princess either."

He limped over to me and his lip was doing that twitching thing again and he wasn't any taller than me so our eyes were dead level. And because he was ugly and unlovable and in pain, all the things I felt myself to be, I said, "This is a crap job to begin with and your nasty mouth's the worst part."

He was shaking so hard I expected to see parts of him spin off, his smeared glasses, maybe, or his percolating forehead. I wanted him to hit me so I could hit him back, but he just told me to get out, and I did, and there I was back on the sidewalk, not two minutes since I'd gone in, and a job was one more thing I didn't have anymore.

School was done for the term, and although I could have found somewhere else to work, there didn't seem much reason to do so. My rent was month to month. There was nobody to tell me not to leave town. I decided I would move back home to my parents' house, take whatever dose of disapproval they'd dish out— as long as I was in school they'd been able to tell themselves I still had potential—and find another crap job that might pay a little better. Out of my group of friends, I was probably the first to give up on all that vague, splendid ambition.

I was leaving town in two weeks, and then it was one, and then it was down to days. I'd already told him I was moving and I watched him say that maybe it was for the best, and I agreed, and that was our story and we were sticking to it. But the night before I left town I called and begged him to come see me one more time, and if there's a more abject word than *beg*, that's what I did. Please, I said, and he said he wanted to as bad as ever but it couldn't happen, the baby changed everything, and Please, I kept saying, and finally we knew who we were. Me who put nothing above the wanting, him and his soldier's honor.

I used to have an album with a picture of him in it but I lost it somewhere. It was a picture I took of him standing next to the motorcycle in his beat-up boots and jeans. His arms were crossed and his chin was up in a tough-guy stare and he wasn't smiling but the second after I snapped the shutter he did, and that's what I remember now. The smile, not the picture.

The blonde girl never did have the baby—it was another thing lost—though I didn't ever learn the whole story. Time went on and he married someone else and then unmarried them, just as I married and unmarried. He had his kids and I had mine. He was married again when he died, yes died, in one of those stupid freak accidents that you think nobody ever dies from, like a giant wave sweeping you off a cliff, or getting struck by lightning. He'd moved to another state so the news didn't reach me right away, and because there was the wife I couldn't be part of any official mourning. He went fast. His heart stopped speaking and I imagine he didn't even know he was dead.

Over the years I'd heard from him now and then, a card or a letter. It was nice that he did that, kept in touch in a friendly way. Once he wrote and told me he was going to be visiting the city where I lived. But he had one of the wives in tow and she was funny about old girlfriends, who could blame her, and he didn't know if he could get away. There was a night when the phone rang late—I was already in bed—and I listened but nobody spoke into the machine and I didn't get up to answer. He told me later that was him. Now if a phone rings late at night when the house is dark, he's who I think of, although I know the dead don't make calls, at least not in that way.

I'm older now than he was when he died. Things happen to the body over time that are God's practical joke, and I don't much like this face I've got now. My life turned out pretty ordinary. Not great, not awful, I'm not complaining. Nobody looking at me now would guess there had ever been anything wild in me, anything as desperate as that loving. I know we're meant to grow from experience, like a tree, send out roots and branches of wisdom and patience and understanding. But my best and truest self was a tree in blossom. All those years since, there's a sense in which they count for less, even as they take up space, crowd out the past. That quick, there goes your life, like a black-haired boy on a motorcycle, looking back until he's out of sight.

THE
INSIDE
PASSAGE

You had to be ready for the bears, the photographer said. You had to be sharp. He pointed to a spit of sand at one end of the cove. They would camp there, he said, out in the open. Sleep away from the cook fire and seal the food. Use a rattle along the trails so the bears knew you were coming. That wasn't all you needed; they had a rifle strapped in with the rest of their gear. The rifle didn't look real to me, although I knew it was. It could have been a child's toy. If I ever saw a bear it probably wouldn't look real to me either. It would eat me up while I was still thinking none of this was happening.

The boat's engines slowed to an idle. I looked around me and I thought, this was wilderness. The water snaked between gray cliffs five hundred feet high, sheer rock at their tops, spruce and hemlock around their knees. Glacier country, not so long ago. Small waterfalls fell over the cliff face like knots of lace. I said they were "spectacular." Oh yes, said the photographer knowledgeably, but the trick was to make each shot different. After a while, a waterfall was a waterfall. He had done this sort of thing many times before. He was a famous photographer, I could tell that, even though I'd never heard of him before. He and his assistant would spend four days in the wilderness, camping and taking pictures. They wore orange Gore-Tex jackets and pants, and they carried tents, maps, a first aid kit, freeze-dried food, a cookstove, and of course the cameras and lenses and tripods and film, all trussed up in waterproof packs. I liked the idea of carrying everything with you, of not needing anything you couldn't carry.

The captain of the boat helped them launch their yellow rubber raft. The water was dark green and glossy, like a polished stone. The boat reversed course and, looking back, you saw the colors, orange and yellow. Then a shoulder of rock cut them off. I was only in the wilderness on a day trip, a few hours out from town. A part of me would have liked to stay there with them. It was the closest you could come to being nowhere at all.

Back in Ketchikan I tried to call Mac from the hotel lobby. I called his office. Both his wife and his secretary knew who I was, but the office seemed safer. I used someone else's credit card number. It was not the sort of thing I usually did. Mac was not the sort of thing I usually did either. I'd overheard an old woman giving the number to an operator two days ago. She said it extra loud for the operator to hear, like it never occurred to her there were people like me in the world.

The connection was clear. Sometimes you got a good connection, sometimes it was pocked with static and echoes and odd metallic whooping, as if you really were calling from nowhere at all. The secretary answered. I pinched my voice through my nose. "Mr. Mackenzie please."

She asked who was calling. I said, "Northwestern Mutual Insurance." I was proud of that one. I figured I could be an insurance company a few more times at least.

The secretary said she was sorry, but Mr. Mackenzie wasn't in.

The secretary was nobody's fool. She didn't like me. She was a fifty-two-year-old divorcée with daffodil hair and poison green eye shadow. She had two daughters, also divorced, who lived with her. I guess there was no real reason for her to like anyone. I hung up the phone. I thought the secretary would know it was me and wouldn't put my call through. I had to tell Mac I had run away to Alaska. It wasn't any good being here if he didn't know.

I walked outside, down along the waterfront. Everywhere you looked was water and spruce-covered peaks. Tiny floatplanes took off and landed in the channel. They looked too small and wobbly, like something out of an old Buck Rogers movie. I had never been to Alaska before. I'd come here because I had the luxury of going somewhere exotic to be miserable. I was going to take the ferry on the Inside Passage, from island to island up and down the Panhandle to see what I could see.

Ketchikan was the first stop. So far I'd seen totem poles, and the old whorehouses, restored and prettied up for tourists, and a stream full of enormous black salmon, grazing in the water like a herd of cows in a pasture, and the lumberjack bars that filled up by nine a.m. I hadn't really met anyone, unless you counted the photographer. I was trying to get used to solitude. I allowed myself two or three conversations a day, the same way I allowed myself meals.

The next morning the police came to my hotel room. It was another thing that was not usual for me. There were two of them, a ladycop and a man, standing in the hall. She did all the talking. There had been an armed robbery across the street and the robber had run into the hotel. Was anyone staying in the room with me?

None of this was really happening. Oh no, I said. It was just me. A robber in the hotel? Was it safe here? Good gracious.

Yes, they hoped it was safe, said the ladycop. They were here to make it safe. She was young, with her hair screwed up in a twist, and a tough little face. She reminded me of Mac's secretary. Was I sure no one was staying with me?

The night before I'd met a man in a bar who said he had cocaine. He came up to the room, and when he kissed me I tried to tell myself that it was like waterfalls, after a while a man was a man and there wasn't any difference between them. But what had come out of my mouth was No, and he went away. Now I thought someone had seen him, or maybe he was the one who sent the police here to get back at me. I was thinking about the phone calls too, the way you think about things like that when the police come. I said, Mercy me, a robber. I surely hoped they would catch him and bring him to justice. No, no one else was here.

The ladycop was losing patience with me. Maybe I was over-doing it. She would have liked to arrest me for something, I could tell. The other cop hung back, as if he were bored or embarrassed or maybe just trying to get the right angle to look inside the room. They could only see a little ways behind me. There was plenty of space to hide a man, if I'd had one.

When she asked me a third time if I was staying here alone, I affected a look of shocked prissiness and said, Heavens to Betsy, I certainly hoped they caught that fellow. They went away then. I sat on the bed for a long time. I guess a woman alone is always suspect, always an adjunct to some man. I would have liked to tell someone how well I'd handled things. I wondered how close I could get to trouble, bears, cops, men, without actually being in trouble. This was a dangerous place to be for somebody like me who had come here for the express purpose of messing myself up.

Before the ferry left Ketchikan I tried to call Mac again, from a pay phone on the street. I dialed the number of a bar where we used to go, and asked for him. I heard laughter and the music of ice cubes before the bartender came back to say he wasn't there.

The ferry was blue and white and clean-looking, big as an office building. People drove cars right into its belly. People had kayaks, bicycles, dogs. Once again I felt underequipped. Cabins were expensive, so I slept on the floor of the lounge. The solarium and the observation deck were full of campers, kids who pitched tents and played guitars and smoked dope all night long. I could have joined them, but I was too busy being alone and tragic.

The only person I would have talked to was the Solitary Traveler. That's what I called him. He looked even more alone than me. He was an old hippie with gray hair down to his collar, a green army surplus parka, and lumpy boots. Little bits of fringe and leather sprouted from his clothes. He sat by himself on a deck chair, smoking a long curved pipe. He sat and smoked and watched the sun go down behind the blue-black hills, and he didn't need one thing from anyone. I wanted to talk to him, though I knew I wouldn't. Where was he from, and where was he going, I'd ask him.

No place in particular, he'd say. No place in particular, coming and going. How about yourself? A woman like you shouldn't be knocking around these parts alone.

I can handle it, I'd say. I can handle most things.

Tough, eh? Come to Nome with me, where men wear guns on their hips, like the old West, and the sidewalks are built of boards, and everyone's running from something. Come to Kotzebue or Disaster Creek. Ever drive the Alcan when the gravel runs out? Ever camp on pack ice at minus thirty? You can be just as tough as you want to be.

Excuse me, I'd say. I have to make a phone call.

I got off the ferry in Petersburg the next morning. Petersburg was this fishing town founded by Norwegians. I heard some tourists complaining that it was not as Norwegian and picturesque as they had been led to believe, and you couldn't buy anything Norwegian. There was a blond here and there, and a few of the downtown buildings were painted with hearts and birds and flowers. That was all. There were a lot of big fish factories and canneries in Petersburg and now, in the summer, crews of kids worked there, living in campsites outside of town. On their day off they all hiked into the Laundromat to wash the fish guts out of their clothes. The tourists contemplated them glumly, their cameras sagging around their necks.

I got sick in Petersburg, a fever and a cough. For three days I stayed in a hotel room drinking a bottle of cheap brandy and trying to call Mac. No one bothered me. It was the weekend so I called him at home, but his wife always answered. Once when I called I was an old woman who had reached a wrong number. Once, and this was the best or worst one, I said I was the hometown paper, and did she want to subscribe. I thought she'd say no, because I always did when I got calls like that, but when she said yes, I had to go ahead and pretend to sign her up.

Mac's wife was a tiny girl with long limp hair falling into her eyes. The one time I met her, at a party, she made absolutely no impression on me. That was before Mac and I began anything, so I didn't have to feel melodramatic about her. At the party Mac's wife drank diet soda and got into a lengthy conversation with the host about the merits of electric bug zappers. Of course I wondered what Mac saw in her. For a long time I wondered what hidden charms or powers she possessed, but I finally figured it out. She was his advertisement to other women: I am available for screwing around.

I thought I could handle it. I thought I was tough and reckless and wild, a real old sourdough. I had handled it pretty well while it was going on, but not now, when it was over, coughing up snot and brandy into a dead phone. I was losing track of who I was pretending to be. I packed up my bag and tottered down to the ferry terminal to wait for the next boat.

I'd missed the scheduled ferry while I was sick and no one knew when one would come through again. Things were like that in Alaska, hit or miss, as if they were too far away from the rest of the country to be bothered by the usual urgencies. I sat in the weeds outside the terminal, waiting. The fever made the sun blare down too hard and everything tilt in odd directions. I talked to a man waiting for a ride back into town. I was talking to him because he was short, though I didn't tell him that. I figured short men were safer, if you had to talk to someone.

I traded him the telephone credit card number for some dope, and we sat in the weeds, smoking companionably. He had a cheery, handsome face, and he wore a plaid shirt and khakis. He looked out of place, like a fraternity rush chairman gone wrong. He'd been bear watching at the town dump, him and a friend, and they'd spotted two. I asked him what the bears looked like.

"Disgusting. Like anything looks when it's going through garbage."

His name was Willy and he was from Connecticut. He was going to Denali, Mount McKinley, hitching the Alcan. He wanted to see Eskimos and glaciers and whales. He wanted to see everything. When he'd used up half his money, he'd turn back. He thought. "Sometimes I'm afraid if I go too far I'll just keep going. End up in Japan or somewhere, you know?"

Willy had been camping out with the fish factory workers, but that was getting old. Those jokers thought it was great to cook fish over a campfire and eat it with their bare hands. As bad as the goddamn bears. If I ever came to Connecticut, I should look him up. If he was there, that is. He knew some pretty nice restaurants. We'd have ourselves a real dinner.

I said I'd do that. It seemed like a good-enough plan to me. When his ride came he hiked off with a jaunty wave. I was trying to get used to people coming and going, popping up and disappearing so fast.

The ferry came at dusk. I stood on the deck and looked around me. It was like no place I'd ever seen. The sky was a bowl of stars held in by the black shapes of the mountains, and the harbor was a pool of the last sunset, and the lights of the little town glittered. I was thinking it didn't have to be so bad, being here. That was a new thought for me. I went down to the ship's purser and bought a bed for the night.

What you could buy cheaply was called dorm space, one bunk in a four-bunk cabin. There were only three of us, me, Vivian, and Rose. Vivian was getting off at Haines Junction and driving a pickup truck to Valdez to meet her husband, who worked on the pipeline. Vivian said it *VAL-dez,* which I guess is how it's supposed to be pronounced. She said she hadn't seen her husband in eight months. I said she must be pretty excited about seeing him.

Vivian shook her head. "Eight months. What kind of marriage is that? I don't know anymore. You ever been to Valdez? They had them this big earthquake. Everything got smashed and they built it up again all trailers. I'm going to drive seven hundred miles to live in a trailer with what's-his-name. I just don't know."

I liked Vivian. She told me all this about five minutes after she met me. She had red hair done up in one of those curly, architectural styles. I was thinking about the photographer, who had a wife but didn't see her much because he was always away taking pictures of mountains and deserts and jungles. I thought about Mac and his wife, and what kind of a marriage was that?

The other woman, Rose, was a lot older. She had white hair cut straight across her forehead, Buster Brown fashion, and she wore plaids and heavy shoes and spent a lot of time brushing her teeth. She had an accent I thought was German, but it was really Scottish. This was a terrible boat, she said. The engines were noisy. The lounges were too crowded. Last night in the cafeteria they had served a really unspeakable piece of veal.

And so on. When she marched off to take her evening promenade of the decks, I asked Vivian if Rose always had this many complaints.

"Since Seattle," said Vivian. "Every blessed day."

"Where is it she's going?"

"Nowhere. She got on in Seattle. She's going to the end of the line, then turning around and coming back. I don't think she's been off the boat for two hours total."

I said it was a shame that Rose wasn't having a better trip.

"Are you kidding?" said Vivian. "She's having a ball. The time of her life. Some people just got weird ways of enjoying themselves."

I climbed into a top bunk and slept like the dead. Except I had a dream about Mac. I dreamed he was someone I didn't recognize. That is, he came up to me on the street and said, Hello, it's me, I love you. But I didn't know his face; he could have been anybody. It's me, Mac, he kept insisting, and I was embarrassed, the way you are when you can't remember people. I love you too, I said, but he could tell I was only being polite. There was a horrible jarring noise. Oh, that's the earthquake, said Mac, or the fake Mac, conversationally. I opened my eyes. Rose was thumping from the bottom bunk, telling me we were in Juneau.

I said good-bye to them both. Rose warned me about taxi drivers and unclean restaurants. Vivian said, "I wish I was going with you. You know what they say about Alaska. Ten good men for every woman."

"Vivian, you're married, remember?"

"Sure. I got this great memory."

The first thing I did in Juneau was try and call Mac. The dream confused me. I thought I had it backward, that if anything, Mac would be forgetting me. I thought something must be horribly wrong and the dream was a psychic signal. I called Mac at work and the secretary answered. Of course he wasn't in.

"This is Dr. Valdez's office," I said. "When could I reach him?"

The line crackled. I imagined the secretary squinting through clouds of cigarette smoke, like a dragon guarding the telephone. The secretary smoked cigarettes that came in long pastel boxes and had snazzy, upbeat women in their ads, the kind of women neither of us would ever be. Look, I wanted to tell her. It's me. You got me. I give up.

The secretary said she thought Mac would be in at three o'clock. That was something to go on. Maybe I fooled her and she figured a doctor, she could listen in and hear something personal and embarrassing.

Juneau was a real city, the capital, with buses and office buildings and even a four-lane highway. It made you feel like Daniel Boone coming into town after a long tramp through the territories. I had some time to kill before I called Mac again, so I took a bus to the glacier. You could do that here. They called it the drive-in glacier and it was just a few miles out of town. I thought I would phone Mac from the visitors' center there. Where are you? he'd ask, and I'd say, On a glacier.

But the bus took a lot longer than I'd thought it would. We

passed a shopping center, houses, a used car lot. It was like a bus ride anywhere, except we crossed a stream so thick with salmon they looked like a wallpaper pattern. When the bus let me out there was still about a mile to walk, and you were still nowhere. All I was thinking about was calling Mac. I could see the glacier up ahead in the notch of two mountains. It looked like dirty snow. I had half an hour to find a phone, I figured.

But when I got to the glacier there wasn't any phone. The visitors' center was the rustic kind, with plaques talking about eskers and lateral moraines and outwash plains. There was a nature trail and a telescope. I was really upset about the phone, like, who ever heard of a glacier without a phone? Right outside was the glacier, like the screen of a drive-in movie a mile and a half wide. The ice was gray and black and crumpled. It reminded you of an old sheet of aluminum foil. The glacier wasn't doing anything at all. It was just one of those things you were supposed to go see, like the Eiffel Tower in Paris. I turned back the way I'd come and stood by the side of the road with my thumb out.

An old man in a big clean car picked me up. I said I had to call my doctor before he left the office, and he could drop me off at the shopping center.

The old man said he always hated to see a girl out there hitchhiking. It was dangerous, there was no telling who you might run into. "I live just down the road a little ways. Not even five minutes. Come home with me, you can call from there."

I looked at him. He wasn't ancient old. He was maybe sixty. He had a wedge of crimped, sandy hair and a pink face collapsing in on itself, and he was dressed like a sporty old man, in checked trousers and a knit shirt. He could have been anybody.

"No thank you," I said. "I could be on the phone for a while."

"I'll be there a while. I go home for lunch. Every day, that's what I do. You hungry? Ham sandwiches."

"The shopping center's fine."

"Five minutes away," he said. "Then I'll take you back to town. Drop you anywhere. I run an upholstery business right downtown."

I thought of calling Mac from the old man's house. Where are you? he'd ask, and I'd say, At an upholsterer's. "It's long distance," I said.

"Talk all you want. What's a few phone calls, what does that cost anybody? Sometimes people just need to talk to each other."

"Turn here," I told him. I had my hand on the door. I figured if I had to, I would open it and kick my way out.

"You girls," he said, sighing, making the turn, coasting up to the shopping center. "One of these days you'll end up trusting the wrong person."

Mac's phone was busy for twenty minutes. When the line was clear the secretary told me he'd gone for the day.

I saw the Solitary Traveler again in Juneau. He was down by the waterfront smoking his pipe, just like before. I was still too shy to talk to him. Where have you been? I'd ask him, and he'd say, Prospecting. On Gold Creek, halfway up the mountain. I'm staking a claim.

But the gold's gone. It's been gone for years and years.

Just because you can't see something doesn't mean it's not there.

The mines closed down, I said. The prospectors went broke.

He shook his head. There's times that people ignore things right under their own noses.

Like what? I said. What things? But he was blowing blue pipe smoke. I couldn't get him to say any more.

There was a place in Juneau where you could buy phone calls, a store that sold phone calls. You paid them to dial the number for you and you sat in a little booth and talked. Travelers used it, and the Mexicans and Filipinos who worked on the big cruise ships, lining up to call home. Two young guys ran the phone call store. I told one of them that I wanted to talk to my ex-husband but I didn't want to talk to his wife. Could he place a person-to-person call for him, and if he was there, let me talk?

The phone call guy got into it. "What name should I use?"

"It doesn't matter. Anybody."

"I'll be Bruce Wayne," he said. "You know, Batman. We'll flash him the old Bat-Signal." He was really into it, and he seemed like a nice guy. I felt sort of bad about telling him the ex-husband story.

So Bruce Wayne called Mac at home, but Mac had just gone out. Mrs. Mac didn't know when he'd be back. No, he couldn't be reached at the office and she didn't know when he'd get the message.

"She's a real sweetheart," said the phone call guy. "What's she got going for her, she rich or something?"

"Something," I said. I liked him. I thought I would have liked to get to know him better, if it wasn't for the effort of being in love.

I took a southbound ferry to Sitka. The boat was almost empty and I sneaked into a cabin, one with a real bed. Nobody seemed to mind. I still had the brandy bottle. I drank a big slog from it. I wondered what Mac was doing right then, right that minute. I thought if I tried hard enough to see him, I could. It seemed you ought to be able to aim desire like a lens, and pass your longing straight through it. Maybe I was simply out of range.

I put the cap back on the bottle. It seemed like a good idea to save some for later and besides, no one would know or care how drunk I got.

Sitka had been the Russian capital of Alaska. It had a fort with cannons, and a Russian cathedral, and women who dressed up in costumes to do Russian dances for tourists. I took a limo van from the ferry into town, and I asked the driver if the Russians had made much difference. He shrugged and said not so you'd notice, but they had killed a lot of Indians.

The hotel this time was sort of creepy. Nobody seemed to be staying there except me, and a couple of old men watching TV on a plastic-covered couch in the lobby. A sign by the front desk said that showers could be rented by the public.

But the room did have a phone. I called Mac's house. I hadn't figured out what to say this time. I was tired of having to make everything up. When Mac's wife answered I didn't say anything at all.

"Hello," she said. "Hello?"

The line whooped and crackled. I couldn't think of one thing to say. If I'd opened my mouth the only thing that would have come out would have been some kind of animal noise, like a dog baying at the moon.

"If this is Sheila," Mac's wife announced, "you don't have to bother calling anymore. He told me all about you. I found the apartment key. It's all over and we're going on with our lives. I think you're pathetic. Plus a few other things."

I put the phone back quietly. My name wasn't Sheila, and I didn't have an apartment.

I walked outside. It was raining, the misty, constant rain that people in the Panhandle called liquid sunshine. I had a fold-up rubber poncho that came down low over my forehead and smelled like the inside of a shoe. I went to see all the Russian things. I went to see all the Indian things. There were still plenty of Indians around, the Tlingits. They were pretty much like everybody else now, after having been beat up by so many white armies. There was even an Indian center set up to teach them how to be Indians again and do things like beadwork and wood carving.

I walked down to the waterfront. The sun was coming out behind the veils of rain. The light came through in rainbow smears. Little islands like separate countries dotted the harbor, and at one end was the extinct volcano, Mount Edgecumbe. This was the Pacific Ocean, I told myself. This was beautiful. I was trying to make myself feel the right way about something for once.

Someone tapped me on the shoulder. I had to fight my way past the poncho to turn around and see. It was Willy from Connecticut. He said, "You know what's out there? Japan. It's a straight shot."

"I'm leaving tomorrow," I said. I'd just made up my mind.

"Leaving? For where?"

"Home. The Lower Forty-eight. The Outside."

"So we'll go out tonight," said Willy. "Live it up. See the sights. This is like fate, you know? We were fated to have dinner."

I told Willy I'd meet him later. I went to the airline office and got a flight to Seattle the next morning. Everything was really over now, I told myself. But it didn't feel over yet. I went back and forth calling Mac names and calling myself names. *Chump. Stupid idiot. Prick.*

I met Willy in a bar where you could watch the sunset over the harbor. "You shouldn't be going into bars by yourself all the time," said Willy. "I worry when girls do that."

"Chivalry is horseshit," I said.

"Aren't you sweet."

"I can't help it. I'm in love. I'm in love with a jerk."

"Is that what's eating you? Listen, love is horseshit. Back in Connecticut is this girl. Talk about love, you can't imagine two people more in love than we are. I mean, it's perfect."

"So what are you doing here?"

"Because sooner or later we're going to have to get married. You know how miserable that's gonna be? Man, it'll be a piece of work. Wretched! Big-time suffering! I don't want to spoil things yet."

"So why get married?" I said. "And by the way, this really isn't helping to cheer me up."

"Everybody gets married," said Willy with conviction. "Everybody's gotta bite the bullet."

We had dinner, Italian, and a bottle of red wine. The food was Alaska prices, that is, it would have been just about as cheap to go to Italy. Willy wouldn't eat the salad. "They put sulfites on everything here," he said. "Somebody told me. That lettuce is probably three weeks old. Eat enough sulfites and your body gets artificially preserved. Archaeologists will dig us up in two thousand years and say, 'These people knew the secret of embalming.'"

I liked the dinner and the red wine. I thought I owed myself one genuine good time in Alaska. "Come on," said Willy. "I'll show you a bar you shouldn't go into by yourself."

"I'm getting tired of hearing that crap," I said, but I went with him anyway.

The bar was down on the waterfront, low-ceilinged and smoky. There was a big ship's bell at one end of the room, and a harpoon and moose antlers and that sort of thing on the wall, all these manly artifacts I guess women were supposed to be afraid of. When I walked to the bathroom the men all cleared a path for me, like the Red Sea parting. It felt good having them watch me. I pretended they were all Mac, and none of them could have me.

Willy and I sat at the bar next to an Indian woman who said her name was Leonora. We shook hands all the way around. Her hand was small but she had a grip. Leonora was about forty, maybe, it was hard to tell. She had one of those great Indian faces, broad and smooth, that creased one way for smiles and another way for frowns. Leonora bought us drinks, whiskey. She said we should drink to friendship. I thought she was drunker than we were, but as time went on it was hard to tell. "Is he your boyfriend?" she asked once, when Willy couldn't hear.

"Who, me? Nope," I said. "No boyfriend."

"He's a cute little thing," said Leonora. She craned her neck trying to look for him and her eyes crossed. "Makes you want to take him home and put him on a shelf or something." I wanted to tell Willy there were some bars he shouldn't go into by himself.

Later Leonora asked me what I'd been doing in Alaska. "This and that," I said. "Being a tragedy queen, mostly."

"Say what?" The bar was noisy.

"Doing some sightseeing."

"She's in love," volunteered Willy. "And she's pissed off about it too."

"No I'm not. In love I mean. I just decided."

"Well good for you," said Leonora. "Love. What's that, just something you hear come out of the radio."

"Willy's in love too," I said. "But it doesn't bother him much."

"You're still cute," said Leonora.

"Everybody thinks I'm cute," said Willy.

I was trying to remember being in love. I knew it hadn't been that long ago, probably sometime before I got drunk.

I shook hands with Leonora again. I shook hands with Willy. "Have a good life," I said. "Watch out for the bears."

"He's a teddy bear," said Leonora.

"Everybody loves me," said Willy.

The Red Sea parted for me again. I couldn't tell anymore if the men were staring at me or not. Back at the hotel I set my alarm for six a.m. and hit the mattress hard. The phone rang. It could have been two hours or two seconds later.

In the dark I knocked it to the floor. The phone was singing a song. "One lil two lil three lil Indians," it sang. "Four lil five lil six lil Indians."

"Willy?" I said. "Where are you?"

"Downstairs," he said. "Heap big fun."

"Let me talk to the desk clerk," I said. The desk clerk was laughing his ass off. "Get my friend a room and put it on my bill," I told him.

The clerk said he'd be happy to oblige, but in fact he needed cash. I shoved my nightgown into my blue jeans and started downstairs. I figured I was still drunk. The lights in the hall were like an old horror movie, dripping with shadows. Willy was glad to see me. He tried to hug me but he missed by a mile. "Where's your backpack?" I said. "Where's Leonora? Never mind."

I paid for the room. The desk clerk thought this was all the funniest thing he'd ever seen in his life. He was an Indian too, a young guy. "We're getting married," Willy told him.

"Just give me the key," I said. I steered Willy down the hall to his room and wrestled the door open. "Here," I said. "Sleep it off. Wake up happy."

Willy fell into my neck. "This is the part where we make love," he informed me. "It's fate."

I was drunk but he was drunker. I pushed him inside and

threw the key after him. Short men really were safer. I started back to my room. One of the old men from the lobby was behind me, rattling a key ring. He must have been the janitor. "How's the heat in that room?" he asked me.

"It's fine."

"You want, I can fix that heat."

"Get lost," I said, slamming the door. There was no chain lock. I lay down to sleep on the floor with my feet up against the doorknob. I picked up the phone. It stretched just far enough. I dialed Mac's number. "Hello," he said, sounding sleepy.

"I just wanted to tell you I'm in Alaska," I said. "And I can whup any two-legged or four-legged varmint in the territory. It's all over between us."

"Lady, you got the wrong number," the man said. "I don't know what time it is in Alaska, but it's five ayem in Missoura."

"Sorry," I think I said, and fell asleep with the phone in my ear.

In the morning I felt bad, but I could have felt worse. The night clerk was still downstairs. He started grinning the second he saw me. "Here," I said, handing over the rain poncho and the brandy bottle. "Give these to my friend, if you see him. If you don't see him, give them to somebody else." From now on I would carry no more than what I needed.

It was only six thirty, but the airport was hopping. Everybody in town was there, it looked like, all the cabdrivers and bartenders and Indians, drinking coffee and eating sweet rolls and carrying on, a party. Everybody seemed happy, wide awake, like they got a big kick out of getting up early, like watching the sun rise was one hell of a good time. It was too soon to decide if I'd had a good time in Alaska. Some people had weird ways of enjoying themselves.

HOLY
WEEK

Arf arf arf. It had been that kind of day. Olivia Snow, hugely pissed, rancid with ill will toward the universe, sat in steamy traffic, laying on the horn. If she were a dog, she'd bite. Some kind of parade was blocking the intersection. Incredible. The universe was hating her right back.

Cars idled or nudged uselessly sideways. But there was an alley up ahead and if somebody would just get it together to turn, or let her squeeze in there, she might reach home before her car overheated. She honked again. Bow wow wow. It felt good to be making her angry noise. They'd tried to make her cry again at work. Ha ha. She was president of the Bitch of the Month Club. The Breaker of Balls. They hadn't laid a glove on her. Still, it had taken its toll. Her head was full of slag. Her neck had turned to lumber. The city sunlight took on a fermented look, bleary and thickened. She needed a drink. She needed a bunch of drinks.

Olivia craned to see the parade itself: a line of people hoisting things over their heads, statues, she thought they were, statues winking with gilt, wreathed in flowers. The marchers wore costumes of the flapping, drapey sort. She had no clue. Then she remembered. Holy Week. Holy Week in Pilsen, and the Mexicans were dressing up like Christ and scourging themselves.

Of course there would only be the one Christ. Everyone else was an apostle or a mourner or a jeering throng. Olivia eased off the horn. What was the point? Traffic had stopped to watch the show. Here were some men in fake beards and gold crowns. Patriarchs of the Church? The Magi? No, those were the Christmas guys. Here was a squadron of women dressed all in black, a suffering sisterhood. She should get out of her car and join the procession. Throw a shawl over her head and beat herself with a rosary. Make a complete spectacle of herself.

Defeated, she switched her engine off and watched the parade's progress, its reverent ebb and swell. Maybe she could be Mary Magdalene. Except there was probably a lot of competition for the part, getting to look bad and willful, like a cosmetics model. Olivia read somewhere that the Bible did a number on Mary Magdalene. She wasn't a whore at all, just another uppity woman who got a subpar job evaluation from the guys who ran the office. The goddamn office. She didn't want to think about it. She couldn't help thinking about it. The place was a stadium for championship dick-waving contests.

Oh but here was Christ! Bare-chested, crowned with real-looking thorns, his expression all pallid and swoony. The cross bumped along behind him in top-heavy fashion. It looked like it had some real weight to it, and Christ was a little too short to be hefting the thing. But then, wasn't pain the whole idea? Two Romans in fierce headgear and scarlet tunics stomped along on either side, sneering and coiling whips. The woman in blue was the Virgin Mother. Had to be. Don't even get her started on the Virgin Mother. Immaculate Conception. Please. What was wrong with these people?

She didn't have a particle of religion in her. Catholic, Mormon, Lutheran, Jew, whatever. She had no clue. Her parents had been hippies given to mushy transcendental thought. Olivia's own daughter, Roberta, had lived through her childhood in a similar unchurched fashion, although that had more to do with absentmindedness than with policy. Olivia was just as glad to have missed out on sin and guilt and piety, but sometimes it put her at a disadvantage. She didn't understand the mindset, God and all. She thought that things were funny when apparently they were not. It was as if she'd been brought up eating with her hands and had to learn about silverware. She bet the guys in the office were all churchgoers.

The parade was breaking up now, everybody heading off for the final gala, the Crucifixion. Simulated, one hoped, though Olivia remembered news accounts of Christs in more fervent countries who actually had the spikes driven in. As if you had to fabricate suffering in this world. The car ahead of her moved forward. Now here was a religious experience. Acceleration!

At home, she dumped her coat and bag and kicked her shoes into a high arc. They landed with a clatter, scaring the cat. She was getting too old to wear heels. Her feet were growing strange knobs, like potatoes left too long in the pantry. She took off everything elastic and pinching—hose, bra, underpants—and walked around for a little while, naked and flabbily self-conscious. She remembered when naked had been a lot more fun. Then, because Roberta and her boyfriend were likely to come in at any time, she put on her old rag of a bathrobe and mixed a pitcher of margaritas. She had a sudden taste for them. Something about Mexico.

She sat at the kitchen table and looked out the window, three flights up, with its view of alley and sooty rooftops and the Chicago sky which even when clear was the color of bathwater. The people across the way used wadded bedsheets for curtains.

Never once had she seen those windows open to the light. The first year she and Roberta lived here, they'd amused themselves by imagining lurid goings-on inside. Now it was just one more unremarkable weirdness. They were going to fire her ass. She didn't want to admit it, but it was coming up fast in the rearview mirror. They'd never liked her much to begin with, and now the veneer of civility, and even indifference, had worn off. They were laying the groundwork. Silky inquiries about her client list. Suggestions, reminders, admonitions. Kissed off, axed, outsourced to some twenty-two-year-old in New Delhi.

She knew her products cold. Everyone acknowledged that, even the jerks. And she was good with clients, did follow-ups and problem solving. She had real relationships with them, not the usual salesman glad-handing bull. One more thing the boys gave her grief for. Today it had been Harris, a kid who probably still got pimples. He'd overheard her on the phone with one of the clients who was having allergy troubles, had hung in her doorway, grinning—she could never decide if these guys were rude on purpose, or if they were ignorant of manners—while Olivia commiserated and suggested remedies. "Wow," Harris said, when she hung up. "What do they call you, Mother?"

"Is that your suit, Harris, or your dad's?"

"Ha ha. Seriously, you waste too much time on these people. Too much of the warm fuzzy stuff."

"And seriously, Harris, you should start shaving. Even if nothing's growing in. Toughen up the skin a little. See if it doesn't help."

Harris muttered something under his breath.

"Didn't quite catch that," Olivia said. "Did you say 'lesbian'? Do you even know what that means, Harris? How about 'vagina'?"

Harris had showed his teeth in an ugly way and taken himself off. She hadn't always been like this. Hostile. At her first jobs she'd been a nice girl, brought cookies to the office, remembered her coworkers' birthdays. It got you nowhere. There were too many nice girls out there, answering somebody else's phone. Now she had attitude. She stood up for herself. She talked back. She took no shit. She was mean as a snake. She tilted her glass back, tasted salt and tequila. Snake food.

Feet on the stairs. The front door opened and Roberta and her boyfriend Larry made their skulking entrance, moving sideways, like a couple of cats. "Hi baby," Olivia greeted her daughter. "Lare."

Larry let a couple of vowels escape his mouth. Roberta said, "Hey Mom." She spoke in a series of exhales, as one succumbing to a great fatigue. Not talking was a teen thing.

"You guys hungry?" Chipper, perky tone, as if she was just taking trays of oatmeal cookies out of the oven. "There's probably something to eat around here. Snacks."

"Maybe a little later." Roberta slowed her pace and she and Larry tangled knees. An almost visible hormonal charge, like static electricity, passed between them. Roberta was a short girl, busty and ripe-bottomed, with white-blonde hair worn in a dandelion fluff. Her eyes were made up with a lot of silver and black. Her beautiful slut daughter.

Poor Larry. He wasn't going to be able to keep up with her for very much longer. The only thing he had going for him was that he'd been her first. He was a furtive boy—but then, all boys his age struck her as furtive—with dyed black hair shaped into a neogreaser forelock. He was narrow-chested and his hips were so skinny that they seemed only a kind of attachment mechanism for his penis. These were not motherly thoughts.

Olivia tried again. "Or I could get takeout. I was thinking bar-becue."

"Yeah, barbecue's good." Roberta continued down the back hallway to her bedroom, Larry stepping on her heels. They had not actually stopped moving since they entered the apartment. A slow-motion beeline for the bedroom. The door closed behind them and their music came on, lots of boom and growl, turned up high to cover the sounds of sex.

Olivia found some tortilla chips and shook them into a bowl. Celery and carrot sticks, prepackaged. String cheese she had to pry out of its plastic skin. The assemblage looked almost healthy. She ate a celery stick and thought about calling Marlon to see if he wanted to go out a little later. She felt both tired and restless. It wouldn't hurt her to get out of the house, hang a good time on the end of this befucked day.

Marlon was her sort-of boyfriend. He wasn't reliable enough for an upgrade. He was older than Olivia, forty-eight to her thirty-six. She thought that explained the sex part of things, how he wasn't all that interested all that often. The penis was a kind of rare orchid that stopped unfurling somewhere between Larry's age and Marlon's. Or one of those old-fashioned window shades that lost its zip after you yanked on it too many times. Or maybe it was the drinking. Marlon drank too much. Well so did she. Probably. She couldn't say she got all hot and bothered these days, not the way she used to. Hormones were draining out of her. No more Magdalene.

She dialed Marlon's number and spoke to his answering machine. "Hey. Me. Call if you want to head out for a drink. No, call anyway."

He was probably still at work. Marlon was a subemployed

musician. He played jazz piano as part of an ensemble that made fitful appearances in small clubs. For income, he worked odd hours, in bits and pieces, in a sound studio, processing homegrown commercials for car dealerships and retirement communities. He lived in a friend's basement, he just got by, he would never make a name for himself, and none of that seemed to bother him. Olivia couldn't decide if Marlon was a true artist, disinterested and detached, or simply lazy. He played beautifully. Olivia loved sitting in the clubs, wedged into a tiny side table, watching his long fingers knit the piano keys into sound. Listening, she felt serenaded. These were their best times together.

Other times they got into fights about things that didn't matter, like who was worse, Bush or Nixon, or they walked out on each other in bars, or fell asleep in the middle of sex, or in the middle of attempting to have sex. She guessed she could do better than him if she tried. But she and Marlon had known each other for three years now and had knocked all the expectations and hard edges off each other. He was someone you could call up for any reason or no reason or when you wanted to forget you'd been summoned to the supervisor's office for another crappy little talk about being a team player, and that everyone else had watched you, knowing you were about to get a good pasting, how you'd walked past them slow and haughty in the elegant shoes that hurt your feet.

It was almost dark when Roberta and Larry emerged from the bedroom. Olivia eyed them covertly, searching for signs of sexual exhaustion, or even gratification. Kids not only had poker faces these days, they had poker bodies. They retraced their earlier path to the front door. "I'm just going to walk Larry outside,"

Roberta announced, and Olivia said OK. She replenished the margarita pitcher, figuring that Roberta would want some. When she came in again, Roberta eyed the food on the kitchen table, picked up a piece of string cheese, and put it back down.

"We can get some real food," Olivia said. "We could go to the grocery." She spoke as if the grocery was an exotic location, a special treat or a place requiring passports. "Or did you think any more about barbecue?"

"No, this is all right."

"How's Larry?"

"Oh, you know. He's Larry." Roberta shrugged.

Olivia knew. The brooding high school boy. The hasty and unhygienic lover. "You guys going out later?"

"I don't know. We might."

Olivia didn't think her daughter was being deliberately uncommunicative as much as expressing genuine indifference to the prospect of more Larry. She watched the girl pour herself a glass from the pitcher, taste, and put the glass down again. "Whoa, Mom. This is way strong."

"Sorry." She guessed you started making drinks stiffer over time, the same way you did coffee. The taste buds turned crispy, the brain dull, and you wound up brewing potions that gagged a normal person. "You could add more mix."

Roberta stuck the tip of her tongue into the glass again, like a swimmer testing a pool. "I guess it's not bad once you get used to it." Her makeup had smeared around her left eye, thick silvery Crayola lines that gave her the look of unbalanced headlights. "So, how was work?"

"It was work. On the way home I saw the Mexican Easter parade. The one with the Crucifixion."

"Via Cruces. That's what it's called."

"You are so smart," Olivia marveled. Her daughter was always coming up with little nuggets of knowledge, things Olivia hadn't known at that or any age.

"Not so much. Half the school's Mexican."

"Sure you are. You have a first-rate mind. You get that from me. I've never seen it from that close up before. The parade. It's a big deal. Costumes, and all the, well, costumes, mostly."

"A girl I knew when I was a freshman? Her mother got to be Veronica."

"Who's Veronica?"

"You know, Veronica's Veil." When Olivia shook her head, Roberta explained, "She wiped the sweat from Christ's brow and her veil took on the image of His suffering face."

"You're kidding."

"Uh-uh. I mean, that's the story. It's in the Apocrypha."

"What? Never mind." *Apocrypha* was probably a word she knew, when she wasn't drinking. "Don't you think that's revolting? Did anybody help him blow his nose?"

Roberta made a face that indicated the exquisiteness of her pained disgust.

"I'm making a point here. There's all this veneration of the body . . ." The phrase rolled grandly off her tongue, and in pausing to admire it, she lost the thread of what she intended to say. ". . . yeah, the body, but they make it disgusting, you know, all the disgusting parts, like blood and sweat, and all the relics, bits of teeth and bone. You don't have to look like that, I'm just telling you."

"It's supposed to be proof of the miraculous," Roberta said primly.

"Like toenail clippings prove anything. The poor old body. It's been my only religion. You live by the sword, you die by the sword."

"What? What do you care what the Catholics do anyway, what have you got against them?"

"Their parade tied up traffic."

"Seriously, Mom."

She liked drinking with Roberta because that was when they had their serious conversations. Olivia said, "Sacrifice. They're all lousy with giving things up and then congratulating themselves about it, but still being all pissy about giving them up in the first place."

"All right," said Roberta. "That's an answer."

"Pedophile priests. There's another."

"I think they feel pretty bad about those guys."

"And isn't a crucifix, a cross, really just another big ole phallus? That means . . ."

"I know what it means. There's something wrong with you, Mom."

"Thank you."

"You turn everything into a dirty joke."

"Eat some cheese or something. Don't keep drinking on an empty stomach."

Roberta picked moodily at the chips. "I wonder what it's like to have a normal mother."

"You'll never know, will you? Besides, I'm so much more fun than normal."

"Sure you are, Mom."

They were quiet for a time. Olivia turned on the light over the sink, a small fluorescent that was the next best thing to sitting in the dark. The drinking was taking her on a familiar ride, extravagant loop-the-loops of emotion that you couldn't entirely trust. But you hopped on anyway, because there were times you needed your feelings to be bright and loud, oversized, even sloppy. She watched Roberta sandwich a piece of string cheese between two chips and raise it carefully to her mouth. "Darling daughter."

"Yeah, yeah, yeah."

"You're a beautiful girl. I'm not just saying that because I'm your mother. It's an objective judgment. Thank God you take after me."

"Objective. Sure."

"And you're smart. You're the smartest little baby girl in the . . ." She had momentarily forgotten which grade her daughter was currently enrolled in. ". . . the whole school."

"I don't want to go to college," said Roberta, as if this was what they'd been talking about all along.

If she really did get shitcanned, Olivia considered, and couldn't find anything right away, and the bills backed up, there wouldn't be money for tuition anywhere decent, even with loans, and she would have to try to extort or beg money out of Roberta's warthog father. That would be one more bad consequence of the truly fucked-up circumstance of being fired. She forced these thoughts back into the subbasement of her mind. "What's wrong with college, baby girl?"

"The people who want to go there, mostly. They are like the major snots. The ones with little outfits and hopped-up computers."

"I'll buy you a new computer, baby. Just say the word."

"Are you even listening to me? Huh?"

"So if you don't go to college, what do you do?"

Roberta's eyes were cat green and thickly lashed. The gunky makeup was one more of those mother-type things Olivia tried not to get into. Roberta gazed at the ceiling in a plea for patience and for forbearance. "Get a job, duh."

"Great. What kind of job?"

"Any dumb old thing to start with. Work at the music store. Waitress."

"Is this a Larry-based decision? You want to hang around with Larry instead of going somewhere else? Because you're going to be so not into Larry someday. Trust me."

"It's not about Larry."

"Jobs like that don't pay many bills." Olivia congratulated herself on sounding abnormally calm. Maybe she was supposed to screech and argue, but she hoped this was just talk, something Roberta was saying out loud to hear how it sounded. Like little kids announcing they wanted to be ballerinas or astronauts. They hadn't yet learned that what you became in life didn't have that much to do with intention. "It wouldn't make you happy."

"Oh right, because your job makes you so happy. Did you get in trouble for coming in late?"

"I can be late once in a while."

"Says you."

A couple of times in the last couple of weeks. She'd been out with Marlon, or maybe she was home, just like this, in the kitchen with her feet up, not hurting anybody, and she'd slept heavily and couldn't get her eyes unglued in the morning. Then had to make a production out of charging into the office full speed ahead, juggling coffee and keys and cell phone, as if she'd been in hectic, productive motion for hours. That was the way you did it. Make an entrance, put a good face on it. She felt bad about being late but not that bad. Other people came in late all the time, and their making a federal case out of it showed you what she was up against.

Roberta said, "You could, like, not drink so much. OK, me neither."

"Did you know," Olivia said, "that your father left and didn't come back for three days? You were still in a crib. He finally called. From Florida. That was the one time."

"All right, Mom. He was a real shit. Go ahead, drink yourself stupid."

"You're the only thing I care about in the whole whole world."

"All right. Jeez. I'm going to call Larry. We'll probably go over to his brother's for a while."

"Don't get pregnant. I wish somebody had told me that when I was your age. So I'm telling you."

Roberta was gone, and then she'd been gone for a while, and the nighttime noises filtered in through the open windows: slower, rolling traffic, scraps of music, raised voices that could have been either arguments or good times. Marlon hadn't called. She couldn't decide if she was mad about that or relieved. Somewhere along the line she went to bed.

Saturdays were for sleep. Neither Olivia nor Roberta got up much before noon. Olivia woke first, dressed, and went down to the corner for coffee and a newspaper. Doughnuts too, in case Roberta wanted breakfast. As a gesture toward nutrition, she added two tough-looking oranges and a banana, and stood in line, waiting for the morose Korean shopowner to ring her up. The register was decorated with red plastic flowers and a small gold bell with a silk tassel and a three-year-old calendar featuring an Asian beauty with lacquered pink cheeks. Olivia had stared at it all without seeing any of it for days and weeks and months, while the dust solidified over everything, the Bic lighters and key chains and snuff and bags of hot chips and breath fresheners, the small, tired items that little by little became the scenery of your life. And then you goddamned died.

That night she told Marlon, "You're lucky you have your music. Nobody can take that away from you."

"Nobody would want to. It's not worth anything to them."

"Oh boy, you can't ever agree with me, can you? You've got an answer for everything."

"If you say so."

"Now you're agreeing just to be a smartass."

"Whatever you say, pumpkin."

"Why don't you just shoot me in the head? Never mind. I want a chili dog. Go get us a couple of chili dogs."

Marlon stood up and headed to the bar. He was tall and he walked with his shoulders carried forward from years of playing the piano. Every chair in his apartment pitched and curved, so that sitting, you slumped too. "I got them with fries," he said when he came back. "If you don't want yours, I'll eat them."

"No, fries are good. Fries are our friend." The bar was one of their usual places. It had a high, unfinished ceiling with exposed rafters, like a barn, and was decorated with Scottish memorabilia, in tribute to the owner's ancestral homeland. There were tartans and coats of arms and framed landscapes of lakes and highlands, moors and fens and glens. What was it with this city, Olivia wondered, that everywhere you looked was a different country?

"What are you so worked up about?"

"The fries."

"You've been in this major mood all night, what's the matter?"

Olivia thought she must really be losing it, if even Marlon noticed. But then, she'd wanted him to notice, even if she didn't want to tell him about work or anything else. The bad part about drinking was how illogical it made you. But then, that was also the good part. She said, "I don't know. Just bored." She made a bored gesture with one hand.

"You ever think about a hobby or something?" asked Marlon,

looking out over the room with his watery, nearsighted gaze. He wore glasses with clear pink plastic frames, like a crippled child on an old March of Dimes poster. "A serious, important kind of hobby. You could join a book club."

"Nobody reads books anymore. It's all movies, television, stuff with pictures."

"Sure they do. Or OK, you could take up weaving. I had a lady friend who became very involved with weaving. First she bought a loom. Then she got way, way into yarn. She learned to dye it and then to spin her own and eventually she ended up at the source, you know, sheep."

"I don't think so."

"You're kind of stuck on no, aren't you?"

"Just say no to sheep."

"You need to work on being a more positive, affirmative type of person."

"Tomorrow's Easter," said Olivia. It was one of the things that struck her as melancholy, the way you could get sometimes on a sad night. "Think of all those little Mexican kids, watching Jesus get whipped."

Marlon snapped his fingers. "What's that book, that book that's so big right now. See, people still do that. Read. It's about how Jesus and Mary Magdalene had a kid."

"You're making this up."

"No, it's in the book. You can read it for yourself."

"Old Mary Magdalene's a mom?" Sure. It made perfect sense. One more thing they'd hold against her. "What else happens?"

"I didn't read it," Marlon explained. "I've just heard people talking about it."

The food came and they settled into eating. Olivia liked the idea of Jesus having a kid. Even if it was just another bullshit story. It made him more human-sized and regular guy–like. She should have married Jesus. All the good men were already taken. Her cell phone rang in the depths of her purse, and Olivia groped for it, cautiously, as if the thing was a little wild animal getting ready to scratch and bite. "Hello?"

"Mom?"

"Honey?" She was instantly alarmed. Roberta never called her on a night out "What's going on?"

"Nothing."

"You better tell me."

"I'm at this guy's house and he's acting kind of weird."

"What guy? Weird how?" The connection kept zooming in and out. She couldn't tell if Roberta was really scared or just drunk. "Where's Larry?"

"Wait a minute." Roberta put the phone down. There was music in the background, loud, techno stuff. "He's from somewhere else," Roberta said when she came back. "Bosnia. Or one of those other places that wasn't a country before."

"Roberta. Where are you? Like, an address."

"His name is Bruno," Roberta informed her, her voice now bright and strong. "He's a friend of these other guys we met, I forget their names. They're all from this same dumb place."

"Is Larry there? Put Larry on."

"Larry went home. We had a fight."

"He left you there alone?" Was the boy good for nothing? Marlon was stealing her french fries. She slapped his hand. "What's Bruno doing that's weird? Is he hurting you?"

"I think it's because he's a foreigner. Stuff he says comes out funny. Where's Tuzla? That's where he says I should go."

"Go where, what are you talking about?"

"Because he could get me a job there."

"Absolutely not."

"I haven't even told you what kind of job it is, you just start right in saying no. It's in the entertainment industry. Americans are very popular over there. Bruno knows some people who could, you know, sponsor me."

"Now listen to me," Olivia said, slowly, overenunciating, as if Roberta was the one who didn't speak English. "I want you to keep your phone on. Keep talking to me. And walk right out the front door."

"Just a minute," said Roberta. The phone made clattering noises, and the music surged again.

"What's going on?" Marlon asked, as Olivia shouted into the phone.

"Some Slavic pimp is trying to sell my daughter into white slavery."

"Oh wow."

"Roberta?" The music roared and bleated. "Roberta!"

"Hello?" A man's voice, furry with accent. "Hello in there."

"Who is this? I want to talk to my daughter."

"Mamma," said the man. "We are good times."

"How much English do you know, slimeball? Police? *Comprendes?* Police?"

"Mamma, this is Bruno. Your daughter friend. Beautiful girl. Very fun."

"She's seventeen. She has no passport. After I shoot your sorry stinking ass, they'll put what's left of you in jail for the next hundred years."

"Mom?" Roberta came back on the line. "Mom, I feel better now. I threw up."

Olivia put the phone to her heart, then brought it up to her ear again.

"We're supposed to go see some guys he knows, so I should get off now."

"Do not go anywhere with this person. Do you hear me? This is not negotiable."

"I never should have told you he was a foreigner," Roberta complained. "You are so totally prejudiced."

"Are all your clothes on? Huh?" Olivia realized she was shouting into the phone. People in the bar were turned around in their seats, listening. "Excuse me," Olivia said to the room. "Does anyone here speak Bosnian?" People turned themselves back around again, grudgingly. "Does Bruno have a last name? Does he have a visa? Where are you meeting these people?"

"Some club. It's not real far from here."

"Where's here? Roberta!"

"Club Veejay. Or it sounds like that." Olivia mouthed the name to Marlon, who nodded. He knew most of the questionable bars in the city.

"Fine, go there. We'll come get you there. Me and Marlon."

"Marlon's such a loser. I don't think you have any business criticizing me when you hang out with him."

"Stay on the phone," Olivia ordered, but Roberta had already shut it off.

"Let's go," said Olivia. She was already at the door while Marlon was still standing at the table, saying his good-byes. Then they were in the car. "What is this place, where is it?"

"Go north on Western Avenue," Marlon told her. He was playing the piano on his knees, an unconscious, irritating habit that she tried not to let irritate her. He said, "I knew a Bruno once, but that was just a nickname. Are you sure you should be driving?"

"Do you want to?"

"I didn't say that." Marlon hadn't driven a car in years. The reason involved something legal, or maybe illegal. She knew she shouldn't be driving. Traffic lights and street lights and car lights careened around them. The shapes of people and cars and buildings were both flat and menacing, like driving through a stage set for a horror movie. Marlon wasn't sure of his directions and they got lost in an evil near-west-side neighborhood, a district of dark underpasses and blind-eyed buildings and lurking figures in hooded sweatshirts. Figuring that crazy speed was her best option, Olivia floored it and the car fishtailed for the length of a block. She was crying by now, crying and hunching over the steering wheel as if the car was a horse that needed urging on. She hadn't thought she was a lousy mother but she guessed she was. The kind whose children appeared in lurid news stories and you thought what degenerate scum the parents must be. She had done everything wrong, not just with Roberta but everything her whole stupid life, and she was sick with shame, knowing she could never make it all right. Yet even her guilt, she knew, was suspect, that same old extravagance of feeling and weepy self-regard. She was disgusting, really.

"Try her phone again," she ordered Marlon.

"I can never figure out how these things work."

"It's a *phone*, how hard can it be? Do you really know where this place is?" Nothing looked familiar to her: gas stations and car lots lit with galaxy-bright floodlights behind chain-link fences. Brake shops, welding shops, exhaust repair shops, all the spoor and fodder of the automobile.

"Just keep going. Or no, go around the block."

This was a neighborhood of tilting, two-story frame houses, each with some kind of appendage—porch, awning, outside stair—haphazardly built and almost visibly separating from the main structure. The yards were narrow lumps of dirt in which the occasional small tree stood, bare as a hat rack. She couldn't stand thinking that her daughter might be inside one of these ugly houses, drunk or drugged or worse. How many lives were carried on in such places, how vast was the world and all its wretchedness and meanness and clamoring greed, and how could she find the one human soul dear to her in so much darkness, ah help her, help her, she was losing her mind, it was peeling away in great sodden chunks, like wet cardboard.

Club Veejay was a building of yellow brick, not much bigger than a garage, with high slits for windows and a solid metal door. "What do we do if she's not here?" Olivia asked, shivering in the chilly night air. It had been spring earlier, but they'd taken it away again.

"Have a drink, I guess."

"You were always one of the smart kids in class, weren't you?"

"Don't talk a lot," advised Marlon. "And act like we just dropped in, we were just in the neighborhood."

Olivia dialed Roberta's phone over and over, getting her languid voice message: *Hi. Roberta. Talk to me. I'll get you back.* What if she never saw her daughter again? It could happen. Things like that happened to people. At the entrance of Club Veejay, they paused, listening, but no sound came to them. Marlon shrugged and pulled the door open.

Roberta wasn't there. It only took a moment for Olivia to scan the dim precincts of the little bar, and another to want to back right out again. But Marlon was behind her, an obstacle to retreat, and besides, maybe they were supposed to stay there, she couldn't remember.

They stood at one end of the bar, which was a block of stained and scarred pine, and Marlon ordered two brandies. He gave her a nudge, a cautionary reminder, and Olivia gave him one back, harder. She kept her gaze down, not meeting anyone's eye. The bartender had hands like lobsters, red and scuttling. Bits of murmured conversation reached her, full of sinister consonants.

When she raised her head for a look around, she saw eight or ten men at the bar and the two small tables, all of them drinking in a steady, businesslike fashion. It was not possible to tell, from observing them, if the alcohol was cheering them up or sinking them further into some expatriate melancholy. The walls were paneled with cheap wood veneer. The furniture, what there was of it, had the same look of dismal thrift. Where was her daughter? Weren't they supposed to be doing something about her? She drank her brandy. It crawled down her throat like something alive. "Let's go," she said to Marlon, but he was asking the man next to them if he had a light.

"You can smoke in the car. Come on."

Marlon said, "Yeah, I've been here a time or two," and Olivia realized he must have been talking for a while, having a whole conversation without her noticing. "I came with a friend, and my friend had this other friend, what was his name, honey?"

"Bruno," said Olivia. She was sweating beneath her clothes. She felt poisoned.

"That's it. Bruno."

"Bruno," said the other man. Olivia tried to get a good look at him. She had to tilt her head back because her eyes wouldn't open all the way. He was plaid. "Big Bruno or Little Bruno?"

"He kidnapped my daughter."

"Oh, that would be Little Bruno." The plaid man laughed, which made her indignant. But then she realized she hadn't really spoken. Something else had been said that she'd missed. Sweat was rolling off her.

"Ladies' room," she said, very carefully, and the plaid man conferred with the bartender, and the bartender's lobster claw pointed to the corner.

"You all right?" Marlon asked, and she would have liked to say something witty and caustic back to him, but instead concentrated on putting one foot in front of the other until she was behind the door of the little toilet room, where she vomited and urinated and vomited again in such quick succession that she had to keep hopping up and down.

She splashed her face with cool water, avoiding the mirror as much as possible. She made a promise to the universe: Give me my daughter and I will . . . What could she promise? Who was in charge of these things anyway?

Olivia loosened the hook that provided the bathroom's minimal privacy. The door didn't close all the way and an inch or so of space allowed a view of someone's stolid backside, shifting his weight from one haunch to another. A thin, indirect current of cigarette smoke filtered through. The bar had grown noisier, more crowded, and she had to push past a layer of thick-bodied men who made amused, possibly obscene comments. Screw you. She was going to learn enough Serbo-Croatian to say that, she was going to make a point of learning it and coming back here to tell them.

"Mom? Hey, Mom!"

Roberta was waving to her from one of the little tables, where she sat with Marlon and the plaid man and a creature who must be Bruno. Olivia fell on her. "Ow, you're smooshing me," Roberta complained.

"I should only kill you." Olivia had been blubbering, but now that was over and she was ready to be furious. "What the hell kind of stunt was this? And what are you wearing?" Roberta had on an unfamiliar blouse, emerald green, made of some shiny, stretchy, cheaply glamorous fabric. "What did you do to your face?"

"It's professional makeup. It's for my photographs."

"You look like a clown." Or like the girl in the Korean shop's calendar, rouged to the eyebrows. "Since when did you do pink? What photographs?"

"This is Bruno, Mom. I told you about him."

Bruno was draped across the chair in the corner. He was younger than Olivia had expected, twenty-five, maybe, with blond curls slicked down with hair goo, and pale blue eyes set a little too close together. His face was long, horsey, with sunken cheeks, but still a face girls might persuade themselves was rakish and desirable, oh yes, she knew a thing or two about girls. "Mamma," said Bruno, nodding and grinning.

"Creep," Olivia said, sitting down across from him. There was some new problem or danger here that she would have to deal with, but she was still too sick and liquor-dazed to see the shape of it and navigate it successfully. "What photographs?" she repeated.

"For my portfolio. Heeheehahahah." Roberta squealed and squirmed. Bruno had made some under-the-table contact.

Olivia said to Marlon, "If I hit him, do you think anyone in here would care?"

"This is Drakko," said Marlon, indicating the man in the plaid shirt. "He's from Bosnia too. He's a doctor. Of philosophy."

"That's not a real doctor, what does that mean? Anybody can call themselves that."

"It is an honorary title," said Drakko.

"What's that you're drinking?" she said to Roberta. "How did you get in here anyway when you're underaged?"

JEAN THOMPSON

Drakko, said, "It is a family place. Family atmosphere." His English was better than Bruno's but still heavy going. He was Marlon's age or older, a big, sagging man with ill-fitting dentures.

Roberta said, "I'm almost eighteen. When I'm eighteen, you can't tell me what to do anymore."

"If you live that long. Let's go home now."

"This is all because I said I wasn't going to college, right? So anything I want to do instead, you won't let me."

Marlon said, "You used to hear a lot of bad things about Bosnia. But I believe that's changed."

"My country is my broken heart," said Drakko, with genuine, if drunken, sadness.

Marlon said, "I think it would be an interesting place to visit sometime. For the experience."

"See? Even Marlon thinks you're overreacting."

"Marlon's just making noise. He's improvising. Tell Bruno it's been nice knowing him."

"I'll come back and see him," threatened Roberta. "You know I will. How come you're the only one who ever gets to have any fun?" She was sitting on Bruno's lap now. This had happened while Olivia had not been paying attention. The despicable Bruno was jiggling and rearranging her for his own gratification. The bar had become impossibly loud.

"Fun?" Olivia tried to get out of her chair, but the crowd hemmed her in. "Show me where I'm having so much fun, what is this place anyway, Little Transylvania?"

"There you go again. Being this *character*."

Drakko said, "In America, everything is always so funny."

"We'll go home and talk," said Olivia. "We'll work it all out. What about Larry, shouldn't you be thinking about him?"

"You don't even like Larry. See? You say whatever you think I want to hear, then you take it all back because you're always drunk."

"Am not. Besides, so are you."

Bruno spoke up then. His mouth was nibbling at Roberta's armpit and his voice came out muffled. "For money, Mamma give permission?"

"For free, Mamma break your face."

Marlon had gotten up from the table to go to the bathroom, and now he was back. "They have a condom machine with international brands," he reported. "Isn't that something?"

"What? Who cares? Roberta! How does anyone even get to Bosnia, I bet nobody you ever heard of flies there." She was aware that she was exhausting all her good arguments.

"*Bosna i Hercegovina*," Drakko said, "is the correct name." His dentures made a sound like a stick rubbed across a picket fence.

Roberta said, "I bet I could take classes there. It would be like study abroad."

"Aren't they all Muslims?" asked Olivia, vaguely. She was trying to stay awake, stay conscious until the bar closed, when one or another thing would surely happen without her needing to struggle further, assert herself again and again. She was so tired.

"Muslim, Orthodox, Roman Catholic," Drakko explained. "Lots of God."

"Here's a deal for you," said Roberta. "I won't go if you stop drinking. And I'll stop too. Can you even think about doing that? Huh, Mom?"

"This isn't about drinking."

"Sure it is."

Drakko said, "My country is where they is try to kill God. Knife and club. Gun and bomb. But here he is back again."

Were everybody's stories just the same old story all along?

About sacrifice, and giving things up? She said, "That's what it's gonna take, huh." There was a sensation in her head of birds flapping. Battering against her skull, trying to get out.

"Right here right now. Promise. And keep promising."

"You know you'd miss the way we are," she told Roberta. "You know we wouldn't be able to be the same. Hang out the same."

"Some," said Roberta. "Sure. But it's no good anymore, Mom." She was crying, and something in the makeup turned her face shiny, as if it was coated in sheets of cellophane. "Look where we ended up."

"Almost in Bosnia," Olivia agreed. It was the universe again, smacking her around, claiming its due. Killing her off and bringing her back again, changed and unrecognizable, no more high old bad old times or raging fun. And she didn't want to do it. That was the sacrifice part. "I promise," she said, not meaning it yet. She guessed that would be one more thing that came later.

A
Normal
Life

She wanted them to have a normal life, she told him, and he said he wanted that too. They deserved it. After all the bad business of sneaking around and trysting in motel parking lots and telling the necessary lies. It had gone on for a long, rotten time and had filled them with loathing admiration for their own slick, dishonest skills. After the expensive wreckage of his marriage and the decertification of hers. It had been hell, their tricky love. Now they were finally together. The awful legalities had been played out. The angry children had said hateful things and transferred their allegiances. That was a sore point but you had to expect some sore points, you had to believe the children would eventually come around. For now they were happy, and free to revel in all the boring, normal things they'd been denied: grocery shopping together, and falling asleep in front of the television, and padding around the house in their sock feet.

Money would be tight for a while with the legal bills and child support, but they agreed that it was brave and freeing to live simply. Melanie had a small import business specializing in Asian gifts and gimcracks, carved elephants, bamboo trays, kites, fans, lanterns, beadwork, lacquerware. Mass-produced exotica for American living rooms. She thought she could squeeze a little more out of the business, now that she was no longer preoccupied with all the apparatus of an affair, the lingerie, the secret phone calls, the cover stories. Chad worked selling advertising for a radio station with a classic rock format. The ringtone on his cell phone played "Layla." It could be a melancholy job, since the station's demographic skewed to middle age and so many of the advertisements were for active retirement communities, investment funds, prostate screening tests and the like, reminders of the march of time, of bodily failure and mortality. Chad was forty-five and Melanie forty-three. They told themselves that they were still a long way from old. With any luck at all they'd have a considerable span of healthy years together. And after all, they had leapt and grasped at happiness, made purposeful, invigorating choices. Surely that was good for a few bonus points in the actuarial tables.

They regarded the grubby corners of their new, undersized home with a certain fondness. Each of them had come away from the marriages with a few pieces of family furniture, a rocking chair or dresser or hutch. Melanie rummaged her business inventory for decorative lamps and shell-encrusted mirrors and embroidered pillows, giving the rooms the look of a struggling carnival. It was like being kids all over again, back when they were just starting out. For each of them had once lived in similar small, lumpen houses at the beginning of their previous married lives. Each of them had arranged (with Diana, with Greg) similar sparse belongings in vacant spaces. They had not known each other then and they were jealous of all the time they'd missed.

"I bet you were nervous about cooking," Chad teased, and Melanie said that she guessed she was, she couldn't remember.

Then, realizing she should make more of an effort to get into the spirit of things, she said, gaily, that she had been a terrible cook at first. She'd burned everything. And when she had managed to put meals together, she'd served roasts and steaks and slabs of ribs, large, shuddering cuts of meat, dripping with blood and cholesterol, the kind of thing she wouldn't even touch nowadays. There had been the notion that men liked meat, great caveman portions of it, and in fact Greg had always gobbled it down. Of course, Melanie added, that was before anybody knew better, and long before Greg's bypass surgery. These days it was all about steamed kale and bran.

"Ha ha," Chad said, and rested one hand casually on his chest so that he could feel his own heart, its reassuring *dump dump dump* sound. He already took medications for high blood pressure and for anxiety. He had a bad knee and a worse shoulder. He was rusting out. Sex would probably be the next thing to go. He struggled with gloomy thoughts. He was beginning to feel he might have launched himself under a false flag, misrepresented himself as bold and resolute, or at least talked himself into thinking he was. There were times he half wished he was still undivorced, back home in his garage, changing his car's oil. He hadn't been happy with Diana but he'd gotten good at ignoring her. He missed the old habits, old routines, being able to find his toothbrush or coffee mug or keys without thinking. Now everything required premeditation. He wondered if his brain was too old to learn new pathways, new responses, if it was already folded into indelible creases like the lines in his palms. There were still times when he woke up in this strange bed in this strange house and did not remember where he was. Then he'd become aware of Melanie's industrious sleeping—she sighed and twitched and burrowed—and reach out for the nearest friendly body part—

breast, crotch, thigh—and fall back to sleep with his hand still there, warm and nested.

Melanie wished there was more than one bathroom in the new house. She was used to privacy for certain bodily functions, though Chad seemed to have no such problem. Well, that was all right, it was all part of the normal life thing. She could and would adapt. She was determined to make this new marriage work. Somehow it was always the woman's job. Fine. She was going to nail the sucker. She stepped lightly around Chad when he sank into one of his moods or broods, gave him back rubs when he came home from work bent into peculiar shapes from driving while talking on his cell phone. She rehearsed sprightly topics of conversation. She pushed sex about as far as it could go, which turned out to be pretty far indeed. Thank God for the reliability of male lust, that handy switch that was so easy to flip on. Who would have thought it, after all those years of good old married sex, or of doing without (often the same thing), that you could still make love with your whole heart and soul, not to mention skin?

Of course, this was something that might change over time.

One of Chad's kids, one of his daughters, was having a particularly hard adjustment to the new marital configuration. The daughter was twenty, which in Melanie's opinion was old enough to roll with a few of the punches the world aimed at you, although she refrained from voicing this. The daughter's name was Danielle. She still lived at home with her mother and attended a local community college. She was studying art history and hotel management. She was stalking them.

Chad and Melanie had been so exquisitely tactful about each other's children. They had understood the pitfalls. They had arranged the initial introductions in neutral public places, casual

restaurants and parks. They had avoided bribes and false enthu-
siasms. There had been assurances and welcoming gestures. Fat
lot of good it had done them. Chad's youngest girl put her hands
over her ears and howled, refusing to listen to Melanie's taking-
an-interest questions about ballet lessons. Melanie's middle son
called her a big stupid slut and stomped out of the Denny's with
his mouth full of french fries. Her oldest boy relayed messages
through Greg. He was writing a rap song in which she featured
prominently. He was going to get a "Mom" tattoo on his biceps
and then cut his arm off.

All that was bad enough, but Danielle was a different kind of
problem, a plump, sad-sack blonde girl with eyes that reminded
Melanie of oysters: quivering, viscous, bruised. Melanie had
never seen her when she wasn't crying, or clouded up on the
brink of crying, or scrubbing her abraded eyes after a bout of
crying. Chad said that Danielle had always been sensitive, always
been a bit of a Daddy's girl. Danielle phoned to say she was in the
middle of some kind of attack—heart? asthma? anxiety?—and
was having trouble breathing. Chad was able to talk her down
from that crisis by getting her to admit she'd been drinking
enough coffee to stun a lumberjack. "She gets all wound up and
doesn't think things through," Chad explained.

One night as they were getting ready for bed there was a knock
on the door. Chad opened it to find Danielle propped against the
doorframe, dripping with rain, her oyster eyes swimming. "I
can't feel my hands and feet!"

They brought her inside and sat her down and Danielle held
her flaccid hands up for them to see, and stretched out her legs to
display her equally afflicted feet. Melanie fetched towels and tried
to mop up some of the water that was streaming and puddling
around her. "How did you get so wet?"

I couldn't walk! I practically had to crawl to the car!"

"Let's see those hands," Chad said, rubbing them energetically between his own. "What was it, like, pins and needles?"

"Knives! Like knives stabbing me!"

"Sounds like a nerve thing, a little old pinched nerve." Chad lifted his head to ask Melanie, "How about you fix her some hot chocolate? Does hot chocolate sound good, sweetie?"

Danielle allowed, piteously, that hot chocolate would not be unwelcome.

Melanie went into the kitchen and put the kettle on. They had some envelopes of cocoa with marshmallows and she emptied one into a mug. For herself she uncorked a bottle of red wine and poured a glass. She drank and watched the crown of blue flame flicker beneath the kettle. Chad came in and began opening cupboard doors. "Do we have cookies, anything like that?" Melanie produced a package of saltines. "Hmm. I guess I could put jelly on them."

"Chad."

He looked up from arranging the crackers in a circular pattern on a plate. "What?"

"There's nothing wrong with her."

"Yeah, I'm pretty sure she's just a little freaked out. They can be pretty scary, these nerve—"

"No, I mean there's nothing wrong with her."

"You don't know that."

"Call it a hunch."

"What am I supposed to do, send her back out into the rain?" The kettle began to whistle. Chad poured the water and took the cocoa and crackers out to the living room. Danielle spent the night sleeping on a futon mattress on the floor and in the morning Melanie fixed everybody blueberry pancakes and cantaloupe and Danielle said that her hands and feet felt nearly normal and wasn't it great that they could all have breakfast together?

The next week Danielle's car broke down at two a.m. and she hitchhiked to Chad and Melanie's because it was closer than home. Then she had a fight with her mother and showed up with a suitcase. This was when Chad had a talk with her about setting boundaries and respecting privacy, and how they would welcome her visits at agreed-upon times.

They began to get hang-up phone calls. They caught odd glimpses of Danielle as they went about their rounds of work and errands: her furtive, peering head, an unexplained wad of crumpled Kleenex. They unplugged the phone at night when they went to bed. They didn't answer the door after dark. Danielle took to pulling her car into their driveway and idling there for long stretches of the night. If they got up to use the bathroom, her headlights illuminated the hallway. Sometimes, if the night was quiet, they heard floating bits of music from the car's stereo, hectic rock songs rendered sweet and blurred by distance. Every so often Danielle would fall asleep in the car and in the morning one of them would have to go out and ask her to move.

The station Chad worked for was taken over by one of the big radio networks and the format changed to religious programming and angry politics. Chad stayed on—jobs didn't grow on trees at his age—as did the control room staff and Liz, the receptionist and bookkeeper. The new shows were rebroadcast from remote studios and intruded only as aggrieved voices buzzing from the building speakers.

But other things were different. A new station manager was installed, The Kid, Chad called him, though not to his face. The Kid was a real go-getter. He liked shaking hands. He hummed along with commercial ditties. He instituted weekly staff meetings where coffee and violently sugared pastries were served. "Who's come up with the next great idea for performance enhancement?" he'd ask, and when nobody had any, he read from the newest round of corporate directives, which always involved doing more work in the same amount of time.

Chad ate a chocolate doughnut—he was never able to resist the doughnuts—and felt his nerves twitch and jangle. "So, Chad," The Kid said, turning to him with practiced, managerial enthusiasm. "How are the ad quotas coming along?"

"Like gangbusters," Chad said. He had the lingo down by now.

"Glad to hear it. How about you work up a few quarterly projections, then give me a shout?"

Chad reached for another doughnut. "Roger wilco." Sometimes he got through an entire meeting speaking only gibberish.

The Kid said that would be super. Chad filled his mouth with more doughnut and gave a thumbs-up sign. The Kid's eyes fixed on something remote and unseen as his brain went through a sequence of calculator functions. You'd think that people like The Kid, working for a corporation representing such stalwart values, might be especially religious, or supernut patriots, or both. But no. His real faith was money.

After the meeting Chad stopped by Liz's desk to sign out before his sales calls. The speakers were playing the current program, one of the preachers. The preacher's voice was full of weepy glissandos that conveyed the consciousness of sin and the hope of redemption: "Oh hallelujah, hallelujah," the speakers groaned. "Hallelujah, hallelujah." Chad strolled out to the parking lot, and the glass front doors cut off the preacher's plangent noise. His account quotas were in the toilet.

The problem, as he explained to Melanie, was that the network had upped the ad prices and also squeezed the local accounts into less and less airtime. He was supposed to bully his clients into ponying up more money for less exposure on the strength of the network's proven high audience share. "Like every day is the Super Bowl. I'm embarrassed to show up in these people's offices. I feel like I'm collecting on juice loans."

Melanie brought him a beer and turned up the air conditioning, although they had agreed to try not to run it until the weather got really hot. Chad tilted the beer bottle and took a big smacking drink. "And the crap they play! It makes you realize the failure of universal public education. Anyone who attended the sixth grade should see right through it."

Melanie made sympathetic noises, although she couldn't help thinking he was overenjoying the chance to be eloquent about his grievances. She was coming to realize that Chad wasn't exactly one of those guys who put his shoulder to the wheel and saw a job through in a stoic, manly fashion. "Could you do sales for somebody else? Another station?"

Chad let out an expiring breath. "There's not a decent independent left in this town. They're all tight playlists and canned slop. Man, I used to love radio, it was the sound track of my life. I ran the campus station back in college, I ever tell you that? We were just kids, sure, but we did edgy, eclectic stuff. Jazz, blues, progressive rock. Nobody does that kind of programming now. Hey."

He realized he had talked his way into an Idea. Well, why not? Well, money. But he was tired of money being the answer to everything. Where was passion, where was delight, wasn't this the brave new self he'd hoped to inhabit?

He might persuade some of his ad customers to get behind

him. The crew at the station wasn't crazy about the new regime. He thought he could get the guys to volunteer a few hours a week, lend a hand, sort of like helping to build a treehouse. After some negotiations with Diana, Chad was allowed to visit the garage of his former home and carry off three cartons of his old records. They were even more peculiar and varied than he remembered. There were piano rags and show tunes, ancient Mississippi bluesmen who sang accompanied only by the squeak of porch rockers. There was folk music and hard jazz and a cache of early rock and roll, the album cover photographs picturing the now-famous bands as baby-faced tough guys.

Melanie pointed out certain fiscal realities. Chad said he'd get a bank loan and give himself a year to turn the station into a moneymaking proposition. After that he'd go back into harness in some kind of sales job. He just wanted a crack at it. In a surge of love and dread, Melanie cosigned the loan application. She wanted Chad to be happy, sure. But why wasn't he already happy, or why hadn't he resigned himself to being a grown-up and settling for finite amounts of happiness?

Now when Melanie drove around town she could tune in to Chad's broadcast, to Gaelic trios or robotic synthesizer music, or sometimes it was just Chad talking. He kept up a chatty stream of commentary, welcoming people to the show and introducing the music and remarking on the weather or whatever stray thought came into his head. "I've been thinking back to when I was ten years old and I had rheumatic fever and had to spend the whole summer in bed." He did? He had? Melanie was sure he hadn't told her about it. Wasn't it the oddest thing in the world, Chad sitting in a little room by himself and sending his words far and wide. Although not too far or very wide; the station didn't have much wattage. If Melanie drove past a certain radius, the signal fizzed out and was lost. She found it disturbing that he was talking to all these unknown people, sharing himself with them. It felt a little like the old days of their affair, when she'd been forced to be jealous of Diana.

"I wonder if any of us can ever make decisions without second-guessing and regrets."

She heard his radio voice say this clearly. Her heart froze. She'd been maneuvering through an intersection and hadn't been paying complete attention. Now the music started up again, hillbilly bluegrass. Had he meant her, the two of them? Moreover, did she have regrets of her own? Maybe. Yes. Sometimes.

She turned the car around and headed for the studio. On the way she stopped at a deli and bought sandwiches and potato salad and sodas. The studio was a storefront on a narrow, edge-of-downtown street. Melanie stepped carefully along the uneven sidewalk, past the bricked-over entrances to disused warehouses, and entered the cramped little office.

Chad was visible behind the glass panel that housed the broadcasting apparatus. He waved her on back. Melanie waited until he had finished speaking ("Let's see if anybody else out there remembers the Coney Island Whitefish") and cued the music before she went in.

"I brought us some lunch." She held up the deli bag, an offering and an excuse.

"Wow, thanks. Is this roast beef? Can I have it?" Chad was wearing a T-shirt and shorts, his new work clothes. Melanie missed his salesman's suits, his beautiful crisp shirts and silk ties. There was something irritating about a man who went native. They settled in to eat and every so often Chad leaned over the console to play an ad or introduce a new song. "So, what do you have to do this afternoon?" he asked her.

"Oh, this and that." She really had nothing to do, or at least nothing urgent. She felt forlorn. A thin stream of air conditioning came from the clanking wall unit and she tried to maneuver herself beneath it. "Hey. Can I ask you something? Do you ever talk about me when you're on the air?"

Chad was surprised. "Well, maybe once in a while, sort of. Like, 'Last night my wife and I had pizza for dinner.' Why?"

"I don't want you to."

"What, I have to pretend you don't exist?"

"No, just don't . . . tell everybody in the world what you think of me." He frowned; she could see him shaping denials, working up resentments. "Never mind. Don't tell me either. If I was some kind of big mistake, I don't want to hear about it."

Melanie marched out before he could answer. She knew she was being childish, unfair, and later there would have to be tears and apologies. She sat in the car for a few minutes to collect herself. When she started the engine and turned up the radio, Chad was saying, "This one goes out to a special lady, she knows who she is." There was a blip of static, then the music started, Janis Joplin singing "Turtle Blues": "Oh I'm a mean, mean woman, I don't mean no one man no good. I'm a mean, mean woman . . ."

As Melanie drove away she thought she saw Danielle's car parked on the corner but she wasn't sure and it would have depressed her to go back and find out.

Melanie decided she was being mopey and fearful, qualities she did not admire in others, and that she should not lose sight of her own goals and sense of individuality in this new estate of couplehood. She resolved to move forward. She made further advances to her children and patiently allowed them to abuse her. She began a diet plan. Her own business needed attention. She sold her import products online, from a website, dispensing jade Buddhas and teakwood salad bowls to people who desired them in places like Tennessee and Minnesota. She had never visited the faraway countries where the merchandise was produced. (For that matter, she had never been to Tennessee or Minnesota either.) She'd bought the business from the woman who'd started it, slid right into the driver's seat. The Internet made it unnecessary to go anywhere anymore. Besides, she'd never been much of a traveler. She was squeamish about insects and diarrhea and discomfort and the general unsanitariness of that part of the world. But she was aware that much of life there was difficult beyond her imaginings. At times she fretted that hers was a largely frivolous existence, lived out in a too-narrow channel. Doting on Chad was not taking up as much of her energy as she had imagined it would.

So that when the letter reached her from Miss Poona Chumnoi of the Christian Relief and Rescue Center, based in Pattaya, Thailand, she read it with attention and then showed it to Chad. Miss Chumnoi sent respectful greetings. Her organization had as its mission the rescue and retraining of women forced to work as prostitutes. The sex trade flourished notoriously in Thailand. Women and girls from poor rural districts were lured to the brothels under false pretexts, then exploited, subjected to horrific violence and deadly disease. They had little hope of ever returning to their families. The CRRC offered safe haven, education, medical treatment, and instruction in skills such as hairdressing and embroidery. Miss Chumnoi knew firsthand the degrading lifestyle and hopelessness that were the sex workers' lot; she herself had endured it until the CRRC had come to her aid and told her of Our Lord Jesus Christ's message of faith and redemption. She offered her personal story as testimony and hoped that Melanie would be moved to aid the CRRC in its important work with a generous donation, she asked it In His Name.

Chad said, "Oh yeah, Thailand. You can book special tours there, sex tours they call them. Never mind."

"They look so young," said Melanie, examining the brochure included with the letter. There was a picture of laughing, sparrow-delicate girls in modest smocks, preparing a meal in a tidy kitchen.

"Could be a scam." Chad had a more jaundiced view of organized religion after his forced acquaintanceship with the radio preachers. "Why do those guys always have their hands out?"

"Well this is actually helping people," argued Melanie. "Not building some kind of megachurch. Besides, I looked them up on the Internet, they're for real. OK, they have a website."

Chad told her she should do what she thought was best, and so Melanie sat down and wrote an e-mail to Poona Chumnoi, congratulating her on overcoming her difficult circumstances, and mentioning that she was sending a donation of five hundred dollars to the CRRC via international mail. Miss Chumnoi answered almost immediately, thanking her in the most affecting and heartfelt terms. "You will receive a blessing," Miss Chumnoi declared.

Melanie loaded the dinner dishes in the dishwasher and tucked the leftovers away beneath plastic wrap. She felt buoyed by her virtuous deed. It was sobering, really, to think how seldom she did anything altruistic. What must it be like to live one's life in the pursuit of good works, trying to make the world a better place? Instead of selfish gratification and underhanded, hurtful behavior of the sort, she had to admit, that had characterized her and Chad's furtive courtship. She was not at all religious, but she did believe in guilt.

They'd had lemon cake for dessert and Melanie wrapped a couple of slices in foil and set them on a plate outside the garage door in case Danielle came by tonight to lurk. They had taken to leaving occasional snacks for her in this fashion; the dishes were always replaced neatly the next morning. She and Chad watched some television and then got ready for bed.

But when they'd turned out the lights and Chad lifted her nightgown to begin his fond, preliminary explorations, she burst into tears.

"I can't help it," she said, still weeping, the tears running into her open mouth. "I keep thinking about those poor . . . the poor little . . ."

It took her some effort to articulate it, that the suffering of the unrescued Thai prostitutes filled her with empathetic sorrow and made it impossible to allow herself untainted pleasure. She knew it was unreasonable. She apologized. Chad was very patient. He pointed out that the Thai prostitutes were entirely unaware of her feelings, and that punishing herself made no difference whatsoever. And that she should feel even less responsible than most people, since she had made a tangible effort to improve their lot. And that given the mass and volume and variety of human misery, the logical extension of her scruples was that no one should ever enjoy anything.

I know, I know, Melanie said, but tonight, could they just lie here together, could he just let her be sad? Chad said, Of course, it was no problem. If he was disappointed he knew better than to sulk and risk seeming like the kind of man who might consider signing up for a sex tour.

And so they fell asleep chastely entwined. Melanie dreamed about a school of tiny glittering fish that turned tail and darted away, transformed into a length of silk fabric, and then into a shower of coins. She woke with a light heart, determined to get another check to Miss Chumnoi as soon as she was able.

Chad had his own preoccupations. The radio station was a long way from turning a profit, or even getting out of the red. It required great amounts of his time, energy, and effort. With the help of his pals from the old station he was gradually building up the number of on-air hours. He recruited a couple of people to host their own shows on weekends, devoted to topics like gardening or pets. But he was still the iron man, the anchor, the one who held it all together. He couldn't tell if they were building much of an audience, beyond the local cranks and oddballs who adopted the station as their own discovery, and who felt free to call with opinions and suggestions or just to chew the fat, mistaking Chad for an idler like themselves instead of the humming nerve center of a growing enterprise.

Where did they come from, his loyal fans, the spidery old men and dough-faced, garrulous widows, the peculiar citizens who wore fuzzy hats and let their facial hair grow into topiary shapes? Or rather, where had they been all along? It was as if they had lived their entire crankish lives waiting for the airwaves to summon them, move them to contribute their life experiences, their wisdom, their expertise. Some number of them took to coming around the studio itself, clutching old record albums so softened with use that the circle shape of the disc was visible from the outside, or a homemade tape of a washboard and mandolin duet. They hung around underfoot until Chad put them to work making coffee or answering the phone or pasting mailing labels. The place took on something of the air of a sheltered workshop. Well, the station was meant to be a community enterprise. You had to take your community where you found it.

Meanwhile Chad was busy organizing a kickoff concert that

he hoped would really get the word out about the station, get the ball rolling, and any other cliché that might have come out of The Kid's mouth. Penguins Don't Fly was an indie band with a growing reputation; they would be the headliner. Different local groups would fill out the program. The station would gain exposure, valuable association with the desirable spectacle and the heat of urban life. The concert was six weeks away. The preparations were killing him, requiring all his old, wheedling salesman's skills.

When Melanie's ex-husband Greg walked into the studio, Chad at first mistook him for one of the cranks, come to loiter unhelpfully and be his newest best buddy. He and Greg had not known each other back in the adultery days, had only met once before, in fact, and that was after the divorce, a glancing brief encounter when one of the children had needed a ride home. It had embarrassed them both.

Now Greg announced his name. Chad got to his feet and extended his hand, making a quick, involuntary scan for weapons. "Hey," Greg said. "It's cool. I just wanted to talk to you, if you've got a minute."

"Sure," said Chad, who didn't really have a minute but could hardly say so. He invited Greg to sit. Greg lowered himself onto a folding chair. He'd lost a lot of weight after the bypass surgery and he had a deflated look, loose in the jowls and chins. He gazed around the studio.

"So this is the setup, huh?"

"It is." Reluctantly, Chad looked too. The desk top was a scramble of untidy papers. One of the cranks had brought in a rainbow-colored tissue garland that drooped across the front window. Another had contributed two African violets in a ceramic planter. The bulletin board was shaggy with thumbtacked notices, everything from program schedules to home-made ads offering art therapy sessions and salsa classes. He was going to have to start drawing some lines.

"How's Mel?"

"Good. She's good."

"Glad to hear it. She's a great gal."

"Yeah, she is," Chad said, trying for the right mix of buddyish, appreciative zest and respect. He didn't know what the etiquette was for such encounters. Greg was shifting around in his too-small chair, either nervous or preparing to jump up and throttle him.

"You know, for a long time I hated your guts."

Chad found himself nodding, as if in encouragement.

Greg let his breath out in a long, horsey sigh. "Man. I must have killed you off about a hundred times. A fantasy, you know? It would just come over me without thinking, I'd be at work, or eating dinner in front of the TV, and all of a sudden I'm seeing pictures. I'm squeezing your head like a grape. I'm watching you spit teeth. You're bleeding from your ears. I'm kicking your ribs and hearing them snap. It was nothing personal, you know? I mean who were you, some slimeball I didn't even know. It was more the whole fucked-up situation. Yeah, I was pretty hot. It took me a while to realize neither of you was worth giving a crap about. So I've calmed down a lot. Not that I don't have flashbacks once in a while, and looking at you up close, I'm pretty sure I could take you. But hey. I've moved on. I stopped by to tell you that. I've got a girlfriend now. Her name is Kendra, she's a personal trainer at the health club I go to. I've never seen a body like hers naked before, and I say that not to brag, but as simple fact. We're going scuba diving in the Bahamas next month. She's got me doing Pilates. I've got a ways to go, but I've strengthened all my core muscles. It's like she's opened the door to a whole new world for me. So maybe everything works out for the best. I sure hope you guys are happy, I mean that sincerely, because if you're not, what's the goddamn point?"

Greg stood and walked out. One of the cranks, who went by the name of Easy Rider, came in from the street with a batch of oatmeal cookies he'd baked. "Hey, Chad? Is it OK if I go sit in the control booth if I promise to just sit there and not touch anything?"

Chad stared out the front window and ate four of the oatmeal cookies, one right after another. What was the goddamn point? Was he happy? Sure. Most of the time. Sort of.

He thought back to the earliest days of his affair with Melanie, the furious emotions, the giddy lust, the feeling that his most ordinary walking-around moments glowed with significance. Of course that had tempered over time. The circumstances had been so impossible. There had been a sense of grinding it out, cycling through all the guilt and frustration and longing. Then had come the momentous decisions to unmarry and to marry. The culmination, the crown, the goal achieved. It was only natural that everything after that might seem a bit—just a bit, and only ever so often—anticlimactic.

Besides, life kept on happening. Little cruddy, annoying things. You never got to the place where you could stand back and admire your happiness like it was a picture on the wall. At least he couldn't. There was something sad and failed and furtive at his very center that didn't allow for it. Chad swallowed the last of the cookies and prepared to reclaim the control booth from Easy Rider, who had taken out a dental hygiene kit and was prodding at his gums.

Melanie and Miss Poona Chumnoi had established an e-mail

friendship by now. E-mail was such a wonderful thing. Here they were, ten whole time zones apart, on opposite sides of the international date line, and still they could send these tiny swarming electrons back and forth, an affirmation of human connection. And though such connection was made possible by technical, mechanical means, wasn't it also mysterious, random, hopeful, almost like prayer?

Sometimes the responses lagged, either because of transmission times or because Melanie was busy or Miss Chumnoi was occupied with her devotions or her relentless campaign of good works. But she never failed to answer. She was a reliable presence in Melanie's inbox. "Dear Melanie friend," wrote Miss Chumnoi, and that locution was charmingly typical of her exotically flavored English.

Dear Melanie friend,

The most superior of greetings to you. I am blessed to be in good health and wish it to you also. Today was a difficulty due to harassment by owner of brothel where we rescue three girls. This is very bad man, threaten and beat the girls. Very bad police take money from him. Sad that so much in the world is money money when there is the love of God and of Christ our Savior, His peace that passeth all understanding.

His light shine upon you,
Poona Chumnoi

My dear friend Poona,

I have to tell you how much I admire the work you do, your courage and your faith. You are one of the people who is really making a difference in the world. You are right, money is never as important as we think it is. I have to admit, I am just as materialistic as the next person and probably more so. My husband and I always seem to argue about money and I must remind myself not to get so carried away.

my very best wishes,
Melanie

Dear Melanie friend,
   Is he a good husband?
            PC

Poona,
   Sometimes. Yes. Maybe.
            M

As the station's big concert approached, Chad worked late every night. Whenever Melanie called the studio he was there, sounding tired and distracted, but she couldn't help remembering all the times the two of them had pretended to be working so they could see each other. It was a sad, unwelcome thought. Maybe she was reaping what she'd sown, maybe it was true what they said, a cheater always cheated. Although she was pretty sure she wouldn't herself. She sat up waiting for him, reading or watching a movie, or sometimes she wandered out into the back yard. When she looked up at the cold stars she felt lonely. It was autumn now and the air smelled of smoke, and soon it would be winter.

She missed her children. She missed the women friends she'd had when she was married to Greg. They had all drifted away after the divorce, either because they disapproved of her or because they had never really been her friends in the first place and couldn't be bothered to pick up a phone. She wouldn't go so far as to say she missed Greg, but at least he'd stayed in nights.

Chad came home very late and was surprised to find her in the yard. "What are you doing out here all by yourself?"

"Good question."

"What?"

"Nothing."

Fighting words, passive-aggressive style. Melanie walked back inside and Chad followed. She felt the hair on the back of her neck prickle, as if in a thunderstorm. Chad was standing in front of the open refrigerator, shoving cartons around. "There's nothing to eat in here."

"Fix a sandwich."

"I don't want a sandwich, I want dinner."

"Then come home at dinnertime."

Chad pushed the refrigerator door shut and stood in the center of the room, looking petulant and absurd in his sneakers and old dirty jeans and sweatshirt. Melanie couldn't stop staring at him. It was fascinating, in a horrid way, to see how unattractive, how *ridiculous,* he had made himself. It was as if he had tricked her into throwing her life away, her dear old, drear old life, and then lost interest in keeping her fooled. He said, "I don't need this right now. I'm beat to shit. Don't you know I've got everything riding on this concert?"

"Well that's a dumb thing to have everything ride on."

"Thanks. Glad to know what you really think. It's only, like, make or break for me. My future. Excuse me. Our future. But I guess you're not very invested in that."

It was a stupid argument. Melanie was already bored with it. It wasn't the fight either of them wanted to have anyway. She said, "You think it was a mistake getting married, don't you?"

She watched him make the familiar, exasperated face which meant that she'd said something messy and distasteful, an expression that had less to do with her than with women in general. Except that now she was the particular woman he was impatient with. No longer a sexy siren, just another nagging, squawking wife, as if he'd been tricked also.

"Could we not do this tonight? I have to be back at the studio in six hours."

"Do you ever wonder if we're being punished? For being dishonest. For hurting other people."

"The only one who's doing any punishing is you." Chad shut himself in the bathroom. There were vigorous sounds of gargling and flushing. Melanie got into bed and turned out the light and when Chad came in she pretended she was already asleep.

The next day she researched airfares and booked a flight to Bangkok with ground transportation to Pattaya. She equipped herself with a map, a Thai phrase book, vaccinations, passport, and travel-friendly clothing. She said nothing about her preparations to Chad; their argument receded and they were very polite with each other. She said nothing to Miss Chumnoi either. She wasn't sure she had the nerve to go through with her plan and she didn't want to risk disappointments. Besides, she kept hoping Chad would seek her out, attempt to close the distance between them, declare his deepest, truest feelings. She imagined the welling up of tenderness, how he would entreat her not to leave his side, and how, since the world was well lost for love, she would abandon her expensive plane ticket for him.

But she had forgotten how good men were at ignoring things. Chad worked, came home, slept briefly, and left again. He insulated himself with work. Irreproachable, virtuous work! Oh, she remembered that one. She was scheduled to leave two days before the concert. That morning she called Chad's voice mail and left a message that she was going out of town on business and didn't know when she'd be back. She drove herself to the airport, half expecting him to appear, brakes screeching, sprinting madly to the gate area, heedless of the pursuing airport security goons, as he realized that he was losing her forever.

But none of that happened. They called her flight, and Melanie boarded, and the plane lifted cleanly off the runway.

She slept most of the trip, waking at groggy intervals to stare out the window at the blue and glowing horizon, the plane hanging level and motionless in the roaring whoosh of the engines. She hadn't realized how very tired she was. They stopped over in Hawaii and Melanie got off to wander around the airport, poke her nose outside and sniff the balmy air. She smelled coconut, probably just someone's suntan oil, but festive nonetheless. Melanie wondered if Pearl Harbor had any connection to actual pearls, which had to come from somewhere, didn't they? She was losing it, going daffy, she was already too far from home. She turned her phone on to see if Chad had tried to call her but he had not.

On the last leg of the trip the Thai flight attendants served an incongruous sunrise dinner of seafood soup, green curry, and chicken with chilies and cashews. The sunrise stayed put for quite some time because it was chasing them down. It was like running the wrong way on an escalator. Melanie had not thought the flight would be so long, that is, she knew it would last fifteen hours but that had not registered on any purely cellular level, as it was doing now. She felt the same sort of hallucinatory clarity she'd experienced during childbirth. She was going to get off the plane, just for a little while, then she'd come right back.

Finally, against all hope, they landed. The airport was gleaming and modern. Corporations had built it in their own soulless image. Customs waved her through without examining her luggage or asking why she was running away from her husband. Oh she was a mean, mean woman. The loudspeakers played tinkly Thai music, alternating with Western pop of the sort Chad disdained. She wondered if the concert had started yet, if today was tomorrow yet back home, or was it the other way around, and if he even missed her. Crowds of people pushed past her, ladies in butterfly-colored silks, men in business suits, teenagers in the most painfully hip American gear, skinny jeans, mincing heels, glitter T-shirts.

Amazingly in all the confusion, she found her driver for the ride to Pattaya. Or rather, it was hardly amazing since the system for the gratification of well-paying tourists was very efficient. The heat outside was molten. She was glad for the expensive, air-conditioned car, furnished with bottled water and flyers for different area attractions: the Floating Market, temples, elephants, dancing girls in traditional garb, monks, monkeys, waterfalls, snorkeling, world-class shopping, none of which was in evidence or she quite believed existed. Traffic surged. The driver swerved and cornered at thrilling speeds, like the streets in a video game. Sheets of light reflected off a glass-fronted office building. As Melanie watched, an ornate red and gold dragon traveled the full length of the building's front. It took her a moment to realize it was an ad pasted on the side of a bus.

"First time you Thailand?" The driver was proud of his English.

"Yes." That didn't seem emphatic enough, so Melanie nodded, yes yes yes.

"First you Pattaya?"

Again she nodded, wondering if it was a trick question, and

why one answer hadn't been enough. But a middle-aged white woman traveling solo to a notorious center of sexual entrepreneurship might require extra scrutiny. Perhaps she was actually a retired transvestite nightclub performer, or else she was in need of some unguessable variety of personal companionship. Melanie fell asleep again and woke a couple of hours later when they arrived at her respectable, extravagant hotel. She was installed in a room carefully incorporating East meets West: rice paper screens, low platform bed with excellent box spring, big honking television.

It was night, but now she was unable to sleep. Twenty stories up, she watched the hectic lights that outlined the crescent of beach and the life beyond, the lurid goings-on at the beer bars, discos, hostess bars, go-go bars.

She checked her phone again but there were no messages.

She lay down and must have slept a little because she opened her eyes to daylight. She ordered an American-style breakfast from room service. Her head felt like a helium balloon, lightly tethered. She dressed and had the concierge call her driver.

The Christian Relief and Rescue Center was on the edge of the pleasure district. Melanie caught glimpses of jumbled, empty streetscapes with signs in different scripts, their neon gone blind in daylight, cartoon posters of winking, come-hither girls, the fake-looking thatched roof of an open-air bar. It was early and there was still a little freshness in the air, a sea breeze that stirred the cooked, garbagey smells. Street cleaners were hosing down the pavement. Vendors were setting up food carts. Here and there some of the aimless, dissipated sex tourists were out for a stroll, looking as if they were afraid of running into somebody else from Sioux Falls.

The center was housed in a two-story frame house with wrought-iron balconies and tall, flamingo pink shutters. Melanie couldn't help thinking it looked rather like a whorehouse itself, except for the cross out front. She told the driver to wait. The front door was ajar; it opened into a long hallway. The cheerful sound of a typewriter encouraged her. At the first door, a pretty Thai girl wearing a plain white blouse and slacks looked up from her typing and smiled. "Good morning," she said, her voice a slight singsong.

Melanie's heart rolled around inside her like a pinball. "I'm looking for Poona Chumnoi."

"Ah," said the girl. "Ah." She got up from the desk, recalibrated her smile, and asked Melanie to wait, please.

So she wasn't Miss Chumnoi. She'd been so sure. Left alone, Melanie studied a framed poem on the wall about God bringing the rain to grow the roses. Girls' voices called out to each other from somewhere in the building. Light feet padded unseen on the stairs. A stout white woman about Melanie's age, with her hair going gray in pieces, came in. "May I help you?"

Melanie introduced herself. The woman's face registered no recognition. "I got a letter from her—Poona Chumnoi—about the center, the work you do. I sent a donation. We've been e-mailing . . ." Melanie trailed off. She really had no good explanation for being here.

"Would you like something to drink?" the woman asked. "Iced tea? Lemonade? I'm Greta, by the way." Melanie followed Greta down the long hallway. An old-fashioned ceiling fan stirred the air. The hall led outside to a small brick terrace, shaded by trees with thick, glossy, unnatural leaves. Greta sat down on a bench and patted the space beside her. "Would you like to try the iced tea? It's good old Lipton's. Reminds me of home."

Melanie said yes, thank you. Greta's growing-in gray hair made her look rather like a badger. Melanie guessed she was some kind of housemother, a missionary, probably. She wore black-framed glasses and had a big pink wart in one eyebrow. Did you have to be homely to live a virtuous life? She hoped not. Greta called out something in Thai and another girl who might have been Miss Chumnoi but was not appeared with a pitcher and glasses.

The tea steadied her though she still felt, and no doubt looked, shipwrecked. Greta said, "You say you got a fund-raising letter from us? How extraordinary."

Melanie explained the import business. She said she guessed she was on all kinds of lists. Greta waved that away. "We're Mennonite," she explained. "We don't solicit outside of our own church family. The letter was from Poona? So you've never actually met her."

"No, we just . . . correspond. Like pen pals. But, you know, by e-mail." The more she tried to explain herself, the more abjectly witless she felt. Something black and harsh and foreboding was taking shape, like a flapping crow. "Is Poona all right? Did anything happen?"

Greta sighed. "This is really most distressing. I have to wonder who else she wrote to. I'm afraid she's gone off the reservation."

"I beg your pardon?"

"Recidivism. It's a chronic problem. The girls can earn so much more as prostitutes than doing anything else. I always believed that Poona was sincere in her religious feeling. And she may well be. A sinner can be every bit as genuinely religious as a saint. They just don't test as well."

"What are you saying?"

"We haven't seen her in almost a week. I expect she's back at one of the clubs. If you sent her any money, I'm sorry to say it's probably gone."

"That's all right," Melanie said. By now any catastrophe was filtered through a thick layer of jet lag and disorientation. She wanted to go back to the hotel and sleep.

"Try not to judge her too harshly. These poor girls. So often they just don't believe they're worthy of redemption. If you'll give me an address, I can certainly let you know if we hear anything."

Melanie produced a business card. Greta studied it. "If you don't mind my asking, why are you here? This isn't your typical resort spot. Well, it is and it isn't, if you take my meaning."

"My husband and I have been having some problems." She had foolishly entrusted her life to love, and it had disappointed her, and she'd had some goopy notion of self-sacrifice, or maybe it was self-punishment, of making amends. Living humbly in service to others. Being worthy of redemption. So much for that. "I guess I needed to get away for a while."

Greta's eyebrows, wart and all, lifted ironically. "I'd say you managed to get pretty far away, dear."

The phone rang in the deep dark dreamtime of Chad's sleep. He was out of bed looking for it before he was actually awake. When he picked it up he was just glad the noise had stopped, and didn't say anything until Melanie's voice detonated in his ear. "Chad! Are you there?"

"Crap." She'd startled him and he'd banged his shin on a table.

"Did I wake you? I'm sorry. I keep forgetting if it's earlier or later here."

"Where's here, where are you?"

"Thailand."

Silence spread like a pool of water between them. "Chad? Hey."

"Thailand, the country?"

"Yes, but never mind that now. I miss you so much. How was the concert?"

He was waking up now, beginning to assemble the various pieces of consciousness and memory. "It was OK. Fine. Good. You're kidding, right? Where are you really?"

He heard music starting up in the background, a boom-boom beat with squalling saxophones, a jabber of excited voices speaking some monkey dialect. "I'm coming home tomorrow. Or is it still yesterday? Anyway, soon."

"You could have told me where you were going."

"Well you could have called me."

"I did! I tried but the phone didn't work." Melanie was saying something the music drowned out. "I can't hear you."

More jabbering, sound of rushing air, things slamming. "That's better," Melanie said. "I'm in the car. Thanks, Niran. Niran's my driver. We've grown very close. Tell me about the concert."

"It was a little crazy. They're one of those anarchy-rage bands." The lead singer had briefly set his own hair on fire. There had been a simulated crucifixion. At least, Chad thought it was simulated. "I guess I hadn't heard about their stage shows." There had been considerable damage to the club, and a minor street riot. They were still trying to figure out liability.

"But you got your publicity, right?"

"I'd say so." There had already been a couple of letters to the editor and a resolution introduced in the city council. Of course none of this would necessarily be bad for business. It would be a great irony if he ended up making money in spite of himself. "Oh, Danielle left town with the band. She put a note on my car's windshield. She said she was tired of watching out for me, and I was on my own, and from now on she was just going to try and be happy."

"She said that? Watch out for you?"

"Yeah."

Melanie pondered. "You know what's strange? I'm going to miss her. It was kind of comforting, having her hang out in the driveway. Like a night-light or something."

"Yeah." But the strangest thing to him was the conjunction of the words *happy* and *Danielle*.

"Girls. They're always running off somewhere, aren't they?"

Chad shifted his weight from one foot to the other. He didn't know what she meant, but he gathered that he wasn't supposed to. He hadn't told her everything about the concert. How he'd been stressed, and worried about her, and feeling sorry for himself, his chickenshit, sorrowful self that always held back, always stopped just short, and what good had it done him? So he'd gone backstage with the band, drinking shots of tequila with them, tequila and God knows what else, things smoked, things ingested, things inhaled. How the memory of the next twelve hours had been snipped from his brain like a piece of film. He woke up on the floor of the band's hotel suite, sick, sweated, shaking, alone. The band's hit song, "The Path of Excess Leads to Wisdom," was blaring from the stereo. He felt the edge of a broken tooth with his tongue.

A little anarchy and rage, he discovered, went a long way. He'd tried, and failed, to commit rock-and-roll suicide. Who knew what he had done, and with whom? Bile crept up his throat. From now on, any stranger on the street might have the goods on him.

"You know what I think?" Melanie's voice broke in on him. He shook his head, forgetting that she couldn't see him. One of her

Buddha statues sat on a shelf in front of him. He'd seen it count-less times before. Or maybe he had never seen it. His vision was adjusted to the dark by now. The Buddha's grave, placid face drew him in and he stood there, his mind fixed on exactly noth-ing.

Melanie again. "I think life isn't supposed to be normal."

"What is it supposed to be?" Chad asked, but the connection failed then.

Thirty-six hours later, Melanie guided her car cautiously along the airport access road. She seemed to have forgotten how to drive, although she assumed this was a temporary condition. There was a certain apprehension involved in seeing Chad. There would be explanations, recriminations, promises. They would have to start all over again and keep starting over. It was possible that they had learned nothing at all.

Melanie turned the radio on and found the station's signal. "Graceland" was playing. Then the song ended and Chad said, "That's one guy I never get tired of listening to. The great Paul Simon." Simultaneously near and distant, absent and present, his radio voice struck her as miraculous. The sky was filled with waves of invisible electronic longing.

"Special thanks and greetings going out to all my clean and sober friends. You're my everyday heroes. Stay strong. Stay in the now. And I've been thinking . . ."

There was a pause while Chad took a sip of coffee and set the mug down again. Melanie could see him as clearly as if she was in the room.

". . . about the big questions and the little ones, and whether there's really any difference between them. The Dalai Lama says that the purpose of life is happiness. Isn't that grand? Isn't that a *relief?*"

It was. But Melanie knew something the Dalai Lama didn't, or maybe he knew everything and just hadn't said it yet, or maybe everything in the world was always and continually being said again and again: that happiness too was something you had to work at. She took a turn and Chad's voice faded. She circled until she found the signal once more, then aimed the car straight toward it.

HUNGER

It's forest fire season and every day the newspaper runs a map of the state to show where the big fires are. These are marked with flames, stylized drawings of flames sprouting up in Los Gatos and Kings Canyon and Grass Valley and Mariposa. Nowhere close, and none of them places that Patsy's ever going to go. But it scares her, ten years in California and she still can't get used to it, land itself burning. Fires are meant for houses or other normal buildings, and fire engines with sirens are meant to pull up and open hydrants and take care of business. That's what she's always been used to and she's too old to change her way of thinking. But in California it's trees and grass that burn, all the dried-up, dried-out vegetation caused by the unnatural way it doesn't rain out here. In California there are smoke jumpers, and planes with bellyfuls of chemicals, and exhausted men with soot-blackened skin and lungs scarred from breathing the smoke from burning poison oak, and whole neighborhoods lost under flames that rise up and crash like ocean waves.

Sometimes when Patsy is on the very edge of sleep, the balance point between thought and dream, she sees the fires behind her closed eyes. Fire has devoured everything right down to the earth itself, a layer of black crust, and in the next instant the crust is eaten too and the fire has turned it into nothing. Inch by inch, the world falls away into nothing. It's the End of Days, the final judgment, the failure of all things hopeful and human, the failure of kindness and courage and faith, of striving and beauty and of love itself, all fallen short, God's great experiment ending in wrath and burning.

This is when Patsy comes awake with her heart going hard, and looks around her to find the room is still here. This room will never change. There are worse things than the world ending. The leather recliner is shaped like some humpbacked dinosaur, the drapes are nubby and overwashed, the television never really changes either, no matter what the program is, if it talks or brays or sings. Time settles over every surface like dust. One more night and one more and one more. She's fallen asleep in the recliner again. It's a bad habit, this early, unsatisfactory sleep that keeps her from any genuine rest. The clock tells her it's only a little after ten. The room is hot, all the heat of the day trapped inside. Waking up to it makes her fretful and heavy-headed. She listens for house sounds, her niece or nephew moving around, but everything is quiet.

In the kitchen, in the back of the refrigerator, is a new bottle of wine that is not, technically, hidden, only placed in this inconspicuous spot. Patsy takes the bottle and a glass and slips back down the hall and settles into the recliner again. The television flickers and changes colors. She knows she'll be awake for hours and hours. What would God do with himself if he destroyed the earth and everyone on it? Really, who would there be for him to punish and push around and be disappointed in? He'd still have the angels but they are perfect and boring, something else that never changes. What's the point of being God if there's no one around to be impressed? What a strange thing to be thinking. *I am getting as bad as Angela,* Patsy tells herself. But this is only a way of reassuring herself that she's not anything like Angela. A kind of superstition or backward good luck charm. She's too old to be so foolish, an old woman now, or maybe because she's old she can be as foolish as she wants because nothing she does matters to anyone.

The house is laid out in an L shape, one of countless ranch-style constructions from the eighties, one story, siding and shingle, attached garage. From the outside the house gives the impression of spaciousness, while inside you are conscious of how narrowly everything is laid out, what sacrifices of space and comfort have been made in order to fit the requisite number of bathrooms, etc., and still come in under the price ceiling. The master suite, so called, which is Patsy's, lies at one end of the L. The kitchen and living areas occupy the middle, and there are two more bedrooms and a bath at the far end. Sliding glass doors look out to the patio and the back yard. Although the patio is equipped with a grill and a picnic table and a movable fire pit and an umbrella for shade, all the apparatus of determined outdoor enjoyment, no one in the house goes out there. The drapes covering the glass doors are left closed.

The grill and everything else date from ten years ago when Angela, Patsy's younger sister, lived here with her husband. Their children, Leslie and Jack, still reside in the house, but neither they nor Patsy ever prepares or eats a meal outdoors, or comes out to sunbathe or tend the yard. Once, soon after Patsy came to live with them, she organized a back yard picnic with hot dogs and corn chips and orange soda and a bakery apple pie with ice cream. The children ate their food while Patsy admired the trellised roses and the hummingbird feeder and the ceramic frog perched on a railing, the verdant grass, the marvelous sunshine, the perfect lack of humidity.

Leslie, who was fourteen at the time, remembers the careless food that was meant to be festive, remembers her heart turning to stone as her aunt went on and on, pointing out the yard's attractive features, as if to convince them that they were fortunate, blessed, the possessors of rare vistas and enviable circumstances. How she hated her aunt for her stupid chirping noise, although she knew even at the time that Patsy jabbered away because of her own terror, her fear that if she let up for a moment she would be overwhelmed by her own inadequacy. Much later Leslie comes to realize just how fortunate she and Jack were, in a perverse, non-Patsy sense of the word, having someone so available for hating when they needed it most. Because the import and refrain of Patsy's caretaking is that one has to look on the bright side, soldier on, do the best with what you are given and consider that many, many people have things far worse. Who wouldn't hate that when all you want is to rage and curse and throw your anger into the air again and again, so that no one forgets for a minute what a heap of unfair crap has been shoveled onto your plate, what a screaming bad joke the world is.

Leslie works in a small insurance office, sending out policies and fielding claims. From time to time she takes classes at the community college, business classes mostly, but once in a while something just for pleasure, like art history or photography or Spanish. She's always hoping to discover some special interest or aptitude in herself, something that will propel her into a different life. On Fridays after work she meets her married boss in a Holiday Inn north on I-5, where they fix drinks from the bottle of Scotch he brings with him, make love, talk in bed for a time, then

shower and dress and eat dinner at one or another of the sur-
rounding chain restaurants. Happy hour, they call it. Her boss is
older than Leslie, forty-two, and he makes sad jokes about how
typical this is, his age and the whole younger woman thing. His
name is Wes and he is prone to depression, and sometimes when
he talks about his two small children, their little hands and their
wise, artless remarks, their innocent joy when he returns home,
he gets weepy. "I don't deserve you," he tells Leslie. "I don't
deserve to be so happy, I'm a bad person, I ruin everything."

Then Leslie soothes him and tells him not to be silly, that he's
a nice man, he's always nice to her. But she thinks he's right, he
doesn't deserve her. He's already hogged more than his share of
normal happiness. He makes all the sounds and gestures of suffering and guilt so that he does not actually suffer or feel guilty.
As for her, she likes the good old sex part of things, the regularity
of it, something you can count on. And more: she takes pleasure
in the idea that she's *getting away with this,* that Wes doesn't
belong to her and she's stealing him the same as you might steal
money or goods. He's partial compensation for all the things that
have been stolen from her, and if that's a sick, horrible way to feel,
then that's what she is, sick and horrible, and it's nobody's business but hers.

Ten o'clock at night and Leslie is in her bedroom, reading a
chick magazine that features advice on diet and career moves
and hairstyles. She consumes such magazines the way other
women eat chocolate. They are her guilty pleasure. Silly, most of
them, their blend of earnestness and zippy prose. She has a store
of knowledge about things like cucumber slices placed over the
eyes, breast self-examination, stitched-down pleats, and how to
handle harassment in the workplace, ha ha. And really, where else
was she going to learn such things? Leslie was still a child when

her mother began having her troubles, and as for Patsy, you might as well ask a nun about boys or mascara or which shoes went with what.

Patsy practically is a nun, with her big, pudding face and thick ankles and churchy exhortations. Leslie and Jack used to wonder, meanly, if Patsy had ever known the love of a man. It was easy fun to pretend she was like one of those dolls manufactured with a seamless crotch, that she was plastic clear through and that no sexual notion ever found means of entry. It is something else to consider she might have started out like anybody else, full of nervous flutterings and fears and bodily secrets and the desire to become one flesh with another being. Maybe there was some-body once, some boy or man that Patsy fancied, maybe there were excuses to brush up against each other, or mouths pressed wetly together, or even fumblings involving zippers and elastic. But Leslie can't go farther than this in her imagination. It simply shuts down, or becomes a vision of Patsy saying *no no no*. If she lets herself think otherwise it might put her off sex of any kind for a long time. So Leslie falls back on her old bitterness instead. Because Patsy—whom she hears in the kitchen, trying to be quiet about getting herself a drink—never allows herself any straightforward human desire. When she came from Chicago to live with them she was full of nice making and solicitude, but it was all a show, this vision of her noble sacrifice, giving up her own life—as if Patsy had any life worth giving up!—to raise her poor young relatives. And surely the part of the equation that Patsy did not allow herself to acknowledge was the calculation that if she took care of them, sooner or later they would have to take care of her.

Most nights Leslie needs pills to get to sleep. Without the pills, she lies on her back and feels each grain of the sheets on her skin, an unpleasant, abrading sensation that she can't get away from. Her thoughts begin to wheel and chase each other. Any stupid little thing will get her going. If she feels herself falling asleep, she catches herself at it, then tries to forget she's done so, and by then everything is spoiled. But when she takes the pills, they bury her under a layer of black unconsciousness and leave holes where her dreams should be. So that every night is a choice, pill or no pill, bad sleep or no sleep, willpower or chemistry.

The sleep problems have come on within the last year, and they are worrisome because insomnia was one sign of her mother's illness. If Angela slept at all it was in the late afternoon, so that Leslie and her brother, arriving home from school, had to tiptoe around, keep the television and their music turned down low, as if their mother worked the night shift.

But Angela didn't work. And at some point she had ceased to cook meals, in any normally understood sense of meals, or make beds, or dust, or go grocery shopping, or remember her children's birthdays, or check to see if they were in bed when they were supposed to be or up and dressed on school days, or kept their doctor's appointments, or much of anything else. She was always unwell in some hard-to-explain fashion that didn't involve things like chicken pox or broken bones. Leslie's father moved the laundry from the washer to the dryer and the children picked out what they needed from the clean pile. He bought groceries on his way home from work, or when Leslie got older, he left money on the kitchen table and she would be the one to shop and fry up the hamburgers or make spaghetti. Her little brother Jack ate all his meals in front of the television. He didn't remember ever doing things differently.

When her mother woke up in the early evening, Leslie would take a plate into the bedroom for her. The bedroom drapes were always drawn and the room had an odor of much habitation, like a hamster cage. "That food hurts my throat," Angela would say. "Bring me something else." She only wanted soft, sweet foods, like cake or iced doughnuts or crumbly tea cakes with heavy lemon sugar glaze, and after a time that was what Leslie fed her. Angela lived on sugar like the ants in the pantry. Her body became a strange combination of stringiness and bloat, and when Leslie was close enough to her, she smelled something that she knew to be decay. The inside of Angela's mouth, dying.

"There is too much population in the world now, and not enough food."

The first time Leslie heard her mother say such a thing, it frightened her because she believed it. The true facts, said Angela, were that human beings had no natural predators these days, and so the law of nature was that we would kill ourselves through our own appetites. Soon it would be necessary to eat in conditions of utmost secrecy.

Once Leslie knew better, or at least realized that starvation would not be happening very soon or anywhere very nearby, she turned impatient, even scornful. "Nobody's running out of food," she said, watching Angela lick the paper tray that contained the packaged cinnamon rolls. "Least of all you." She was, after all, still a child, and no one had instructed her in kindness.

Angela's eyes rolled inward, her concentration shifting to the bubbling and squeezing of her digestion. She yawned like a crocodile. "Wait and see," she said, nodding. "Wait until everybody lets their hungers loose all at once."

Leslie's father took to sleeping on the couch in the den. "What's wrong with Mom?" Leslie asked him once, timidly. They did not make a habit of talking about Angela. Her father gave her a look that was nearly unfriendly. "She worries too much," he said. "About things she can't change or do anything about. The doctor is giving her a new prescription so she won't worry all the time and wear herself out."

Things like hunger? Leslie wondered. *Like the world filling up with other people's hungers and crowding you out? What could be changed and what couldn't, and why was it so bad to think about it all?* Soon after, her father begins, the process of leaving their lives, spending more and more time at work or anywhere else that is not home, culminating in his packed suitcases and a call to Patsy. The new prescription doesn't help her mother—pills, it's always pills—and eventually other measures are taken. The thing that all of them worried about was Angela. The thing you can't change is the past. Leslie decides she'll read a little while longer before trying to sleep.

Leslie's brother Jack will turn nineteen next month. He wanted to go into the navy but the time or two he got into trouble over pot caught up with him. Jack never thought of himself as the college type and nobody else did either. When the navy didn't work out he got on with Caltrans as a flagger, traveling the state highways a quarter mile at a time. But it was hot and deadly boring and his ass was always hanging out there, waiting to get taken out by the next drunk or meth freak who didn't believe in slowing down. Caltrans couldn't find him a spot doing anything else, not that shoveling asphalt or jackhammering or baking your skin until it turned maroon was such a great deal either.

So he quit and came back home, and now that he's pissed away his money, he's thinking of hiring on as a firefighter. They need more crews all the time, it's good pay, and so what if it's dangerous, at least you're doing something important. He's stirred by news accounts of firefighters working thirty-six-hour shifts and collapsing into sleep on any available surface once they have the chance, how they dig fire lines and light backfires and keep roads open and rescue the lost and singed pets left behind when people evacuate. Jack has never had a pet of any kind, but he imagines how he'd find a dog or cat, cradle it in his arms, soothe its terrors, and maybe, if the owners couldn't be found, bring it home with him. If it was a dog, he'd name it Ranger.

Jack has taken up residence in the garage. The cars are parked in the driveway to make space for his weight bench and his boom box and the couch where he sleeps and watches television. His clothes are in piles among the paint cans and antifreeze and busted garden hose and all the other garage junk. He keeps a fan running for coolness and that works pretty well. He still uses the bathroom inside the house, but as Patsy suspects, he often goes out the side door of the garage to pee in the yard, especially at night.

The house has come to seem unfriendly to him, he can't explain it. He never felt one way or the other about the place. It's not like he has any store of happy memories or crap like that. He doesn't even remember that much from being a little kid. Isn't that weird? He wonders if there's something wrong with him, if he's short-circuited or incomplete. Other people always seem to expect him to be different. He's too goofy, too flaky, meaning he doesn't always take serious things seriously. If he's asked about his parents and he says, "My dad's down in L.A. My mom's in a nuthouse," people's faces go wary, like they are waiting to be told it's a joke. "No, really," Jack says. "OK, a hospital. A hospital for mentals."

If he's supposed to sound all choked up about it then he guesses he's got it wrong. Jack knows, because he sees it on television and other places, that parents, families, are a big deal, that they are, in general, important, and the occasion for much carrying on. Well that's great, and he's always polite when people talk in that way. His "family" is Leslie and Patsy, but neither of them, either separately or together, has enough substance to bear all the weight the term implies. Jack doesn't think he'll ever get married or have kids, but he likes the idea of a steady girlfriend, of always having someone around, different girls, probably, but always someone.

This thing with the house came on unexpectedly. When he got back from his Caltrans job and tried to sleep in his old bed, he couldn't get stretched out, couldn't make his body fit the well-worn groove of the mattress. The air seemed stale, and the familiar noises coming through the walls—his sister moving around in her own room or flushing the toilet—kept him wakeful and irritated. Then the den, the place where he sat to watch his television, started getting on his nerves. Patsy was always sticking her head in to ask, "Oh, what are you watching?" Not that she cared. She was only looking for a hook to hang a conversation on, an excuse to park herself and complain about the heat or her foot troubles or make useless comments about why anyone would want to watch a program where people ate bugs off a plate or just sat around their living rooms talking, why, the television people might as well show up with a camera at their own front door and put her, Patsy, on a show!

Patsy laughed to show how silly that idea was. Jack said, Uh-huh, and kept his attention on the television screen. If you ignore Patsy, she eventually goes away. Jack does not really dislike his aunt. It's more that he spends so much time alone, in his own head, that he can't climb out of it to make the kind of noises required to engage with her. He's a target of opportunity for her, a sitting duck. One more reason not to be there. But even when he's alone in the house there's something about it that makes him . . . sad? Restless? Whatever it is, it has a different, vaguer shape than a memory, more like an animal coming across a scent and backing away from it.

Jack buys a twelve-inch color TV and takes it out to the garage, where his weight bench is already set up. He watches his shows while he lifts and does arm curls, ten sets of ten reps, keeping it slow so as to build longer muscles. He has an old boom box for music. The couch is one he finds on a curb with a sign that says Free. It's a little funky but he covers it with a bedspread and it's not so bad. The kitchen is only a place where food is stored, so it's easy enough to fix his morning cereal or his frozen dinners and carry everything out to the garage. Most nights Jack gets stoned and stays up watching kung fu movies or cop movies or billiard tournaments or infomercials, whatever's on. He tells time by the television, if he keeps track of it at all. There's a blank and tinny feel to anything after about three a.m., a sense that the world has been left in the care of machines that click and cycle through their mechanical paces.

Some nights he goes out the side door of the garage and gets in his car and drives everywhere and nowhere. Sacramento is now just one big suburb, a metropolitan area, it's called, towns placed along the freeways like knots on a string, Rancho Cordova, Citrus Heights, Roseville, each one with its acres of sprawl, its attendant shopping malls and schools, everything dead asleep, shimmering with heat haze. There's grass where people water it, and back yard swimming pools scented with chlorine, and oleander hedges, and lilies of the Nile, and other stuff he doesn't know the name of but it's all baked dry and powdery. On these drives he sometimes finds himself wondering how hard it would be to kill somebody, in the purest physical sense. He thinks it's probably not as easy as it's portrayed on television. How long would you have to cut off their air supply, or how hard would you have to hit them and where, in order to stop their heart, or maybe it was the brain you had to go for, since it controlled all the other systems. And these thoughts don't particularly alarm him because they are so curious and remote and impersonal. He gets back home before there's any light in the sky, he's like a vampire or something, and beats off so he can fall asleep.

His sister tells him he shouldn't stay cooped up like this, he should get out and do things. What things, Jack always counters, stalling, and Leslie says, "Call somebody up, go to a movie or just hang out. Don't you know any girls? You're not so ugly that you couldn't get a girl to go out with you."

Good old Les. He gets a kick out of her, he really does, the way she's always trying to nag him into having fun, which he doesn't mind. Jack thinks she could use a little fun herself but he can't come up with suggestions. The truth is he doesn't know any girls anymore, or much of anybody else. He never had that many friends to begin with, and they've all receded since high school. As for girls, it would feel like a big dorky deal to call one of them up out of the blue and make the sort of conversation that would get him one bit closer to getting laid. He thinks he'll wait until after he's done the firefighter thing so he'll have something to talk about. He won't have to go into details, or maybe after the details have already happened they'll come out of his mouth on their own in some effortless way. He figures he can get by with saying, "It was pretty tough," and by then he might have some attractive wound or scar that would speak for itself. Tomorrow, he promises himself, he'll find the number you call about the fire crews. He hears Patsy in the kitchen—she has a particular sound, like a mouse in bedroom slippers—and when she's receded back down the hallway, he goes in and fetches himself a couple of beers.

Patsy is writing a letter to her sister Angela. It is unclear if Angela can still do any such thing as read, but Patsy always tucks her letters inside cheerful greeting cards. There isn't anybody who doesn't like to get mail. *Dear Angela,* she begins. *How are you? I hope you are well and feeling fine. We are all getting along pretty good. It sure is hot. I never thought there was anything hotter than a Chicago summer, but I see I didn't take Sacramento into account.*

Patsy measures the remaining space on the page with her eyes. It's always a challenge to fill it up with enough cheerful news of the sort appropriate for a disturbed person like her sister. Patsy is the only one who writes. Neither of Angela's own children do so, and as for Angela's husband, he hasn't had anything to do with them in years. He lives with another woman without benefit of clergy. He's never divorced Angela, even though you are allowed to do that once someone is certified disturbed. Maybe it's guilt, the same thing that keeps him making the mortgage payments on the house, well, he should feel guilty. What kind of man deserts his family in time of trouble? Or maybe that's the nature of men, to run off and leave the hard work to women.

Writing to Angela is another one of those things that Patsy has taken on herself. None of them visit Angela anymore, not since that single, scarifying occasion when the children were still genuine children. Patsy makes sure to send special cards on Angela's birthday and at Easter, and gifts at Christmas, sweaters or scented talcum powder or calendars or extra-warm socks. Patsy has struck up a friendship with Diamond, who is one of the nurse's aides at the hospital. Diamond and Patsy talk on the phone on a regular basis, and Diamond tells her that Angela is about the same, poor soul. "Why they call that place a hospital I surely don't know," says Diamond. "Not nobody's leaving there cured."

Although they always begin by talking about Angela, Patsy and Diamond are in the habit of staying on the phone and chatting. They are about the same age and they share certain attitudes, such as their frequently expressed observation that the world has changed, and not for the better. They lament the failures of the body that come with aging and they compare maladies. Diamond has a husband, Willie, who has his own absorbing health problems, and four grown children and numerous grandchildren and an abundance of other relations, cousins and great-uncles and her cousins' kids and everybody's mates and ex-mates. All of them enter the conversation with regularity, so that talking with Diamond is like following a particularly well-populated television series.

Patsy wishes she had more to contribute than Leslie and Jack, who never really do anything worth repeating, or even complaining about, except in static and uninteresting ways. Compared to Diamond's stories of hernias and diabetes and asthmatic babies and trips to the emergency room and domestic disturbances and the inadequacies of health insurance and landlords and law enforcement personnel, Patsy feels as if she has no right to her own unhappiness, as if she's never lived at all.

And that's ridiculous, because of everything she's been through with Angela. It's a tragedy, and if someone hadn't experienced it themselves, you couldn't hope to describe it and do it justice. True enough, but everything's already happened, hasn't it, and there's no longer any urgency in it. It's like a war fought a long time ago that everybody's forgotten, and that's so unfair. "Our Lord holds us all in the palm of His hand," says Diamond, finishing her account of large and small misfortunes, indignities, setbacks, taking comfort in the profession of faith. And Patsy hurries to agree. But does she believe it? So much of life is unfairness. God could fix it in an instant if he wanted. A wave of his enormous, God-sized hand, and evil and sickness and death would be banished. God is supposed to love us, but sometimes it seems like he's just not paying enough attention.

Patsy takes out a new sheet of paper. *Dear Angela.* The wine makes her writing spiral out and out, uphill and downhill. *Are you glad you went crazy? I don't mean you did it on purpose because I don't think people can choose to be that way. And even if they could if you laid it all out for them the parts about hospitals and not looking very attractive after a while they'd say no. That's because they aren't crazy! But say once you are good and crazy you might find some advantages to it like you don't care what anybody else thinks and say you felt like a thing or didn't feel like a thing say you feel like you're a scream walking around on two legs*

Patsy stops because this is foolishness, she's a fool. She can't even drink enough to sneak up on crazy. Her body is a clock that says *late late late* and it is the outrageous truth that your whole life can turn out wrong sad wasted and no one else will think twice about it.

It sucks, Jack tells himself, that he can't get cable out in the garage. There's some way to hook it up without the cable people knowing but he isn't sure what that is. It's not worth the trouble because he won't be living here very much longer. He's on the brink of something new. His life, his real life, is about to start, he's positive. Tomorrow or the day after or the day after that, anyway, not long. He felt like this when he was getting ready for the navy but that was only a practice drive, a test run, and now he's ready for the real, the serious kick-ass version. Leave his loser self behind and step up to the plate. "Loser" is a little harsh; "non-player" is more accurate. Never got his head in the game, but that's about to change big-time. He's going to surprise a few people.

Nobody who knows him would think he's ambitious but he is, in a secret-identity sort of way, like Spider-Man. He wants people to say, "You're kidding, the same guy we went to school with?" The way Jack figures it, everybody starts out not famous, and his odds are exactly the same as everybody else's.

Of course the best thing would be if he got famous for doing hero stuff, like the firefighters, or say he managed to get into the military. You were always hearing about guys in the military who were heroes because they saved their buddies or killed especially large numbers of the enemy in spite of personal danger. Sometimes he has a whole movie going on in his head, where he's a navy SEAL on a special-ops mission, crawling on his belly at night over rocky ground. It's an ambush and everything depends on keeping the muscles of his body under hair-trigger control. His mind is calm, zero calm, because he's trained himself to be emotionless about a kill. Take out the target. Do it by the numbers. Part of it's training but part of it's instinct, and he's a natural. Even the old-timers acknowledge this, the hard-asses who never have anything good to say about anybody. But he doesn't let this give him the big head because you can't use up brain space when every cell has to focus on the moment of contact, impact, killing pressure . . .

Jack snaps out of it to find himself on the couch with his dick in his hand and the television yelping and it's embarrassing, really. He needs to get the hell out of this rut he's in, and that should be easy, he's thought it through a million times so why can't he just do it? What's it going to take, what's wrong with him that he can't pry himself loose, execute, act? It's late, he's not sure how late or if it matters, and when he opens the door to the kitchen the house is quiet. He walks a circuit from the kitchen and the den and the living room where no one ever lived and the dining room where none of them ever dined. Again and again, the same track, letting his fingers brush against the walls like he's still a kid, a dumb little kid who doesn't know anything.

The walking hypnotizes him and when Leslie comes out of her bedroom saying, "What? What is it?" he jumps.

She's standing in the doorway, she has on the same old stretched-out T-shirt over a pair of underpants, what she always wears to bed, and he tries not to look at the soft parts of her body, she's his sister, for Christ's sake, but he can't help noticing what he notices, and that makes him feel weird, like now there must be something else screwed up about him, he's a pervert. He calls to mind certain images from porn sites so as to redirect his sensations.

He says, "Nothing, go back to sleep," though he knows she hasn't been asleep, none of them sleep anymore, not normal sleep. The puckered skin just below the elastic of her underpants draws his gaze. Although Leslie isn't fat, there is a fatty look to this part of her leg, like a chicken drumstick, what's wrong with his head? He has to quit being a total freak.

"What are you doing?"

"Exercise," he says. "Cross-training."

"Funny guy." Leslie starts to scratch her ass through her T-shirt, then stops, as if she just figured out she's putting on a show. "Are you OK?"

"Super." What is he supposed to say? *I'm way fucked.*

She yawns. "It's too hot in here. The whatsit, the attic fan, broke. Like, shorted out."

"Yeah?"

"Guess who says it's not worth fixing and we should just wait until winter."

"Figures," Jack says, and for a moment their old alliance

against Patsy unites them. But he's never hated Patsy like Leslie does. He doesn't feel one way or the other about anyone anymore. "Sorry I got you up," he says, ready to stop talking.

"Hey. What's going on with you? I mean, really."

"Nothing. Relax." *What happened that I can't remember? Why am I the way I am? Was I supposed to be different? Was I supposed to be a hero?* All of a sudden it seems stupid, the hero stuff, everything's stupid, and you might as well cut loose, rip the world a new asshole, because it sure as hell isn't going out of its way for you.

"Nothing," he says again, and smiles his goofy smile to reassure her, see, it's only me, little brother, the flake, the screwup, the one nobody thinks is ever paying attention.

Leslie has chosen No Pill tonight, which she decides was a mistake. Although there's a good chance that Pill would have been a mistake as well. She's too tired to sort it out, this puzzle that has no solution or right answer. She's too tired to worry about Jack, who seems even spacier than usual. He needs to get his act together, get out of the damned garage, and most of all quit prowling around the house in the dark, which always spooks her because of Angela. Even after all this time, footsteps in the dark remind her of Angela.

One two three ten twenty thirty eighty ninety one hundred. Counting sheep or anything else never works, neither does rolling from her left side to the fresher territory of her right, or rearranging the flattened pillows. She's going to be a zombie at work. Plus tomorrow (today?) is Friday, and in addition to work she'll have Wes to deal with.

Deal with: that's not romance talking. But this thing with Wes has been going on for months now. She wonders if she should start looking for a new job. Affairs like this never come to good ends, she knows that from her magazines. Surely it won't be long before Wes comes to her, sprinkling tears, and tells her how bad he feels about everything, how it's killing him to live a lie, and even though she's the most incredible, amazing girl, etc. etc. blah blah blah. It's a scene she really wouldn't mind missing. First, though, she should check and see how many vacation days she has coming.

Angela said, "It is the natural order of the world for children to devour their parents." She was eating a bowl of chocolate pudding that Leslie brought her and Leslie can't stand to watch the way she sucks and tongues to get the pudding down her throat, it's disgusting, and it's disgusting to have to listen to this kind of talk.

"You're nuts, you realize that," Leslie said. She felt free to say whatever she liked to Angela, since it was always just the two of them.

"Life uses up life," Angela said. "And that is the essence of hunger." She had a ring of chocolate pudding around her mouth.

"Nuts," Leslie repeated. "If you weren't nuts, you'd wash your hair once in a while. And get out of bed long enough to change the sheets." It felt righteous to be scornful. She wanted nothing to do with anyone so revolting. It was odious, beyond belief to think that she had once grown inside Angela's body, like a stone inside a swollen fruit. She had all the normal squeamishness of a girl her age and then some. It made her ill, ill, ill to think that everyone walking the earth had parents, and all the fat old boring old moms and pops had done vile, naked things to each other.

Everybody she knew complained about their parents and thought they were gross, but none of them came home to Angela, none of them had mothers whose scalp showed lines of dirt, like a planted field, or who forgot to flush the toilet. Her father was no help. He acted like nothing was ever his fault. Angela began leaving her bedroom at night to prowl the house. She was quiet; it was the smell that woke you.

"If you don't get in the shower I'm going to take you out in the yard and spray you with the hose," Leslie threatened. It was always just the two of them. Leslie hated being this close to her. She hated breathing the same air Angela breathed. "Would you like that, huh?" Angela smelled of something rotten being burnt, not just sweat and musty hair, something more, as if all the sugar inside her was subject to combustion. Leslie turned the shower on, set the hot water drilling, made Angela peel off her crusted sweaty pants and underpants and sweatshirt and nasty yellow ropelike bra. "Soap," Leslie said. "Tell me you still remember what soap is." Angela's abdomen hung down in loose folds, like something tied around her waist. It was outrageous, all the different things that could be ugly about the human body.

One of the advantages of the hospital where Angela now resides is that minimum standards of hygiene are adhered to. Attendants in raincoatlike gear guide the patients into chutes resembling those used to handle livestock. Every surface is tiled, and nozzles set at different levels spray jets of water and soap. By the time Patsy took Leslie and Jack to see Angela in the hospital, they had scrubbed her down to nothing. She was dressed in the pink and white pajamas they had sent her for Mother's Day. Her skin had broken out in acne, patches of it on her chin and forehead, and her hair had been cut short. Someone had parted it in the middle and secured it with two pink plastic barrettes. She was shapeless, like a lump of cotton stuffing left out in the rain.

It was the medication that made her skin break out. There were always side effects, but they were minor and controllable. At least, this was what one of the nurses said to Patsy in a loudly whispered conversation while Angela was quiet in a chair and Leslie and Jack sat at a table playing cards.

By then they had been told that Angela was sick, that she couldn't help the things she had done, and they must be patient and understanding. It was implied that their positive attitude and support would be an important part of Angela's recovery. Leslie couldn't stand hearing it, one more installment of Patsy's sappy Christian noise, always insisting on the way things should be and ignoring the way they really were. At such times she felt an unwelcome kinship with Angela. Who would have thought it, after everything. But in this at least she was her mother's daughter: she knew the power of hatred. The card game she and Jack were playing was go fish. Leslie had just asked Jack for all his sevens, and he'd said, "Go fish," so tickled that here was a game he could win at, when Angela flew without wings from her chair and threw a set of grinning upper and lower dentures on the table like a party trick and Leslie screamed and screamed. Every one of Angela's decayed and festering teeth had been extracted.

What are little girls made of, what are little girls made of? Sugar and spice and everything nice. Leslie remembers someone singing that to her when she was very small. Was it Angela? Had she ever done mother things, held and rocked her, sung songs, counted her fingers and toes? It's nothing Leslie can call to mind, but she thinks it must have happened. You had to know a thing in order to miss it. Her mother is the thing lost, the shape of her hunger.

Sugar and spice and. Maybe she used to be. Sweet. Dimples, curls. Not anymore. She's a blowtorch, a barbed wire fence. At work she takes phone calls from policyholders who have suffered insurable accidents: car crashes, trees fallen through the roof, flooded basements, ruined furniture, injuries, theft, loss, disaster. The women speak through clogged tears, the men are often testy, irritated, rigid with worry. Leslie is always polite, she always uses expressions of sympathy, but none of it touches her. That's the breaks, folks. People need to toughen up. Not every loss can be repaired or compensated. Some things are best left ruined.

Leslie gets out of bed to go to the bathroom. She listens hard, but the house holds its breath.

Once she gets back in bed, she means to stay awake. There's not much point in sleep so late/so early. She wants to stay alert, vigilant, guard against sleep, because there is an expectation of something about to happen. There is always the expectation and dread of things that come to you when you are asleep. Leslie's closed eyes begin to see dream pictures, little cartoon scraps of things, and she fights to come awake. The pictures go grainy and slide away and she's alert, waiting, her heart gulping and her skin tight.

When the burnt smell reaches her, she says, *Stop, Stop it,* because she knows it's Angela. She rolls away and flails her hands, but it's like moving through glue, and sleep is still holding her down. Or no, it's Angela crushing Leslie beneath her weight and stink, Angela on a night ten years ago and how many nights since. Angela's teeth rip a long piece of skin from Leslie's collarbone, then worry the flesh farther down, the place where Leslie even now has scars, rubbery welts and ridges, she is being eaten! *What are little girls made of, what are little girls made of?* She doesn't feel her own blood but she sees it on Angela's mouth, black like pudding, in this her dream she can see in the dark. Angela says, *You are my perfect food,* and Leslie knows it's true, she is only perfect when she is a part of Angela.

Leslie has sobbed herself well and truly awake by now. There's a little gray light outlining the edges of the windows, and she stares at this, her mind floating.

But the burnt smell is still there, and Jack is pounding on her closed door, calling her name. "I'm awake," Leslie says, as if that is the most important thing.

Jack is rattling the doorknob but it's locked. When Leslie opens the door she sees him looking both scared and important, and a moving, shifting darkness behind him. "What are you, deaf?" he says. "Come on, we need to get out of here."

"Crap." Leslie stares into the smoke-filled hallway. She can't come up with anything better to say and that bothers her. She pulls on a pair of jeans and her shoes and looks around her, wondering if anything here is worth saving. She finds her purse and her keys and fills a pillowcase with stuff from her dresser and desk drawers, she doesn't stop to think what, and takes the blanket from the foot of the bed and later there's probably more she'll miss but everything is right now.

Jack pulls her by the hand down the hallway and through the thickening air. In the middle of everything she marvels at how large her brother's hand is, how big and manlike he's become: when did all that happen? The house is talking. There is noise like a hailstorm, popping and banging. Fire is trying to break through the walls. The smoke reminds her of an amusement park ride, the kind meant to scare you, clouds of it rushing up or falling back, and if Leslie isn't scared it's because nothing seems more natural than the house burning.

When they get outside they cough and rub their stinging eyes and try to get the smoke taste out of their mouths. Patsy is already there, at the end of the driveway, untidy in her old bathrobe. She looks at them briefly when they join her. "Well," she says. "I guess that's that." It strikes all three of them as a strange thing to have said, but no one offers any further comment. They watch the fire poke its way out of the roof in a column of pure flame that rises high into the air. One of the excited neighbors has called the fire department by now and there's a great commotion of sirens and trucks and hoses as the firemen aim jets of water at the flames, producing angry white steam.

"It must have been the attic fan," Jack says. "An electrical short." But none of them can remember turning the fan on. Leslie says something about insurance, about calling her office, making a weak joke of it. The fire keeps finding new ways to burn. It twists and licks and there are small and large explosions as it encounters gas lines, plumbing lines, fuel sources. It is such a transfixing sight that it's startling to realize the sun is up and if you look in any other direction, it's a bright day with a hard blue sky. Leslie opens her mouth, she's about to remark on this, when the roof gives way and the noise of it blots out everything else.

THE WOMAN
TAKEN IN
ADULTERY

I had two daughters and a husband who didn't notice things. I was lonesome. Sex isn't always about sex. Besides, sex was now meant to be the province of my daughters, who were sixteen and fourteen. Their moon waxed while mine waned. Great hormonal waves rippled from them. Their hair shone, their skins were as fresh as the inside of a good apple, and every cell of their bodies was deranged with sex. This wasn't always obvious; sometimes it took the form of tears, or moping, or playing loud music, but I knew all the symptoms. The boys prowled around them, while sour old Mom tried to keep Ms. Egg and Mr. Sperm from congregating. My daughters flounced and preened and every moment of every day was a drama and they were the stars. Funny old fussbudget Mom! Comic secondary character, equipped with apron and feather duster!

My husband was no trouble. Never had been. I'd grown used to stepping over and around him the way you might a large dog sound asleep in a doorway. You start out being married together and you end up being married apart. I'm convinced that's the truth for most people, if they were honest about it. "What's for dinner?" he'd say, and I'd put his plate down, and he'd eat what was set before him. It wasn't our only conversation, but there were times when it seemed like our most important.

I'd tried to cultivate other interests, like everyone said you were supposed to. I signed up for a symphony series, I took enrichment classes at the community college. These were activities that proved useful later, once I started needing excuses to get out of the house. And I actually did learn how to perform CPR, and a thing or two about investment strategies, and thanks to the art appreciation class, I came to know and admire a number of the major painters, notably Gauguin. Gauguin, who trampled his settled life for the passion of art. Like most people, the tropical paintings were my favorite. All those flat bright pools of color, all those dream beaches and brown-skinned lovers. I liked the whole idea of painting, turning the hidden speech of the heart into a picture in a gold frame, hung on a wall for everybody to see.

Because after a while the thrilling part of secrecy wears off. At the outset of an affair you look at crowds of dreary people, and you know you seem just as ordinary as any of them, and yet you have this whole hidden life blazing up inside you. And maybe they do too, maybe the world is full of jolly secrets, and people are more interesting than you believed. But they aren't. Artists make you think they are, or maybe they are only interesting once the artists turn them into subjects.

Infidelity became my work of art. I wanted to make myself remarkable. Of course, vanity and spite and other unattractive motives were involved. But what if the sweet and reckless part of life was declared over for you? What if you lived in a house with people who never saw you, what if your skin was dusty from disuse? Wouldn't you want to hang a gold frame around yourself?

I met his ex-wife before I met him. It was at a happy hour with a few women friends, and the ex had tagged along with someone. She didn't know anybody else, and her being there made us all polite, at least for the first drink. Then we started talking mean about the husbands.

"He won't close the bathroom door. It's like living in a kennel."

"Is nose hair growth a side effect of Viagra? Anybody know?"

"I work out recipes while we're having sex. The other night I thought, 'Chicken breasts with gorgonzola and walnuts! Yes! Yes! Yes!'"

The ex-wife had been quiet, listening. She was pretty, I guess. She had a small, sweet face, like a doll's, but with something lopsided or off-center about it, so you had to keep looking at her, trying to figure out what it was about her that made your eyes cross. She said, "I ran over my husband with the car."

We all stopped talking. She took another sip of her margarita, put it down again in exactly the same spot. "It was the Subaru."

When she didn't say anything more, someone else said, "Those are supposed to be nice cars."

"I had a Subaru once," said another woman. "Not a great car, but a good car."

We all examined, with apparent interest, the surface of the tabletop, the wet circles from our drinks, the drowning cocktail napkins. "So did your husband, you know, die?" someone finally asked.

She looked at us with her flat, doll's eyes. She seemed to have trouble remembering who we were. I wondered if she should be drinking, if maybe there was medication involved. "We're divorced now."

Not dead, then. "Was he, uh, seriously hurt?"

The friend who had brought her jumped in then. "He is such a jerk." And went on to say how faithless, feckless, and cadlike he'd been, and we all made sympathetic noises about men and their beastliness, hoping all the while we'd hear something really lurid.

Finally the ex roused herself. "I hit a UPS truck first. That slowed me down."

We wondered if the UPS driver had come out of things all right, but she didn't say. She finished her drink, tipping it up to drain every last drop. "I don't drive anymore," she confided.

She didn't say anything else, and pretty soon after that her friend took her away.

So when I finally met him, some time later, I remembered the name, made the connection, and the first word out of my mouth was "Subaru."

"I see you've met Marianne."

"Just in passing."

"She likes to tell that story. She usually finds some way to work it into the conversation."

We were at a dinner party. Me with my husband, who I had trained to sit up and beg food from the table. Him with some date, the kind of date you find right after a divorce. She spent the appetizer, entrée, and dessert courses squeezing her boobs together over her plate. I said, "So how bad did she get you?"

"Just winged me. I sort of bounced."

"She mentioned a UPS truck."

"Those are solid, solid vehicles. I'm impressed by how well they hold up."

We stopped speaking for a time as the wine was passed around, and his date claimed his attention. My husband was eating his shrimp cocktail. He finished it, then started in on mine. When we turned back to each other there was already a current of interest between us, that agreeable pelvis-to-pelvis speech that I remembered from so long ago. Yes, he was a good-looking man. But it was probably the car thing that got to me. It was rather thrilling.

He knew I was married. He was sitting on my left, my ring hand, plus there was Old Shep gnawing away on my right. He said, "I suppose people think I deserved to get run over."

I said I wouldn't know. That I hadn't heard even one side of the story, let alone both. "How fast was she going anyway?"

"She floored it, but she didn't have that much room to get up to speed. So probably not much over forty-five. Then, of course, the UPS truck kind of took the starch out of things."

"Still . . ."

He said, "It was a hard one to explain to the insurance people."

No one was paying much attention to us. My husband was happy with his steak kabobs. His date was flexing her chest muscles in another direction. I said, "Was it any one thing you did, or was she just mad in general?"

He shrugged. He had fine dark eyebrows that knit and unknit in an expressive fashion as he came up with self-serving explanations. "It was a gradual disenchantment on her part."

When we got home that night, the daughters were having an argument about Diet Coke, who had drunk the last can of Diet Coke when there were clear proprietary rights. "It was mine and you knew it," said the older. "Mine mine mine."

"You need it more, that's for sure," said the younger.

My husband trudged past them on his way upstairs. It was nothing new, only the girls fighting again.

"You're always taking my stuff."

"That's because you think you own everything in the whole entire house."

"Mom, tell her to leave my stuff alone."

"Mom, tell her how big her ass is getting."

"Jerk!"

"Bitch!"

"Hah! You haven't even seen bitch yet."

"Ooh ooh ooh. I'm so scared."

"Enough," I said. "Zip it. You got no problems. Neither of you."

The older daughter swished her hair in contempt. She was a tall girl with a figure like something carved, like one of those majestic painted ladies they used to put on the prows of sailing ships. She always thought she was too big, but everything about her fit together so perfectly. "God. I can't wait until I'm old enough to get out of this cruddy cruddy house and away from you people."

"I bet she's already old enough. Huh? Isn't she, Mom?" The younger daughter was smaller, and if she wasn't a serious beauty like her sister, her looks were prettier, more accessible.

"Nobody's going anywhere," I said. "I wouldn't turn either of you depraved hussies loose on an unsuspecting world."

They looked at me with that dour, suspicious expression they got when I agreed with both of them about how unpleasant the other one was.

"I'm gonna be so out of here," said the older. "By the time I'm twenty-five, I'm going to have my own magazine, like Oprah."

"By the time I'm thirty-five, I'll own the corporation that buys out your stupid magazine."

"Nice," I said. "You'll both go far. But it's not so great, getting older. It just means your outside dries up while your insides keep boiling away in an unseemly, undignified fashion."

"You're weird, Mom."

"Thank you," I said.

I called the man I'd met and asked him if he wanted to meet for a drink and he said, Sure, why not. I could think of a lot of different why nots, but I sailed right past them. I dressed up a little. I put on perfume, but not the killer variety. I wanted to keep all my options open. I felt guilty and a little sick, but I set my nervous feelings on a shelf where I wouldn't have to bump into them at every moment.

"So tell me," I said, once he and I were twinkling at each other over wineglasses. "How long were you married?"

"I'd say seven or eight years. The exact dates escape me."

"Any kids?"

"No. Just as well. The divorced dad thing is messed up."

"I have two daughters. If I ever got divorced they would have the deep satisfaction of hating me forever."

"That sounds a little harsh."

"Trust me on this one."

"You're a very attractive woman."

As a compliment, it was about a five on a scale of ten. Maybe that's what he thought I was, a five. "Hmm," I said.

"I feel this connection between us. I know it's wrong, but I can't help it."

"Oh please," I said. "Try harder."

"I don't usually have to," he admitted.

I was beginning to think that in spite of my resolve, this was all a bad idea. Or rather, I knew it was a bad idea, but now it was looking shabby and depressing as well. I said, "I'm supposed to be at my art appreciation class. If I hurry, I think I can get there for part of the discussion on Velázquez. I already did the reading."

"Hey, could I tell you something? There's times I honestly miss my wife."

I mistrusted the sadness of men in such instances, although he probably was sad, in a self-absorbed sort of way.

"Sure, things got rocky between us. I guess I could have tried a little harder there too."

I just looked at him.

"I stayed out late and didn't call. I screwed around on her. I didn't show appreciation. I forgot things she told me. I'd see her mouth moving, making shapes, and I knew I should be listening, but it was like hypnosis. This complete out-of-the-body experience. I'd snap out of it and she'd be stamping her little foot and screaming, 'Frank! Frank! You didn't hear a word I said, did you?'"

"I wonder if the whole business with the car was just to get your attention."

"That's possible," he admitted.

"What is it, exactly, that you miss about being married?"

He pushed a hand through his hair. I liked the way he did it, without vanity. His hair was going thin at the temples and the skin beneath was smooth and worn. It wasn't at all attractive, but it was a human thing. "I hate coming home to an empty house. I hate having to make all my own noise. My wife, she was always doing something, running the garbage disposal, talking on the phone. Vacuuming. I'm thinking of getting a parrot. Do you know anything about parrots?"

"There's so much noise where I live, sometimes I pretend it's all in Italian, like opera, and I only have to focus when somebody screams or falls down."

"So I guess we have that in common," he said, brightening.

"No offense, but I'm not sure I want to have anything in common with you."

"Look," he said. "I'm that guy. The one they come after with the car, or the gun, or the lawyer. But it's also true that they never seem to leave me alone. If you like we can try it a time or two, see how it works for you."

"Try what?" I said. "Oh."

We tried it a time or two. And then a few times more. It took some getting used to. I don't mean it wasn't godalmighty pleasurable. It was, especially after the sleepy routines of married sex. I give the man credit. He could have made love to a potted plant. But there were times I felt strangely disassociated from it all. I could never entirely believe what I was doing, at least not in the exact moment I was doing it. It was a failure of the imagination on my part. You catch a glimpse of yourself in some naked and enthusiastic state, and the believing part of you just shuts down. Maybe that's what they used to call conscience.

I'd spend a couple of hours with the paramour, then shower, dress, run back home to unload the dishwasher and find the jeans that one or another daughter couldn't find. My husband would ask me how class was, and I'd say it was OK, or else he'd already be asleep, a familiar lumpy shape beneath the blankets, rather like the famous photograph of the Loch Ness monster, and I wouldn't have to say anything at all.

I decided that maybe this was a workable solution, sex as a kind of Happy Meal, nicely packaged and available at your con-

venience. Somebody to look at you with honest, if venal, appreciation. Meanwhile, the rest of your life would stumble along as
usual, and nobody would ever be the wiser. But of course that
was not what happened.

The instructor for the art appreciation class was one of those
women who always look like a graduate student, no matter that
they have been out of school for a decade or more. Her name was
Leslie Valentine, a lovely name that, sadly, didn't fit her. Leslie
wore droopy cardigans and corduroy pants and desert boots. She
should have done something to her hair. The black-framed
glasses were either meant to be funky, or else they were the same
kind she'd been wearing since sixth grade and she saw no reason
to change. This is all superficial stuff, and it sounds catty as hell,
when in fact I liked Leslie. It just seemed that anyone so involved
with aesthetics would think to arrange themselves better.

Leslie worked as an assistant curator at one of the big downtown museums. It was an underpaid job of the sort that dooms
you to life in an apartment with a cat. The little bit of money the
community college teaching paid her probably came in handy.
But she really seemed to love coming in with her trays of slides
and showing us how to see the things she saw: the elaborate narrative of a Brueghel, the arching patterns of a Bottiicelli, the delicate locket around the neck of the lady in the Renaissance
portrait, its inscription reading "Amor." The course was titled
Masterworks of European Art, which suited us all fine. Leslie was
an old-school gal, devoted to her cherubs and frescoes, while the
rest of us were just simple enough to want a picture to be *about*
something, something we could recognize.

Even when I started skulking around and living my secret life,

I tried to make it to Leslie's class. She'd rush in with spots on her glasses, and a splash of tomato soup on her front from one of her hurried and inadequate meals, and start talking full-speed about da Vinci's sketchbooks. She was so enthusiastic, and so convinced that her enthusiasm mattered, it halfway convinced you. Why not spend your life endlessly circling museum corridors like a fish in an aquarium, harmlessly gratified?

It was Rembrandt week. Rembrandt loomed pretty large for Leslie Valentine. Rembrandt, one of the truly masterful Old Masters, a really big dude. Rembrandt, the painter of light, he was called, although you couldn't help noticing how many of his pictures were all varnishy dark. That class session we'd worked our way through the self-portraits and *The Night Watch* and *The Anatomy Lesson* and some others. I was drifting a bit in the pleasant half-dark of the classroom as the slides clicked and the projector emitted its comforting bland whir. I was thinking of the last time I'd seen the paramour, and already looking forward to the next time, when Leslie's instructive voice reached me. "...typical of his work from the sixteen thirties in the small scale of the figures and the use of dramatic illumination, *The Woman Taken in Adultery* ..."

"The what?" I said, stupidly and out loud.

My fellow students shifted around to look at me. We never said that much in class. We were content to be passive vessels, filled by Leslie's agreeable, lilting voice. But Leslie was happy to stop her lecture for a footnote. "*The Woman Taken in Adultery.* Dated sixteen forty-four but most probably from the sixteen thirties. It hangs in the National Gallery, London."

I peered at the slide, which showed what might have been a gloomy, half-ruined church, and a crowd of people in smudgy darkness. And since I felt stupid for saying anything, the only thing to do was to keep right on talking: "My goodness, it looks like a very public sort of adultery."

Everybody laughed at that, Leslie too. "It's the aftermath," she explained. "It's from the New Testament."

As she told us more, I began to recollect it, vaguely, from some lost Sunday school time. A woman was discovered being unfaithful to her husband (Caught in the act? Incriminating cell phone records?) and brought before Jesus. Jewish law decreed that she be stoned to death. It was a setup, with the priests in the crowd wanting to see if Jesus would either condemn the woman or go against the law. Instead he knelt in the dust and wrote, "Let he who is without sin cast the first stone." And everybody slunk away.

"How about the man, you know, there must have been a man involved," a classmate, another woman, asked. In fact the class was entirely made up of women, matrons like myself. We were the only ones bored enough and hopeful enough to devote one evening a week to culture.

"I bet he was the one who turned her in."

"He deserved better than some slut."

"Oh honey," another woman drawled. "They wrote him a ticket, and if he goes to traffic school, it won't stay on his record."

We were all cracking up, even Leslie. It felt liberating, in a witchy kind of way. I squinted at the slide. The figures were tiny and I couldn't make out much. Leslie recovered herself enough to say, "In fact, a great many artists from that era chose to illustrate this particular text. You must remember, other audiences would have recognized the subject. Maybe they just knew their scriptures better, but they also knew the kinds of things they could expect to find in paintings. Like we know that picture postcards are going to show the Statue of Liberty or the Golden Gate

Bridge. Tell you what. Next week, as a bonus, I'll bring in slides of some other artists' versions."

Oh, goody.

The paramour and I were lying in his bed, waiting for the clock to tick down to when I'd have to go. He reached beneath the sheets and found something he liked, a breast. "Sexy," he murmured.

"Did you know that in biblical times I would have been stoned to death?"

"Whoa. That would be a definite buzz-kill."

"Do most people get caught doing this? I bet you know. I bet you've had experience."

"Some do. Sure. Law of averages. How come you're asking, you starting to get bad vibes at home?"

"I don't have the kind of marriage where you get vibes."

"Well, that's a good thing."

"Yes and no," I said. I wondered how much longer I would be able to keep the whole affair going, at what point I'd grow bored or sated or scared. I figured that once it was over I'd go back to being a normal wife again. I'd cash in some guilt coupons and cook my husband his favorite meals. I'd overfeed him like a goldfish.

He said, "Marriage just doesn't seem to be cutting it anymore. Have you noticed? Everybody's thinking they got a bad deal. So they get married a second or third time and the whole unhappy business starts all over again. Nobody learns a thing."

"The painter Gauguin," I said, "left his wife and children and set out on a series of travels to Martinique, Tahiti, and the Marquesas. Although he was in his forties and fifties by then, and ill with syphilis, he took a series of very young girls, thirteen and fourteen, to be his mistresses."

"That's the kind of guy who probably should have just stayed home."

"But he produced sublime paintings. You know. Art." This was only argument for argument's sake. After all, fourteen was the age of my youngest daughter.

He shook his head. "I don't know beans about art. But believe me, not everybody who screws around is an artist."

"Honey," my husband said, "I thought you were going out to pick up the dry cleaning last night, and here I can't find any clean shirts."

Leslie Valentine was as good as her word. The next week she brought in another ten or twelve representations of *The Woman Taken in Adultery*. "There were more," she said, "but this is a pretty good sample."

It looked like everybody had wanted to paint me back then. Part of the appeal was the ready-made dramatic tableau, sure, but part of it was obviously the lady herself. She was most often shown in fetching dishabille, as was appropriate for someone who'd just been in between the sheets. In a Jobst Harrich painting, there was even an exposed nipple. The woman and Jesus were surrounded by a crowd of men, some of them outright leering (Lorenzo Lotto, Lucas Cranach the Younger). Other artists (Poussin, Polenov) were more interested in rendering movement, all the pointing and arguing. Valentin de Boulogne painted each face as an individual portrait, after the style of Caravaggio.

Brueghel's version was populated by spooky, pallid creatures who seemed to have lived their entire lives underground. Only in the Tintoretto, the Poussin, and the Veronese was there anyone recognizable as the paramour, and he was always being hustled offstage. No stoning for him. The beautiful Veronese was the only one to include numerous female figures, as well as a dog, the symbol of fidelity, and a naked child (Cupid?) hiding in shame.

Leslie Valentine guided us through the slides with her usual skill. After last week's gigglefest, we were all loosened up and talkative. "Draperies," a woman said. "It's too bad we can't all walk around wearing nice flowing draperies anymore."

"They hide so many figure flaws," someone else agreed.

Leslie Valentine said, "They were a showing-off thing for painters. How well they could render all the folds and creases." Leslie seemed to be enjoying herself too. She'd freshened up her look and was wearing a pink blouse with a red fabric rose in the lapel. I wondered if it wouldn't be a kindness to suggest some new glasses, maybe contact lenses.

"Are you supposed to feel sorry for the woman?" somebody asked. "I mean, the story's all about Christian charity and forgiveness, but there seems to be so much ogling going on."

"Ah," Leslie said, nodding so hard that her flower quivered. "That's the thing about artists. It's all showing off. You're meant to ogle the whole painting."

I was trying to envision me in a painting. It would never happen, I was too plump and saggy. The women in Leslie's slide show were young and sweet and rosy, even in their shamed and artistically rumpled conditions. Nobody ever thought or wanted to think about the middle-aged, the unpretty, the fair-to-middling among us doing interesting carnal things. Maybe a more updated approach was called for, something more abstract and nonrepresentational. Here was a streak of vermilion shading into dismal brown, and that was the arc of passion and its inevitable flaming out, here were green questions and blue doubts, and a lot of stippled blank gray that represented the future . . .

"There's no specific mention of the husband in the biblical account," Leslie was saying. "If he's one of the accusers, the pictures don't distinguish him."

"He's been playing golf all weekend. He doesn't even know what's going on."

"All along he'd been telling his girlfriend he was divorced."

"He didn't start to suspect until he began running out of clean shirts."

"Ladies, ladies," said Leslie, laughing along with everyone else, except, of course, me, "you are such perceptive critics tonight."

I raised my hand. "I think that in spite of all the shouting and the threats and the nastiness, the woman kind of likes being the center of attention."

My oldest daughter and her boyfriend were sitting in his car, parked in front of the house. The engine was running and shreds of vicious music leaked past the closed windows. I pulled in the driveway and my daughter rolled her window down to wave. "Hi, Mom."

I walked over to them. "Hi sweetie. Hi Josh." I nodded at the boyfriend, who was busy rearranging his shirt. There was a hard-on in there somewhere. "Don't stay out too long, OK?"

"We were just talking about, you know, school, stuff at school." My daughter looked over at the boyfriend, who tried to assume an expression of detached scholastic inquiry.

"If that's your story and you're sticking to it, fine."

"Ha ha." The boyfriend laughed gamely. He wasn't a bad kid. Just too full of sperm.

When my daughter came in the house, I observed her closely for evidence of violation. But she merely looked pensive. "So, how's Josh tonight?"

"Boys are like the aliens in old sci-fi movies, aren't they? The ones who try to invade the earth by covering it with giant pods or something. All that swarming and spawning. Oh relax. I'm just talking."

"Not really relaxed yet."

"Mom? Does sex come naturally?"

"Really not relaxed now."

"I'm asking a serious question here. Is there something wrong with you if it all seems kind of icky? I mean, penises. What's the big deal? Yuck."

What to tell my good girl? Close her eyes and think of England? "There's definitely an ick factor involved." I considered remarking on the high ick ratings among fumbling teenage boys. "But there's a wow factor too. The whole concept takes some time to process. And there's really no rush."

"I guess." She looked unconvinced. "So did you and Dad—"

"Please. Not now. Maybe in about thirty years."

"All right, never mind. Thanks." She stooped to hug me. She was a couple of inches taller than I was, and the flood of her hair enveloped me. I could smell her shampoo, a meadow full of synthetic flowers. Then she stepped back. We were both a little teary. "By the way," she said, "your blouse is buttoned wrong."

The paramour and I were having an argument. In bed, of course. He said that someone was calling him and not answering when he picked up. No heavy breathing or anything, just dead air, and the certainty that somebody else was on the other end. "It's Marianne. She's stalking me."

"You have no idea who it is. It could be random. It could be anybody else you've pissed off. The usual suspects."

"I know it's Marianne," he insisted. "I know what she sounds like not talking. There were whole months when she didn't talk to me."

"Hang up. Call the police."

"You don't understand. It's a test of wills, to see who cracks first. I have to get her to talk. She has to get me to admit I know it's her. So I say things like, 'Anita honey, speak up, I can't hear you.'"

"Who's Anita?"

"Nobody. It's just a name. Then I start telling 'Anita' how hot she is, and how I can't wait to see her again, and all the things I'm going to do to her. It's practically phone sex."

"Maybe it really is Anita," I said.

"What?"

"Nothing. You should call Marianne. Tell her you've been thinking about her. Say any old thing. Ask how she's doing these days."

"Why would I want to do that?"

"Because she's still trying to get you to pay attention to her. How about some normal, human, civilized conversation."

"I don't have to pay attention to her. That's the whole point of divorce."

"She didn't get her money's worth. She thinks you still owe her."

"Women," he said, making one of those unfortunate faces, the kind that moves you to thoughts of smacking them with something heavy or maybe not heavy but merely disgusting, like a whole trout. "You're never satisfied until a guy totally capitulates. You don't understand that men are warriors. Our natural instinct is to fight back. Steer our own course. Scratch where we itch. Seek the far horizon. Roam free."

"Sounds like a job for Animal Control," I said.

"Honey?" my husband said. "We've been getting all these calls for Frank. Do we know anybody named Frank?"

We were coming to the end of the term in art appreciation class, and since we'd all been having so much fun, Leslie Valentine suggested an outing to the museum where she worked. She'd get off a little early and show us around, a special guided tour, then we could go out for drinks. It sounded great. An evening of Art with the girls. I told the paramour I'd have to skip our regular session. I told my husband there was a special occasion planned and I'd be away most of the afternoon and evening. He seemed surly, even suspicious, and I felt an actual sense of injury, of being unjustly accused. This was purely innocent, no fornication involved, though of course I couldn't say that.

"Since when did you get so interested in Art?"

"It's one of those things that sneaks up on you."

The paramour wasn't very happy either. "It's a bunch of paintings. They aren't going anywhere. Can't you see them some other time?"

"Don't be such a big baby."

"Well maybe I'll just find something else to do," he said, all injured and snotty. "Or someone."

"Like you need an excuse for that," I said, in my own nasty tone. We seemed to have reached that phase of things.

On the appointed evening I drove downtown and entered the echoey marble precincts of the museum. We had been told to meet at the Mary Cassatt, and several of my classmates were already there. Everybody had dressed up. We admired each other, we admired the paintings behind their velvet ropes, each with its halo of light, its beautiful frame and informative label. We were too excited to pay them any real attention at first. They were only bright windows of color, letting Art into the room. Then we settled down and our talk quieted and we began to look in earnest.

Here was the brushwork that gave the little landscape its depth. And some notable foreshortening in the portrait of the Spanish gentleman. An impressionist's sunny dream of light on water. We had learned to see things. The windows had opened for us. As we took our slow promenade there was a sense of other audiences, the ones who had viewed these same paintings in this or other rooms. Powdered ladies with fans, men with swords. Bustles and furs, canes and slouch hats.

Leslie Valentine had dressed up also, in rather remarkable fashion. She came tripping toward us, wearing real, grown-up shoes. The heels made a light, scattered sound on the tile floors. "Hey guys!" She had on a short little skirt. Her glasses were still in evidence, but swinging on a long chain. She'd slicked her hair back into a gleaming knot. She looked smart and knowing and artsy-chic.

"Wow, Leslie," we all said. "Makeover city."

"Oh come on," she said, self-conscious now. "It's all just stuff I already had in the closet. Are you ready for your tour?"

I'd checked and the museum didn't have even one incarnation of *The Woman Taken in Adultery.* So I felt serene and detached, ready to give myself over to the pleasures of the occasion without any melodramatic personal thoughts. There was a small Gauguin, and that got me going for a moment, but it was only from his Sythetist period, not one of the dangerous tropical visions. I wandered in and out of the range of Leslie's voice, contented, serene, the temporary owner of all I surveyed, by virtue of my discerning eye.

Someone fell into step beside me. I looked up. "Oh crap."

"It's a public place," said the paramour. "Anybody can pay their money and walk right in."

"Apparently so."

"All this is Art, huh?" He swiveled his head from side to side, bunching up his face as if trying to sniff out the source of a smell. "It looks pretty much the way I imagined it. Old."

"The moderns are in another wing." I couldn't believe he'd shown up here. It was juvenile and stalkerish, more of the same old inevitable messy romantic wreckage.

At the same time, it was kind of cool.

Several of my classmates had already noticed him. He was the kind of man you noticed. I said, "I'm going to go on about my business and pretend you aren't here."

"That's fine. Don't mind me." He trailed after me a little distance as I stood in front of an eighteenth-century portrait. "Who's this?"

"A lady who had her portrait painted."

"Is she supposed to be hot or something? Because she looks pretty average to me."

"I want to go listen to my teacher. Either go somewhere else or don't say anything."

"You won't even know I'm here," he promised.

We made our way over to where Leslie was standing next to a

Crucifixion scene labeled School of Giotto. Everyone moved over so as to make space for us. Of course they'd been watching. I could tell from the overpolite way they averted their gaze that they assumed the worst about us. If the crowds in the adultery paintings had been all women, no one would be making eye contact.

The Crucifixion featured solid gold halos, like platters, and flat-faced saints. Even Christ on the cross had an expression that was barely sketched in. He looked like somebody who might be having a bad day. Leslie was talking about the difference between realism and representation, how it had never even been a goal of these earlier artists to reproduce what the eye saw. How painting progressed, if that was the right word, to the near-photographic quality of, say, Vermeer, and how over time it had gone in other directions entirely. How realism was consigned to illustrators. How Christ on the cross might be represented by a congruence of shapes or of colors.

The paramour nudged me. "She really knows her onions when it comes to this stuff, doesn't she?"

I told him to hush. The group was moving into the next room and I didn't want to miss anything. "So are you going to stick around here for a while?" the paramour asked. "Do you have to look at every single picture?"

"Go away. Go watch sports or something."

He was standing behind me as I tried to focus on a Corot landscape. I could feel the twitchy heat he was giving off. "You look so damn sexy tonight. I really like this little lace thingie."

"It's a bra strap. Put it on ice. I'm busy."

"I can't help myself," he murmured, pawing at the ground with one foot.

"I think you have me confused with Anita."

He pulled me backward into the room we'd just left, and

started kissing me. "Unngh," I said, protesting. His teeth felt too big. I didn't even have time to close my eyes. Which is why when my husband appeared in my field of vision, sauntering along, consulting a program, I saw him.

My husband paused in front of us as if we were another exhibit. I attempted to make eloquent facial expressions over the paramour's shoulder. "Oh my!" I tried to convey. "This is certainly one of those absurd situations you wish was happening to someone else."

The paramour released me from the liplock and I peeled myself away from him. "What are you doing here?" I asked my husband. Which is just about the guiltiest thing you can say.

My husband said, "So I'm guessing this is Frank."

I introduced them and they shook hands. They were very gentlemanly about it. I guess it was the ultimate guy thing. Keeping your cool. I wasn't sure what I was supposed to do. I seemed necessary to what was going on, but not especially important. The paramour said, "I'm afraid there's been a bit of a misunderstanding."

"That can happen," my husband said.

"A regrettable lapse of judgment on my part."

"I appreciate your saying so."

"Let me assure you, it was a more or less trivial episode."

"Hey," I said at that point, but they were ignoring me.

Some of the women from the art appreciation class had drifted in to watch, along with a couple of the security guards. "It's OK," I said to the assembled group. "We're way past stoning."

"Personally," one of the women told me, "I like the husband better."

"I'd rate it a toss-up," said another. "Depends on how you feel about unibrows."

"Looks aren't everything," a third insisted. "There's a lot to be said for a good sense of humor."

My husband and the paramour were standing around with their hands in their pockets, giving each other sulky looks. To tell the truth, I wasn't that crazy about either of them at that moment. The paramour's scenes and demands were becoming tiresome. My husband was still pretty much the same old him, with the same old insufficiencies. Neither of them had much of a sense of humor.

I tried to see myself as they must see me. An exasperation, a painful reminder of ancient male failures. A woman who wouldn't stay inside a frame. Then Leslie Valentine came tripping toward us, sweetly awkward in her new shoes. Both men gave her an alert, dazzled glance. She was, after all, a new, unknown woman, a wealth of imaginative possibilities.

I gave them both a light shove in her direction. They started toward her, moving like sleepwalkers. Oh resilient hearts! Oh mad recurring drama! Did no one ever learn?

I slipped away when no one was watching me. I didn't know what came next. I knew I wasn't an artist or anything like that. But maybe I was finally starting to get the picture.

PIE OF
THE MONTH

So much of the world had changed and kept
on changing. But you could count on the pie list to remain the
same. January was always custard, February chocolate, March
lemon meringue. There were no substitutions. The absoluteness
of this was comforting, since there were, in general, many rules
now, which were often superseded without warning by new, con-
tradictory rules. In the matter of coconut cream (April) it was
true that Mrs. Colley had persuaded Mrs. Pulliam to allow, if not
a substitution, at least a little flexibility. There were people who
had really violent feelings about coconut. Mrs. Pulliam was not
inclined to humor them. She was an artist. There were aesthetics
involved in the choice of pies, the harmonies of taste and
weather. The cycle of seasons gave rise to the cycle of cravings, for
tart or smooth or juicy. Mrs. Colley had to frame it as a question
of allergies, and only then did Mrs. Pulliam relent and offer (on
occasion, and by special request) a banana cream alternative. But
it always set her to brooding, and Mrs. Colley had learned to walk
wide of her at such times.

The Pie of the Month Club's motto was Easy as Pie! With an
exclamation point in the shape of a rolling pin. Pies were deliv-
ered to subscribers on the first or third Friday of the month.

Although Hi Ho was not a large community, the reputation of the pies was such that the ladies had no lack of business. The crusts were perfect marriages of shortening and flour, so that each bite simultaneously resisted and gave way. The fillings were piled high and handsome. Of course only the best-quality ingredients were used. Nowadays, when there was so much concern about contamination (air, water, crops), a pie harkened back to simpler, more wholesome times. No one had yet cast any aspersions on pie. People in Hi Ho were sensible folks with their feet firmly on the ground, not inclined to sway with each new panic. Still, Mrs. Colley was afraid a day might come when even pie would turn up in one of those ominous newspaper articles, accused of causing some disease you never knew existed until then.

Mrs. Colley tried to avoid the news as much as possible. It was all so worrisome, and all so completely beyond your control. She much preferred the kind of magazines that had recipes instead of news, and television programs where people lived in nice houses and had glamorous problems. But sometimes the news seeped in anyway. She'd be settled in her chair, her front still faintly damp from the evening's dishes, her iced tea and Kleenex within reach, and instead of her program there would be a news bulletin you couldn't avoid. Usually it was about something blowing up. And since whatever blew up was in a place you'd never been, or sometimes never even heard of, you first thought what a terrible thing it was, followed by relief that it had nothing to do with you, really, followed by a vague guilt at feeling relieved.

It was all the fault of the War, or Wars. One ran into the other nowadays. Mrs. Colley couldn't keep them straight. Wars were different than they used to be. They were all fought in hot places, for one thing. The current War had begun back in October (pecan), and they were trying to get it wrapped up before summer, when the great parade of fruit pies (cherry, blueberry, peach) began. Fruit pie season was not a good time to be fighting a War in a hot place. The War news was always about how we were winning, but the enemy was refusing to admit it and was fighting back in dirty, underhanded ways, such as blowing things up or poisoning (or threatening to poison) some vital resource. How were you supposed to deal reasonably with people like that?

When the phone rang at a certain time of evening, it was always Mrs. Pulliam. Mrs. Colley pressed the mute button on the television remote so she could still follow her program as she conversed. Mrs. Pulliam said, "Tell me this rhubarb was meant as a joke."

"What's wrong with it?"

"Aside from being so woody you can whittle it, nothing."

When Mrs. Pulliam was in this particular mood, you had to let her run on for a time. Mrs. Colley murmured that people these days did not understand rhubarb as they used to. She thought this was true. Certain vegetables, peas for example, no longer got the respect they once had. Mrs. Pulliam sniffed in disdain. "The only thing to understand about rhubarb is you pick it before it gets old and tough. It's not rocket science."

Mrs. Colley's program required her attention just then. Something was being explained, some important part of the story that you wouldn't get if you couldn't hear. She clicked the volume up to the first level and said, trying to sound more concerned than she was, "It's what, just six pies tomorrow? Couldn't you mix them three-quarters strawberry, one-quarter rhubarb instead of half and half?"

"It's the rhubarb that gives it body," said Mrs. Pulliam, not ready to stop being irritable. "Without enough rhubarb, it's like jam."

"Well Joyce, why not let me make them? Then if they don't turn out, everybody can blame me."

"Absolutely not," said Mrs. Pulliam, just as Mrs. Colley had meant her to. "You know very well I always do May. It's my responsibility and I'll see to it, thank you very much."

After she put the phone down and got caught up with her program, Mrs. Colley thought, not for the first time, that Mrs. Pulliam made things more difficult than was necessary. She attributed this to Mrs. Pulliam's divorce and the fact that her only child, a boy, had a bad character and had gone off to live in Chicago. Mrs. Colley was a widow. Her daughter, Margery, lived right here in Hi Ho. Margery and her husband had two precious babies, well they were hardly babies anymore, four and six, but that was how she thought of them. Mrs. Colley's son John and his wife lived in Des Moines, which was too far away for Mrs. Colley's liking but at least in the same state. John and his wife did not have any children yet, even though Mrs. Colley dropped hints from time to time about how much she would love to have more grandbabies.

The news said that before they went to the War, some soldiers had stored their sperm in freezers, in case something chemical happened to them in battle. You were really better off not knowing a thing like that.

Mrs. Colley had grown accustomed to widowhood. It had been a terrible thing, of course, her husband's heart attack, and the anxious tug of hope while he lingered, and then the press of large and small events necessary to accomplish a man's death. Everything after that was slower. Slow march of hours and days, months and years. Nothing much changed, except she grew older and more settled into her leftover life.

She got by all right. Sometimes she turned on a football game so she would have a man's voice in the house. And sometimes, if she was shopping at the SuperStuff and found herself in the automotive or hardware or electrical aisle, surrounded by all the mysterious items men used to keep the world running, she missed her husband terribly. Then she would feel so down and blue, she would start thinking bad, crazy things, like what if her grandson, Ronnie, grew up and went to a War and they did something to his sperm? That multitude of little unformed pearls inside him, all doomed. Or what if something in Hi Ho were to blow up? The grain elevator, for instance, or the American Legion. Hi Ho would be the last place you'd expect something like that to happen, and that was exactly why it would be targeted.

At such times Mrs. Colley turned to the Rainbow pills her doctor had prescribed. Of course the pills had a longer, medical name, but they were advertised on television with rainbows. The commercial began with a gray, drippy cartoon sky, which gradually gave way to arcs of violet, red, yellow, green. Cartoon flowers sprouted and cartoon birds sang. While you understood that this was a commercial and was not meant as a literal representation—when it came to advertising one both resisted and succumbed, like pie crust—it was true that the pills made Mrs. Colley *feel* more rainbowlike. Peaceful and sort of glowing. And what was the harm in that, as long as your side effects (headache, nausea, gas, bloating, diarrhea or menstrual pain) were the exact same ones the commercial reassured you were normal?

Mrs. Colley went to Mrs. Pulliam's house in midafternoon, when the strawberry-rhubarb pies were scheduled to be done. Mrs. Pulliam had not disappointed. The six pies sat cooling on the kitchen table. The crusts were delicate brown with scroll-shaped cutouts that showed the deep jewel color of the filling. The pies smelled of May, of blossom and warm wind and sweetness. Mrs. Colley leaned over to drink in the smell. "Oh, heaven," she murmured.

Mrs. Pulliam stood at the sink, washing up. "That rhubarb gave me fits."

"Joyce, they turned out perfect."

"*Perfect*," said Mrs. Pulliam, angling the spray hose to scald a glass, "is a word cheapened by overuse. In the course of a normal lifetime, I very much doubt if anyone encounters perfection."

Yet Mrs. Colley knew that her friend relied on her appreciation, even as she grudged and pushed it from her. Mrs. Pulliam's tall figure bent over to scour a cookie sheet. She wore a hairnet while baking and with her hair skinned back her profile was severe. If you were uncharitable, you might even say it was witch-like. Fretting had kept her thin over the years. Mrs. Colley didn't think that Mrs. Pulliam was unhappy, not in any active sense. More like she'd grown into the habit of mistrusting happiness and had to call it by other names.

A breeze ruffled Mrs. Pulliam's blue curtains. Outside the window a bumblebee lumbered in the white flowers of the spirea. The new grass bent and tossed like a herd of green ponies at play. One of the Mexican families who lived in the trailers across the field had put out a line of wash, children's small bright shirts and pants.

The Mexicans were something new. Hi Ho had been founded by industrious German and Swiss farmers, just the sort of people you would have chosen yourself to found a town, if you'd had any say in it. There were streets in Hi Ho named Hoffman and Schroeder. In the fall there was a Heritage Day when children were dressed up in dirndls and lederhosen and performed Tyrolean folk songs.

But in the last few years, a portion of town had come more to resemble Guadalajara. The Mexicans mostly worked in the meatpacking plants two towns over. Although they were from a hot country, we were not at War with them. There was a new Catholic church to accommodate them, an addition to the many flavors of Protestant. The Hi Ho Market now sold chilies and cans of hominy and packets of Mexican spices. Mrs. Colley did not know any Mexicans personally. She thought they were all right as long as they kept to themselves and didn't go jabbering Spanish at you when they knew you couldn't understand it. She was not the sort to be prejudiced about people just because they came from a hot country.

Mrs. Pulliam looked out the window, where two of the Mexican children had come outside and were kicking a ball around, soccer-style. "Those people won't ever be subscribers. They don't have a tradition of pie."

"We could take some pies by the Catholic church sometime. A free, introductory offer."

"I don't see them going for it, in a business way."

"It would be neighborly," said Mrs. Colley, but they let the idea pass. Being neighborly was a good thing, of course, except there was a sense in which the Mexicans were not real neighbors.

Mrs. Pulliam took her apron off and poured two cups of coffee. She set the cream jug in front of Mrs. Colley's chair, although she herself continued to stand. "Maybe it's just as well we don't add subscribers. Who knows how much longer I'll want to keep on with the baking."

Mrs. Colley tried not to show her alarm. In all of Mrs. Pulliam's history of complaint, she had never mentioned quitting the pies outright. "A long time, I hope. Otherwise, people would be so disappointed."

"Would they," said Mrs. Pulliam. She reached up to pull the hairnet off, though her hair stayed in the same crimped, hairnet shape. "Oh, I suppose. Yes, they would at first, sure. Then they'd adjust. It's only pie. I keep thinking that. All the fuss and bother for something people gobble down in a day or two."

Mrs. Colley knew better than to approach any issue with Mrs. Pulliam head-on. She said, "I saw the most interesting recipe in one of my magazines. Rustic plum tart."

"Gaaagh."

"I'm just saying. Maybe something different once in a while. Perk you right up. They had another one, peanut butter pie with an Oreo crust."

"If I'm going to start down that road, I might as well bake *cupcakes*. I make pies the way they're meant to be. I have to believe there's still an audience for that. Now you'd better get this batch around to people."

Mrs. Colley always handled the deliveries. She had certain people skills that Mrs. Pulliam, being an artist, lacked, and besides, she enjoyed getting out and about. She loaded the pies in their special baskets and set off in her old car, motoring carefully down the quiet streets. Tree shadow from the new leaves cast lace patterns on the pavement. There was a cloud at the edge of the beautiful day. For reasons of her own, or for no reason except temperament, Mrs. Pulliam might decide to end Pie of the Month. It no longer seemed to give her satisfaction to make pie for pie's sake. Mrs. Colley wished she could get Mrs. Pulliam to see how sociable a pie really was, how it brought people together, gave them something to look forward to, talk about, share.

The first delivery stop was Jeffy Johnson. He was out watering his grass seed when Mrs. Colley pulled up. "Hi Jeffy, how are you today?"

"Wonderful and blessed, Mrs. C., wonderful and blessed."

Jeffy always said that. There was a sense that you were meant to answer back, "Hallelujah," but Mrs. Colley never could bring herself to do so. Jeffy was short and round-bottomed and cheerful. Like all the other black people in Hi Ho, he went to the A.M.E. church. He drove an Oldsmobile Cutlass with a license plate that read PRAY MOR. He was a bachelor and the A.M.E. ladies were always trying to marry him off. Mrs. Colley thought that Jeffy enjoyed all the fuss and attention and would hold out as long as possible before he got himself a wife, and then he would say it was the Lord's plan. Mrs. Colley attended the Lutheran church and would have called herself religious, although not to the point where she thought religion made any actual difference in the world.

Jeffy set the pie basket on the porch and said that strawberry-rhubarb was his favorite pie. "Until you come along with next month's, that is." It was the joke he always made.

"Pray that there is a next month, Jeffy," said Mrs. Colley, trying to make it come out humorous instead of small and quavering, as it did. Jeffy clasped Mrs. Colley's hands in his big brown ones and when he bowed his head she felt obliged to do likewise. When Jeffy raised up again and said, "Amen," Mrs. Colley felt embarrassed, as if she'd taken advantage.

The last stop on the pie route was always her daughter Margery's, so that Mrs. Colley could visit with the grandbabies. Margery did not bake her own pies because she worked part-time, in addition to chasing after two kids whenever she was home and never having a minute to herself.

Mrs. Colley tried not to pass judgment on any of this, or on the state of Margery's house, which today as usual was at sixes and sevens. Cheerios floated in the kitchen sink. Every towel in the house seemed to have assembled on the bathroom floor. The television was on, although no one was watching it. The President was doing a commercial for the War. Ronnie and his little sister, Crystal, were playing chase. Ronnie had a potato peeler in his mouth and his arms spread out, airplane-style. He made *rat-tat-tat* noises as he tried to trap Crystal in a corner and dive-bomb her. "Look, darlings, Grandma's here! I brought you a strawberry-rhubarb pie!"

"I hate strawberry," said Ronnie, talking around the potato peeler.

"I hate rhubarb," Crystal chimed in, although she didn't really. She was just being cute.

Margery cleared a space for the pie on the kitchen counter but didn't go out of her way to act appreciative. Margery sometimes sneaked cigarettes. Mrs. Colley was not supposed to know about this but she did anyway. Margery still wore her red smock from work. She was a sales associate at SuperStuff. Margery said, "They cut back my hours again."

"I'm sorry."

"Ronnie, knock it off," Margery called, but without energy. The thunder of feet kept shaking the house. "Yeah. I guess I should be glad, since it's only the worst job in the world."

Mrs. Colley watched as Margery took a number of items out of the freezer to start supper: a bag of Tater Tots, package of corn, fish fillets stuck together in the shape of a brick. Mrs. Colley said, "I saw somewhere that fish can give you mercury poisoning."

"Not if it's frozen, I don't think."

They didn't say anything else about the hours cutback, and after a while Mrs. Colley took herself home.

It didn't used to be that husband and wife both had to work to put food on the table. She and Mr. Colley had managed. But there had not been so many things to buy back then, and there hadn't been a stock market, or there had been but it wasn't full of crooks who sucked all the money out of the world overnight. Times were hard. Jeffy Johnson said it was the seven lean years like in the Bible. The President said there were always sacrifices in time of War. Mrs. Colley took a Rainbow pill and slept for nine and a half hours.

June was cherry pie month, one of Mrs. Colley's favorites, even though cherry juice stained like the dickens. Mrs. Colley still got up on a stepladder and picked cherries from her own tree. There was nothing quite as pretty as a cherry tree, the sprays of red fruit against the green leaves. The birds were never happier than in cherry season. June was always good. June was fireflies and brides. Crops were planted and there had not yet been too much or not enough rain. School got out and children planned long campaigns of play.

Mrs. Colley and Mrs. Pulliam ran cherries through the hand-cranked cherry pitter, saving the juice to can later. Mrs. Colley used a plastic form to stamp out the lattice crusts, which was cheating, sort of, but couldn't be helped. She knew her crust was not the equal of Mrs. Pulliam's, although only a longtime subscriber might notice the difference. She flattered herself that she had a better flair for the fruit pies, a more generous hand with the fillings than Mrs. Pulliam. Her best cherry pies made you wish there was such a thing as a cherry pie tree.

The last few weeks she'd kept a close eye on Mrs. Pulliam, watching for signs of discontent. But Mrs. Pulliam pitted cherries and weighed out sugar and did her share of the chores without complaint. Just as Mrs. Colley was taking the last of the last batch of cherry pies out of the oven, Mrs. Pulliam said, out of nowhere, "Bobby called."

Bobby was Mrs. Pulliam's bad son in Chicago. He did not often call. Mrs. Colley, as she was meant to, kept her eyes on the pies as she asked, "Well, how's Bobby?"

"He's part of a group now."

When Mrs. Pulliam didn't say anything more helpful, Mrs. Colley was forced to ask what kind of group.

"It's a No More War group."

You might expect as much from long-haired, pot-smoking Bobby, and Mrs. Colley was about to murmur something by way of consolation, when Mrs. Pulliam spoke again. "Bobby says we aren't winning the War, we're losing it."

This was such an unexpected idea that Mrs. Colley had no response, only stood there with her hands in oven mitts. Mrs. Pulliam went on. "He says we keep having Wars just so everyone stays all stirred up and scared."

"Now what possible reason would anyone have for wanting that?"

Mrs. Pulliam only shrugged and went back to balancing the month's accounts.

The last week in June the meatpacking plant fired all the Mexicans. The government said it was not safe to have foreigners, people of unknown, undocumented backgrounds, motives, and sympathies, at work in the sensitive area of food supply. Many of the Mexicans just disappeared. Overnight, it seemed, they were gone. They left behind cars, the children's bicycles, food in kitchens, shoes in closets. It was hard to get new workers to replace them. The worst job in the world wasn't at SuperStuff, in spite of what Margery said. Everyone knew the worst jobs were probably in the meatpacking plant, in the slaughter room, or the hide room, or the rendering room. The Texas bank that had already bought up a lot of the farms took over the plant and cut back on the shifts.

Mrs. Colley found that she missed the Mexicans, the black-eyed babies, the snatches of Spanish radio on Main Street. Some people said they must have done something criminal, clearing out like that, but Mrs. Colley wondered if they weren't just afraid. The Mexicans who remained behind were having a hard time making ends meet, and the churches in Hi Ho organized a food drive for them. The Lutheran pastor, young Reverend Higgs, gave a sermon about charity and brotherhood and overcoming differences, which made everybody feel better, since that was exactly what they'd done. Summer baseball leagues started up. There was a bank robbery in Des Moines and Mrs. Colley was terribly worried about her son, John, who worked in a bank, until she reached him on the phone and found out it was a different bank. The War was said to be winding down, although things still blew up now and then. For whole days at a time you could almost forget there was a War going on; there was too much else to crowd it out. But the War was like a pie you'd left in the oven, something nagging at you, a task left unfinished.

July was for blueberry pies. Blueberries were grown in cool places, and when you sifted through the fruit, washing and straining and picking out stems, you thought of pine trees, of gray, chill lakes and seagulls. Blueberry was the easiest of the fruit pies, nothing to pit or peel, and that was a mercy. July was always so blamed hot. The sun rode the sky all day long. There was no rain (the drought had been going on almost as long as the Wars), except for those times when a black storm swept in and sent forks of lightning and crop-shredding hail.

There was a Fourth of July parade, with the fire truck going five miles an hour and running its siren, the high school band, the Veterans of Foreign Wars (by which was meant the old-fashioned Wars that were already in the history books), marching in formation, and some convertibles donated by a car dealership. Mrs. Pulliam got her hands on a quantity of nearly flawless blackberries and donated a dozen pies to the Freedom Celebration picnic. When you cut into the pies each blackberry was still perfectly shaped, glistening with grains of undissolved sugar. No one had ever seen or tasted anything like them.

Mrs. Pulliam stood beneath the awning that covered the picnic tables, accepting compliments. Mrs. Colley was pleased to see her friend getting the recognition that she deserved, pleased also that Mrs. Pulliam seemed to be enjoying herself, after a fashion. She had even dressed up a little, for her, in a new red and white blouse that seemed more cheerful than Mrs. Pulliam herself. For there was a kind of formality, even aloofness, to Mrs. Pulliam as she acknowledged people's thank-yous, and that was to be expected. There was for every artist the awful moment when they stepped out from behind their splendid creation and revealed the meager, human-sized self that was bound to disappoint by comparison. People filled their mouths with sweet corn and potato salad and fried chicken and pie, pie, pie. The excellence of the food was some consolation for the fireworks show, which everyone agreed was not as good as last year's.

In mid-July it was announced the SuperStuff would be closing. The national chains were all cutting their losses, tightening their belts. The store hired a number of the Mexicans to stand on street corners with red, white, and blue signs that said Everything Must Go! Prices were reduced by twenty, then thirty, then forty percent and more. For a time the SuperStuff's parking lot was jam-packed and they did more business in a weekend than they might have in a month. Mrs. Colley stocked up on those items of apparel which a lady of her age and size required. People wandered the aisles. There was a pleasant sense that everything in the store was available for the taking, for free or very nearly free. Everyone in Hi Ho had new dish towels and sheet sets and garden hoses and CD players and fishing rods and generators, and then the store was shut for good.

Margery found work a few hours a week at the dry cleaners, running clothes through the machines that tumbled them and took out spots and gave them that dry cleaning smell. A while back there had been some kind of alarm about dry cleaning, about the chemicals used, but then it was determined that exposure was within acceptable limits. Mrs. Colley babysat Ronnie and Crystal to help out. Ronnie said he wanted to be a baseball player when he grew up. Crystal said she wanted to be a television lady. There was a scare about eating beef, something that had nothing to do with the Mexicans, and just like that you couldn't give beef away. Everyone knew the scare would wear off sooner or later but before it could, the Texas bank closed the meatpacking plant and hauled all the equipment down to Texas or who knows where and padlocked the gates. Most of the local farmers had long since sold off their cattle because of the drought, but still it was a blow. For a time there was talk that the state might build one of its new prisons in the county and bring back some jobs, but nothing ever came of it.

You wanted so badly to believe that life was basically good, that people were basically good. And Mrs. Colley did believe it. She might not go around announcing that she was wonderful and blessed, but she reminded herself often that there were many terrible places she could have been born into but had not. Nothing abnormally bad had ever happened to her personally or was likely to happen except for, eventually, dying, oh well. But nowadays there was so little you could trust to stay good, as if there was a pinhole at the bottom of the world and all the best things were leaking out of it.

In August, everyone's water bills doubled. It came out that the water utility had been bought up by a company in Belgium. Belgium! Most people in Hi Ho were unaware that you could do such a thing as sell the water, and it was unclear why anyone in Belgium should own a lot of the water in Iowa. It was some consolation that Belguim was not one of the hot countries; when people looked it up on maps, it was right up there with normal nations like France and Germany. The new Belgian water company said the increased bills reflected higher costs for security, that it was now necessary to guard against the possibility of the water supply being blown up or poisoned. That was odd, since the workers at the filtration plant still kept the side gate wide open in summer. That way they could leave their cars in the shade of the adjoining park, and take their lunch coolers out there at break time.

"Bobby says it isn't really countries that fight Wars now. It's corporations. The corporations are bigger than the countries."

"I just can't keep up with all of Bobby's ideas," said Mrs. Colley, which she hoped was a tactful way of saying she was tired of hearing about them. Bobby and Mrs. Pulliam talked a lot these days, and after every conversation Mrs. Pulliam offered up some new, outlandish opinion.

"Bobby says everything's global now. Things that happen on the other side of the world, even small things, affect everyone else. He says we are a global village."

"Well that sounds nice," said Mrs. Colley, still trying to be agreeable. "I think I would like to live there."

Mrs. Pulliam shook her head darkly. "The news we see these days isn't the real news," she began. Fortunately the oven timer went off just then.

They were in the middle of the August peach pies. Peach pies were murder. The fruit had to be perfect, firm enough to handle but ripe enough to juice up. The skins almost never came off easy, and by the time you dug the pits out, you threw away more than you saved. August was murder. Ponds turned green and stagnant, the ground dried and split into thirsty cracks. Only the air was humid, like breathing through blankets. When Mrs. Colley and Mrs. Pulliam baked peach pies they didn't even try to run the AC, just set up big fans to blow the heat away. It was a lot of effort, but a good peach pie was a triumph. Mrs. Pulliam always cut smiling sun faces into the top crusts, because the pies had the sun in them, that was what you tasted, everything yellow and ripe.

When they'd finished the last of the pies and done the washing up and put everything away, they sat on Mrs. Colley's screened-in porch to let the house cool down. It was nighttime. A haze of heat blurred the stars. The fireflies were mostly gone by August, but here and there one sent up a faint, greenish spark. Cicadas and mosquitoes bumped against the screens. Mrs. Colley had put sprigs of mint in the iced tea and they let the ice melt a little so it was good and cold. If you raised your eyes beyond the lights of town you saw, or imagined you saw, the outline of the grass-covered hills that had been there, exactly the same, for a thousand thousand years.

"What's got into you lately?" Mrs. Colley heard herself saying. It just popped out. She held her breath.

Mrs. Pulliam was silent for a moment, then she said, "I think I may have gone about as far as it's possible to go with pie."

"I don't understand. Going farther? Why do you have to go anywhere at all?"

"Maybe the world makes you restless. Maybe you just get older, and wonder if you should have lived a different life. A bigger life."

Mrs. Colley thought that all the things she loved were small. They were all close by; she could practically reach out and touch them. She muddled her words trying to explain that this was not a bad thing. She only managed, "Well mercy sakes, Joyce, you talk like life was already over and done with." Although even as she spoke she had a sense that so many things, if not over and done with, had long since been determined for her.

In the darkness Mrs. Pulliam turned toward her and gave her a look, although the look itself was invisible. "I expect you're right. Now I'd best be getting home. This heat! You could wring out the air like a dishrag."

At the end of August, the President said the War was over, and there was general public satisfaction at a job well done. But the very next week there was a new War, or rather, a return to one of the old Wars already won. It was breaking out again, like a rash, and once more there were flags and headlines and airships named after birds of prey. The following Sunday the Lutheran pastor, young Reverend Higgs, climbed up to the pulpit made of varnished blond oak and preached a sermon whose text was

"Blessed are the peacemakers, for they shall be called the children of God."

The Lutheran congregation sat as if they had been given orders not to flinch. Sunlight poured through the stained glass window depicting Jesus the Shepherd of His Flock. Oblongs and lozenges of red, violet, gold, and green moved imperceptibly across the blond oak floorboards. There was a vague sense that someone might come to arrest them all on the spot. When Reverend Higgs finished his sermon and the benediction and the organist played the first chords of the recessional, there were people who went out the exit without staying to greet and visit. There were others who filed out and shook hands with the pastor without knowing what to say.

Mrs. Colley was one of these. Reverend Higgs looked pale and exhausted and noble, like Jesus. "Oh Pastor," she began. Foolish tears brimmed in her eyes. A great confusion of words was welling up in her, but she only said again, "Oh Pastor." The crowd behind her inched reluctantly forward, as if in line for vaccinations. Reverend Higgs murmured a blessing, and Mrs. Colley let her hand drop.

That night she felt unwell. She slept fitfully, and had extraordinary and disturbing dreams. There was a rainbow in the sky that drifted closer and closer until you saw that it was really poison fumes in lurid, neon colors. Margery took packages of frozen sperm out of the freezer for supper. Mr. Colley appeared, dressed in the coveralls and straw hat he always wore for gardening, asking her where she put the. The. She couldn't make out what he wanted because it was a small thing on the other side of the world. Mrs. Colley woke up with a fever and chills and a sore head and called Margery to take her to the doctor's.

The doctor said there was a lot of this going around lately and gave Mrs. Colley some new prescriptions and told her to stay in bed. Mrs. Colley dozed with her windowblinds closed against the heat and the air conditioner whispering to her. Margery fixed her meals of toast and fruit Jell-O, though she didn't have much appetite and was content to sleep. The doctor said there was a lot of War sickness going around lately. Now wasn't that silly. She knew she was dreaming. The cool sheets lulled her, the air conditioner sighed. How could you get sick from a War?

By the time Mrs. Colley felt well enough to get out of bed and open her blinds, it was already September and the yellow heat had dropped out of the sky.

"I'm still weak as a kitten," she fretted to Mrs. Pulliam over the phone. "I've never been so useless in all my days."

"Then there's no point in you even leaving the house. Make yourself sick all over again."

"But the apple pies!"

September was apple. A for apple in the children's schoolbooks. Red apple barns and wagons, the promise of fall. Apple pie being what it was, there were people who doubled their September orders. Apple was the queen of pies. A baker's reputation rose or fell on it.

"I'll manage fine," said Mrs. Pulliam. "The last thing I need is you getting your old germs all over the place."

"I don't have germs anymore, don't be rude."

"Or falling face down into the flour bin. I'm not going to argue with you."

"I've got the rest of the week to get my strength back," said Mrs. Colley stubbornly.

But when baking day came around she wasn't much better,

still short of breath and unsteady on her feet. "I can still do the deliveries," she told Mrs. Pulliam when she called. In the background she heard water running, pans clashing like cymbals.

"Get Margery to help you. I'll leave some money for her trouble."

"Leave? Where are you going to be?"

"I'm going to visit Bobby." There was a whirring, grinding sound that Mrs. Colley knew was the device that took off apple peel in a long thin spiral, cored and cut the fruit into slices. "Don't worry, the pies will be ready."

"You're going to Chicago?" The enormity of this was enough to make Mrs. Colley wonder if she was having another fever dream, as if her sickness had loosened the top of her head like a box lid and now strange things were always falling in and out. "For how long?"

"For a spell. If a grown woman can't take herself on an occasional trip, then I don't know what. Now shoo, I have work to do."

"What is it you aren't telling me? What don't I know?"

The clatter in the background stopped. "You already know everything you need to know. You just have to let yourself believe it," said Mrs. Pulliam, and then she hung up.

Mrs. Colley woke early and drove herself to Mrs. Pulliam's house. It seemed like a long time since she had been outside, and the season had changed. There were dew-covered spiderwebs in the long grass. She noted here and there an early tree, ash or elm, getting ready to turn. The sky was still pink from sunrise. Far overhead a plane pulled a line of silver from west to east. You knew these things because you saw them. Wasn't seeing believing?

When she parked the car in Mrs. Pulliam's driveway, a cinnamon wind enveloped her, wafting from every chink and window. The back door was open. Two pieces of knowledge registered with Mrs. Colley at the same time: that the house was full of pies, and that Mrs. Pulliam was gone, like the Mexicans.

Or not really like the Mexicans, since everything was scrubbed and ordered and cleared away. There were bags of clothes with labels directing them to the Goodwill, tags on furniture, boxes of household goods stacked in the laundry room. And everywhere there were pies.

On the kitchen table, lined up on the counters. The cupboard doors were open to make space for pies. The dining room table and every chair, the bookshelves and dressers. The mattress was covered in a thin, clean sheet, and two dozen pies were set out on it. There were even pies in the bathtub, wrapped up in plastic. And on every top crust, words had been cut out, one hundred, two hundred times, pie after pie after pie:

NO
MORE WAR

Mrs. Colley both knew and believed that if she counted, there would be a pie for every household in Hi Ho. On the kitchen table was an envelope filled with money, all the proceeds from this year's subscriptions. The pies on the table were still warm. Mrs. Pulliam must have left only minutes before.

Mrs. Colley removed a pie from a chair so she could sit down. She cradled a pie in her lap as if it were a living thing, a bird or a lamb or a child. In a little while she would call Margery and they would begin their chores. Mrs. Colley would take baskets of pie to the trailer court and ask the Mexicans how you said it in Spanish, NO MORE WAR. All over town, people would be eating apple pie, swallowing the words down, NO MORE WAR, and they would put it on the license plates of their cars, and pastors would spell it out on the brick-framed billboards in front of churches, it would deck the marquee of the old Cinema, NO MORE WAR. Farmers bringing in their crops would carve the words into the earth with tractors, so that the President himself, aloft in the great sleek airship that signified the power and swiftness of eagles, could look down and read it in the green Iowa hills, NO MORE WAR.

And in this way a small thing might become a big thing, easy as pie.

Throw
Like
a Girl

The night we got the news about Janey I
dreamed I was a ghost, like her. In the dream I kept shouting with
no breath in my lungs, kept jumping up and falling back down
again, as thin as a piece of paper curling over on itself. No one
noticed me. It was desolate, being dead. My heart, or the bitter
space where it used to be, flooded with salt tears. All of this was
absolutely and purely real, the way any dream is, so that for a little space of brain wave activity I knew how profoundly lonesome
it was to stand outside the living world and watch it go on without you. Then I woke up, ashamed at having turned her death
into my own commonplace fears.

In the bathroom I stood in front of the mirror. I didn't look
like a ghost, which I imagined to be something wan, unearthly,
and refined. My face was frowsy with stale sleep. Its every heaving
pore and blinking, rheumy aspect seemed to give testimony to
the ongoing internal combustion process we call life. Janey used
to say I had the face of a gun moll in an old black-and-white B
movie. Gee, thanks, I told her, and she said she meant it as a com-

pliment, meant I was tough and savvy and sexy. You know. A broad. A dame.

I never quite bought into it. Janey's compliments often had that little dig to them. But this morning I looked like nothing so much as a mug shot, and I have to say I didn't mind.

When Janey got sick again she went back home, to the western city where she'd grown up. She moved into her mother's house and slept in the little upstairs bedroom with the slanting ceiling that had been hers as a child. Later the dining room was converted into her sickroom, with a hospital bed and a potty and all the accumulating cards and flowers and teddy bears. There was hospice care, and visits from the clergy, and casseroles dropped off at the back door. This we knew from the one friend who'd been in that town on business, and whom the mother had not been able to prevent from coming to the house.

The rest of us had not been allowed to come visit. The mother controlled access, and kept everybody out except her own circle. When we called, the mother told us that Janey couldn't handle distractions, she needed all her strength to fight this thing. We fell all over ourselves saying that we understood. She was our first death, after all, and we were cowed by the family prerogative.

But Janey and her mother had never gotten along very well. Janey had been a disappointing daughter, willful and careless about living her life in any way that would have gratified a certain kind of mother. There was a sense that this final episode of illness, the fight Janey wasn't going to win, was the mother's chance to turn Janey into a better, if tragic, story. Maybe that's what a dying person needs, a bossy mother in charge of everything. But we were her friends, and we resented being kept at a distance and not even getting the chance to talk to Janey on the phone until the morphine drip had already done most of the work of stealing her away.

Now there was going to be a memorial. None of us was going. Why would we want to sit in the mother's church and drink tea from her cup and saucer set and listen to a lot of talk about God's will and how suffering made us more Christlike? I thought that suffering only made you suffer, and I'm pretty sure Janey did too. She'd never bought into religion, or the kind of backward explanations you got from religion. I didn't like the idea of all the praying that must have gone on, and her too weak to tell them all to shove it.

It was so unfair that the cancer had come back, but maybe fairness is one more word that belongs to the realm of explanations. What I mean is, four years ago Janey had been through the diagnosis, the disfiguring surgery, the rehab, the debate about treatment, the hopeful statistics, the chemo, the survivor group and their cheerleading, the checkups, the cautious prognosis, the pink ribbons, the encouragement and the false encouragement. "Boobs," she said, exasperated. "How much time do we waste worrying about them, one way or another?"

We'd known each other for twenty-five years, which is some fraction of a life. More than half of Janey's, as it turned out. The whole group of us went back to college days, back when nobody had even thought about dying. Janey was the wild child, the one who couldn't wait to do too much of absolutely everything. It wasn't appetite or depravity, just the fear that she might be missing out on something. She had a mass of frizzy orange hair, like carrots run through a shredder. She weighed a hundred and eight pounds. She could dance all night and never come up for air. For a while she dyed her hair black, to go along with all the Goth stuff, but it made her look like everybody else and she changed it back. In spite of all her costumes and poses and ostentatious bad habits, she wasn't at all hard or tough. That would come later.

"Is sex supposed to hurt?"

She asked me that one day. We were hanging around her apartment, the way all of us used to do. Everybody knew where she kept her spare key and that she didn't mind if you came in and played her records—we had actual records back then—or smoked whatever you found in the ashtrays, or anything else. It was one of the nicest parts of life back then, feeling at home in someone else's space.

That day it was just her and me, killing time in between classes, or maybe instead of classes. It was spring but still cold, and we'd been watching the wind push the clouds around in the blue sky, and talking about nothing in particular. Maybe trying to plan exciting lives for ourselves. We did that a lot. We were convinced that the real world, brightly colored and meaningful, lay just beyond the boundaries of our own.

So I had to shift gears when she spoke. "What do you mean?"

"You know. Hurt." She made an impatient face.

"Well it can," I said, trying to sound like a judicious expert. We were both twenty years old at the time, and pretty sure we knew everything about sex, just because we were off to such a roaring start. I wondered who she might be talking about. We always had boys we kept company with, some we were serious about and others who were simply experiments. "Sure. Especially if a guy's real big."

She shook her head. The window was behind her, and her hair looked like an orange cloud against the sky. "Not really. Kind of average. God. That's exactly what they're afraid we say about them, isn't it?"

"So what was . . ."

"I think he was trying to make it hurt."

That made me queasy, I guess it shocked me. We didn't like thinking of ourselves as vulnerable, breakable, controllable objects, even if that was exactly the way some people saw us. I said that it wasn't right, what he'd done, and she said, Yeah, she knew. But she was still mulling it over, keeping something back. "What?" I said.

"I let him think I kind of liked it."

I didn't want to hear that either. Because I understood why girls did such things, even a bold, harum-scarum girl like Janey, understood why we went along with so much, were so anxious to please, laughed when nothing was funny, kept silent when we should have spoken, bent ourselves into obliging shapes, did the things that shamed us, even as Janey was ashamed. There was some desperate and unlovable creature that lived inside us, and we had to keep it fed.

It's always easy to find solutions for somebody else's problems, so I told Janey she shouldn't see the guy again, or at least she shouldn't fuck him again, or at least she shouldn't act as if she liked it when she didn't, and she said I was right about everything. I guess I was looking pretty steamed by the time I finished my speech, because she waved a hand in front of my face to bring me out of it, and laughed a little. "Hey. It's all right. It was just one of those stupid things."

"One that doesn't count." That was our agreement about any kind of episode too hideous to want to remember: it didn't count.

"We should have been religious or something. Kept ourselves pure."

"Too late now."

"I wish I was a lesbian. Can you just decide to be one?"

"I don't think so." It wasn't like I knew or anything. Lesbian, in my experience, was only a word guys used to insult you when you weren't interested in them. "You don't really want to be, do you?"

"Why not? Women are so much easier."

"Sure they are. But I don't think I could do naked things with one."

We were probably a little high, but I remember it being in the spirit of determined inquiry, rather than any sudden passion, that Janey scooted across the couch and pressed her small mouth against mine.

I didn't kiss her back, just let it happen, out of politeness, mostly. Her mouth took the tiniest taste of mine, like a mouse nibbling. I shifted my weight, trying to be accommodating—I wasn't shocked or mortified, still going along with things—and she crawled right up into my lap. I put an arm around her, since that seemed like the thing to do, and her entire restless weight pressed against me, a heap of bird bones and warmth, and then I did kiss her back, a little. Some of her hair caught in my mouth. It tasted powdery.

Janey pulled away. "You didn't close your eyes," she accused.

"Sorry." I was still trying to sort out what had happened, if it was any kind of a big deal.

We looked at each other for a moment, then burst out laughing.

"So OK, not a lesbian."

"Pretty sure," I said. "You?"

"I don't think so. Or maybe you're just too butch. Kidding," she said, though with Janey you were never sure. But we had another laugh, and then we let it go, and it didn't cast any shadow between us.

Now she was dead, my first and only girl kiss. Thinking of it was just one more way to grieve.

Another friend from back then called me. We were still actively mourning Janey, making our donations to the cancer people, checking in with each other regularly, remembering the old stories. She asked me if I thought Janey had been happy.

"You mean ever? Or in general?"

"With the way things turned out," the friend said. "Marrying What's-his-name. The drinking. All that restlessness."

Janey had only been married for a couple of years, in her twenties. Everything else had lasted longer. I said, "That's not fair to ask about anybody. It's like saying you knew what you wanted, and either you measured up or you didn't."

"So you don't think she was," the friend said, ignoring my words, knowing I was only trying to be loyal.

"No," I said. "She wasn't."

After we finished school, Janey moved to New York. She got some dinky job at one of those hipster publishing ventures that launched themselves like rockets and lasted just about as long. The rest of us had gone on to more ordinary things like grad school (me), or teaching, or jobs with various corporate masters. We didn't have much to crow about compared to Janey and her new life of clubbing and near-encounters with celebrities (including some names we were too out of it to recognize as celebrities) and cocaine-filled nights. We got used to saying things like "That sounds so exciting." When I went to visit her in New York, a year and a half after graduation, I was sure I'd be wearing the wrong shoes and talking about crop forecasts.

I flew into LaGuardia. There was construction going on and when we left the plane we had to march through dim, temporary corridors and up and down miles of narrow stairs just to reach the gate. The flight had been bumpy and I was chilled and half sick and wishing I was back home in my own dull bed. I emerged blinking into an open, overbright space and there was Janey, her hair cut short and sleeked down, more auburn than red, wearing a striped skirt and high boots that were clunky, nearly orthopedic. She looked peculiar in a way that I recognized as highly fashionable.

She squealed and hugged me and I was very glad to see her, even unwashed and unwell as I felt. The next minute she was pulling a tall, droopy-looking blond boy in a down ski jacket out of the crowd. The boyfriend. He was new, I'd only just begun to hear about him. "Gail, this is What's-his-name."

Of course he had a name, and we all remember it well enough, but we never liked him or the way he treated Janey, and so his name has been erased.

"Hey," he said, not bothering to shake hands or look my way. Already I didn't like him.

We got my luggage and headed out to What's-his-name's old beater car. It was the week after Christmas and the night was black and glassy cold. Janey made the boyfriend carry one of my suitcases. He acted aggrieved about it and stalked ahead of us through the parking lot. Janey said, "I can't believe you're finally here. We are going to par-*tay!* She's never been to New York before," she informed the boyfriend's unresponsive back.

Cold entered me from all directions. At the last minute I'd decided to wear my more stylish coat instead of the uglier, heavy-duty one, and now I was paying for it. When we reached the car, Janey insisted that I sit up front with What's-his-name, so he could ignore me from close up. At least it positioned me next to the inadequate heater. "So what do you want to do?" Janey asked from the back seat. "You hungry, or you just want to hang out?"

JEAN THOMPSON

I said I was sort of hungry, make that really hungry. I was still trying to orient myself, both to the unfamiliar nightscape of freeways and traffic and to Janey herself, who, like anyone you haven't seen for a while, was both recognizable and strange to me. She'd added a new layer of mannerisms, a brittleness I mistrusted. And I was feeling out of place and diminished, though that was not really anyone's fault. I doubted if I could measure up to New York, or to the high life, even temporarily.

The boyfriend was driving too fast, steering viciously in and out of the passing lanes. I remember thinking that maybe it was a New York thing, the way you were supposed to drive here. Janey said, "How about we go to Louie's? That's Italian, is that OK? Because then we can go right down the street to this other place that is completely amazing. You sit in these alcoves and there are these phones on the tables and you can call up the other tables. Or what about tandoori? Babe, what's that tandoori place?"

"Tandoori sucks."

"It does not. You like it."

"Says who."

He was still driving like he was mad at us, or trying to scare us, leaning over the steering wheel and forcing the little car into terrifying, narrow spaces between thundering trucks. Janey didn't say anything about his driving. Either she was used to it or she was trying to avoid one more fight. "Oh come on," she said. "We were there three weeks ago and it was great. You thought it was great."

"It was shit." He punched the gas and the car shimmied and whined in such a way as to suggest metal fatigue, and I thought I probably didn't want tandoori, whatever that was.

"You ate everything on your plate."

"No I didn't."

"Fine. You didn't." Janey and I shared a glance in the rearview mirror. I knew she was embarrassed, and I was embarrassed for her. You always wanted to show a man off, and here he was being a total jackass.

What's-his-name gave the steering wheel another spin that made me brace myself against the door. "Like Indians know anything about food anyway. They're all starving."

"Please. That's just ignorant."

"Maybe you should keep your stupid opinions to yourself."

"Hey," I said. "Don't drive so fast."

He gave me an evil look, but he did slow down, and they let the argument drop. We were coming into the city then. I saw enormous blocks of apartment buildings, some kind of projects, looming up on all sides, surrounded by metal fencing and narrow, waste-filled lots. I felt dizzy-sick at the sight of those huge, ugly buildings, each window representing a human soul trapped in this glooming world. New York, on my first viewing, looked a great deal like some apocryphal, science-fiction version of itself. I never got oriented, never got my mind around New York, either on that trip or any other. It's stayed oversized and outlandish to me in a way that other cities have not. Janey's town, not my own.

We went to Louie's, a mom-and-pop place where you walked back to the kitchen to see what was cooking on the stove, and we drank a great deal of wine, and What's-his-name improved slightly, at least to the point of offering some conversation about his plans for promoting music festivals. Janey told me later he was hypoglycemic, he got irritable when his blood sugar dropped. And he did get more cheerful as the meal progressed. He even made a joke or two that I laughed at. He was fondling Janey under the table and she seemed to like it, she'd let it drop that the sex was "amazing."

Janey talked about her newest job (she kept moving from one little magazine or broadsheet to another) and how crazy it got sometimes, everybody going off in all directions and arguing and never enough time or money. But it was great too, she said, it was *great*, the wine making her babble, to be in on something new, something that was inventing itself as it went along, she couldn't explain it but she loved it. And maybe she was happy then, right then, for however long it lasted, right at the beginning of everything. I couldn't have told you what ideas or aesthetics were served by those publications. They were like Janey's new boots, in that their function was mostly to call attention to themselves.

"So how's school?" Janey asked, finally, when we'd run out of anything else to talk about. She had an encouraging smile that I didn't like.

"Oh, you know. It's school."

"Well, do you like it?"

"It's not that bad." I didn't want to talk about it. After all it was only school, the same dull thing we'd already done, and nothing in it made for bragging.

When I didn't say anything else, she said to the boyfriend, "Gail was always the smart one."

"Yeah?" He was rummaging around in Janey's stocking tops. I give him this much credit: he didn't pretend to care about my vaunted intellect. It wasn't too long ago that I'd been notable for more exciting reasons, and I resented losing that.

"So do something else instead," Janey said. "Go somewhere you really want to go. Don't waste your time on something you aren't excited about."

"I didn't say I wasn't." I was getting contrary and irritated, unable to explain. It was childish of me not to have more to say for myself, not to defend the choices I'd made and genuinely wanted. I felt I had nothing she could envy, and there was always between us a need to be envied, a burr that rubbed us when we got too close.

"Oh come on," Janey sighed. "You could write. Go somewhere and write about it. Hey!" She brightened. "The magazine could publish it."

What's-his-name leaned across the table to address me confidentially. "They don't pay dick."

I said, "How about you don't worry about me, OK? I'm going to get my degree, and then I'm going to get a job. It'll be all right."

"Jeez," Janey said. "Don't bite my head off. If you're fine with it, then I'm fine."

What's-his-name said, "You know who pays real money? *Rolling Stone.* If you can get a foot in that door."

The visit got better after that. It was simply our first time trying to bridge the gap of our separating lives, and we let everything matter too much.

My last night in New York we went to see a band they were both excited about, and we took a cab, a real extravagance. As usual I had no idea where we were going, and neither did anyone else, including the cab driver, and I guess it was low blood sugar time again, because What's-his-name started arguing, first with the driver, and then with Janey about whether she'd gotten the address right.

"We'll find it," Janey said. "Just hold your horses."

"Hold what horses? Why do you say crap like that? It's simpleminded."

"God," Janey said.

The cab driver said, "We can drive around all night if you want, but it's gonna cost."

"Hold your horses," said What's-his-name. "No, keep looking. Giddyap."

"That's it," said Janey. "Really."

The bad boyfriend. We've all had them, we keep trying to prove some point with them. If we're lucky, they go away on their own.

It ended with the cab dumping us out blocks and blocks from anything recognizable, an ugly neighborhood of industrial buildings and broken, icy sidewalks. What's-his-name stomped on ahead of us. It was the thing he was best at.

"Asshole!" Janey shouted at him. "Wait for us!"

Of course he didn't, but he didn't try to lose us either. The whole point was to let us witness his silent tantrum.

Janey was the one who picked up the first small stone and heaved it at him. It skipped off to one side. Her second try fell short too. We ran a few steps so as to get in better range, and by now I was kicking up chunks of sidewalk and taking aim at him too, and he couldn't ignore us any longer when we hit him, pretty hard, once between his shoulder blades and then beneath his ear.

He yelped and turned around. "Just keep it up, bitch!"

"Yeah? Yeah? What're you gonna do, huh, did you even pay for your part of the cab? Do you ever do anything you talk about doing?"

Janey clutched at me when he took a step toward us, and I hoped something worse was going to happen so I could punch him out. But Janey had him figured right; he only curled up his hands and yelled, "You're crazy, you know that? Besides, you throw like a girl!"

It was supposed to be some killing insult but it only made us screech with laughter, and pick up more rocks, and throw them whatever limp-wristed, elbows-up, sissy-pitch way we felt like, and eventually he took himself off and Janey and I found another cab.

When I was back home, she called to tell me he'd moved his stuff out of her place, and we had some long phone talks, the kind we hadn't been able to have many of when I'd been there, with What's-his-name hanging around. She said, "He was like having the flu. You forget what it's like to be well."

"Good riddance," I said. "Adios. So long, it's been good to know you."

"Why do I always end up with the jerks?"

"There's a lot of them out there."

"You're so much smarter than me. I don't see you with a jerk."

"That's because I'm alone," I said.

A little more than a year later, she married him. None of us wanted to believe it. She didn't tell me herself, someone else had to call me with the news. That hurt my feelings, but of course, she knew what I'd say. They'd gotten married at City Hall, no ceremony, no reception. The antiwedding.

We hadn't talked very much in that year, the way a friendship can go slack. Still, she should have told me. I didn't call to offer congratulations, just sent a card. Maybe we can't help who we fall in love with, and then we come up with the reasons for it afterward, but I didn't want to hear how she'd found new, retroactive virtues in him, or how I'd misunderstood their unique and intimate bonding. It depressed me, the way women could keep hanging on to the same bad idea.

Janey didn't write back, and I went on with my own life (graduation, job, new city), and along the way I met the man who well and truly broke my heart. He loved me until it was inconvenient for him to do so, and then, full of soft regrets, he took his leave. I tried to call Janey then, but I got What's-his-name's voice on the answering machine and hung up. Once again it was somebody else who told me that they were either separated or divorced, it wasn't clear, and What's-his-name had either stolen a lot of Janey's money or simply gone through it, and she'd left New York and gone back to the disapproving mother. A marriage that didn't count.

Time passed and passed and passed. You're supposed to say the years flew by without your noticing but that's not true; I felt their shape and weight at every step. I thought of Janey whenever I thought of my younger self, and marveled at how distant they both seemed.

When I turned thirty-five, I got a birthday card from Janey. She said she'd lived in different places out west, I'd heard that, and then she'd spent some time in Florida. She'd worked different jobs, "or not worked," in media, in PR, always trying to put something together, never getting very far, and now she was back in New York, "the scene of the crime":

> Do you feel old? I'm starting to. I got fat! Old and fat! I'm sorry I haven't been a better friend. One stupid, busy thing always led to another, and then there were times I didn't feel like I had anything that great to say about myself. But I still think that you and me and everybody else from back then are like the crew of the *Starship Enterprise*, you know, all part of a mission, and all part of one big story that keeps going on.

It was another year before we actually saw each other. I had some business in New York, a convention, and we arranged to meet in the bar of my hotel. She hadn't offered to let me stay with her, and I hadn't asked. Another friend who'd seen Janey issued a warning. "There's something going on with alcohol. And some messy behavior, the kind you read about in AIDS statistics. Trust me, you'll want to get a hotel room."

When I met Janey at the hotel bar, the first thing I said was "You're not fat."

"I'm round. Well-rounded. Been around the block a few times. You look good. Like a gun moll in the witness protection program."

We had some drinks. The cancer was still five years away. Janey wasn't fat, exactly, but she'd filled out, and there was the beginning of a roll under her chin. Her skin, that fair, fragile, red-head's skin, was loosening, as if a potter had pulled and stretched wet clay. She smoked, that was something new, and she drank enough for me to notice. She wasn't taking care of herself very well. The vivid hair still caught your eye, but she'd clipped it back without much style. She wore a black sweater and pants, good clothes but untidy and stretched at the cuffs and dangling loose threads. She hunched and shifted on the bar stool, a small person making herself smaller. From time to time she looked around the bar, squinting through smoke, as if she might know someone else there. Part of this was nerves, though I didn't realize it until later. She would still have been pretty except for her careless lack of vanity.

We talked about work for a while. She'd started a new job and she said, vaguely, that she hoped this one would "stick." We talked about our friends from the old days, who was doing what. Janey asked if I was in love or anything and I said no. That I'd gotten too critical, and if I found one thing I didn't like about a man, imperfect teeth, say, or if his car had a Ross Perot bumper sticker,

I crossed him off right away. I was talking lightly. I wasn't ready to make real confidences to this strange little person who had once been my friend.

I asked her the same question, love? and she shrugged and said that once in a while somebody came along, but something always went wrong with the transaction, didn't it? And that she had gotten really serious about a man who turned out to be bipolar. It hadn't come out until he was arrested for carrying a gun to work. Talk about dodging a bullet. I asked how she knew him and she said from the bar she hung out at. "Oh, don't raise your eyebrows that way. Drunks can be good company, if you stay away from the dual diagnosis guys."

Besides, she added, being a single girl wasn't so bad these days. Look at us, right?

It wasn't so bad, I said, not really meaning it. I didn't tell her that I was becoming too used to being on my own and having things my own way, and that this felt like a kind of death, narrow and ungenerous.

We ordered new drinks. I was getting a little drunk, trying to keep up with her, a morose drunk that might end as tears. Janey turned her head to blow her cigarette smoke away. "Filthy habit," she apologized, not really meaning it. "Oh love love blather blather. I'm sick of the whole damned subject, why is it always so important?"

"Biology. The baby thing."

"Who needs men for that, we can put their stuff in jars. I know plenty of women who went to the sperm bank, made a withdrawal, and they're perfectly happy with their lives."

"Good for them," I said, and then we were silent for a time. I didn't want to start talking baby talk, the whethers and the whys. It was one more morose thing. I was pretty sure that if I had to go to any extraordinary measures to have a child, say, opening a phone book, then it wasn't going to happen.

The bar was getting crowded and the talk around us helped to fill in the silence between us. I was leaving town tomorrow. Pretty soon one of us would say it was time to call it a night, and how great it had been to see you, and that would be the end of any sentimental effort at reconnecting. Janey said, "OK, I have to ask you something. Were we always really competitive with each other?"

"I guess so."

"Don't wimp out. Yes or no."

"Yes." I didn't like where this was headed.

"All *right*," Janey said, as if she found my answer encouraging. "Because you really really were. You signed up for ballet the same time I did and then I sprained my ankle and had to drop out and you said it was just as well, the combinations were pretty hard. Like practically telling me I couldn't do them."

I couldn't tell if she was joking or not. "I did?"

She glared at me, full of soggy anger. "And you know what, it was my idea to take ballet to begin with! You flat-out stole it!"

"I can't believe you even remember this shit." But as soon as she'd started talking, a wave of something close to relief came over me, as if I was guilty of this or of other forgotten transgressions, and guilt fit me like a pair of old shoes.

"You always acted like everything you did was so much more important than what I was doing. Like you were a big deal and I was some spacey lightweight."

"How did I do that? Tell me one specific thing I did."

She mentioned the magazine she'd first worked on, more than a dozen years ago. "When I told you about it, you said it sounded 'interesting.' Which is patronizing and dismissive and it's code for 'completely uninteresting.'"

"That's just stupid."

"Maybe you could quit calling me stupid, huh? See what I mean?"

I know better than to argue with a drunk; there's no way either of you will ever be right, you just stagger round and round in the same dumb circle. But I wasn't entirely sober myself, and she was really pissing me off. "How about the time you patted me on the back and went, 'Oh, I thought you were wearing shoulder pads, but those are your real shoulders.' How about all those snotty little putdowns, you think I don't remember them? Look, I'm sorry your life hasn't turned out the way you wanted it to, but it's not my fault. It never was."

She stared at me, so red in the face and her expression so unchanged that I didn't at first realize she was crying.

I said, "Oh crap. Janey."

"My life," she said, bawling now, the words coming out in bursts of sobs and snot, "isn't through turning out yet."

"Of course not. I'm sorry."

"Now you hate me. I'm a big sloppy mess and everybody hates me."

"I don't hate you," I said. And I didn't, I was pretty sure.

"Have you ever thought about the best way to kill yourself? I have. Lots and lots."

"Stop it," I said.

She flicked her cigarette lighter open and held it up like a torch. "I want to be burned alive," she announced. "An inch at a time."

"Give me that thing and sit back down."

"A ceremonial thing, a kind of performance art thing. A holy barbecue."

I slapped the lighter out of her hand and it skittered sideways across the floor. A man sitting at the other end of the bar retrieved it and brought it back to Janey. "Thank you," she told him. "You have a kind face."

I said, "If you're trying for pathetic spectacle, this is the way to go about it."

She started bawling again. People were looking at her. I was aware of the bartender standing in some calculated, professional proximity. "It's all right," I told him. "We just haven't seen each other in a really long time." He put the check down in front of us and walked away.

I got Janey out of there, and we went up to my room, and drank some more, and talked some more, and we were sorry about everything. There's something about people you knew when you were young that lets you fall back on that early common ground and retrace your steps to the present.

Janey passed out on the other bed. When I got up to get ready for my flight, she was still asleep. I was out of the shower, I was already dressed and packing when she sat up, wild-haired and blinking. "Apache mouth," she croaked, and I got her a glass of water. She got up to go to the bathroom. When she came out, she flopped onto the bed again, face down in the pillows. "What time's checkout?"

"Noon, I'm pretty sure."

"I'm going back to sleep."

"Don't you have to go to work?" I said, but she waved that away. "You drink too much."

"Yeah. You're probably right."

"Don't just agree with me. Do something about it."

"Glib. You were always glib."

"This isn't about me." I waited, but she didn't come back with anything. "Go to a doctor. Go to AA. Start somewhere."

"Oh what do you care what I do. You only drop in every ten years or so."

"I will come back next month and kick your drunk ass down the stairs."

Janey rolled over and refocused her eyes to peer at me. "I guess we're stuck with each other, huh?"

"Not if you don't get your stupid act together."

"God, you're a pain. Kiss kiss hug hug." Janey buried her face in the pillows again, and I wrestled my suitcases out the door.

After that, I'd call or Janey would call. She started going to AA. She said she didn't buy into all of it, the praying parts, mostly, but it was all right. She hadn't had a drink for a couple of months. She was losing weight and her brain felt less like an old sofa with sagging spots where the springs were giving way. I said that maybe she could find herself a nice recovering alcoholic boyfriend. Janey said call her a snob, but she wanted to steer clear of guys who lived in their vehicles or at the YMCA.

"Besides," Janey said, "we should quit talking about boys all the time, it's dumb. We're getting to an age where some fantasies are insupportable."

I told her I'd come see her again but she put me off, and I could tell she didn't really want me there. From long distance it was hard to tell what was really going on. I knew that untruthfulness was a part of alcoholism, and that it was perfectly possible for Janey to tell me one thing and do another. But the fact that I was hearing from her regularly seemed hopeful. She was holding down a job. She wasn't making any more resentful accusations about indignities she'd suffered at my hands long years ago. I was glad we'd found our way back to each other. There are some friendships that come to be more about longevity than anything else. Like Janey said, we were stuck with each other.

I was pushing forty, and then I was past it. I'd settled and slowed into my own routines. There was work, and work had allowed me a little of the world's goods, and there was the house I'd bought and the things the house required. There was the occasional love affair, though more and more often they took place only inside my head. Sometimes I was lonely, sometimes not. I realized I'd never been able to imagine any other life for myself.

I didn't see Janey until a couple of years later, at a wedding. Our friends who had been married were all starting to get divorced and to pair off again, the hopeful process of serial monogamy. Janey didn't drink, or if she did, I didn't see it, and I didn't press her on it. She looked both a little better and a little worse, that is, she was no longer untidy or bloated, but it was as if she'd had a pin stuck in her and was shrinking down to some wizened core. But then, we all looked older. We made droll jokes about it. We professed admiration for (but were secretly appalled by) the friend who'd let her hair go entirely gray and chopped it off short.

Janey and I went out for coffee. She said there were still times, plenty of times, when she felt like drinking, it didn't go away. Any more than the desperate and unlovable parts of ourselves had ever gone away. But she hoped now that she could feed them something besides alcohol. "I was pretty mad at you there for a while. I felt you were looking down on me for drinking, the way you always looked down on me. Oh don't worry. Blaming other people is just part of being a drunk. I blamed my mother. Every guy I ever fucked. Then once you take away the alcohol, you start to get it. None of those other people are wasting time sitting around bitching about you, well, my mother probably is, but the point still holds."

She said that she felt lucky to be getting sober right when it was turning into an industry. She meant, look at all the paper- back books, look at all the rehab places and talk shows, it was downright trendy to be in recovery. And AA meetings were rol- licking, really; they were the best free shows in town. I said that she had always been a trendsetter. She thought about that and said, Yeah, she guessed so, but she wished they were better trends.

She was the first one to get breast cancer. She called to tell me she'd already had the biopsy, she was scheduled for surgery, fol- lowed by chemo, radiation, the works. They were hopeful, the treatment team. That's what they called them now, a team. Rah rah. There had been all sorts of medical advances. They had really come a long way.

I said I was sorry, not knowing, in the shock of the news, where else to begin, and Janey said impatiently that it wasn't my fault. I asked her how she was doing, really, and she said, "How do you think? How do you think you'd feel?" The mass—tumor, whatever—was deep inside, you couldn't tell it was there, but she kept trying. It was compulsive, she said. She'd lie in bed and prod and poke and squeeze, as if it was something she could pinch out. There was the sense of the body's betrayal. It was dizzying, really, to think of all the thousand thousand things that could, and did, go wrong with the human physical plant. It was another compul- sion, the enumeration and cataloguing of them all. Diseases of the brain, the blood, the skin, the bones, the circulation, the mus- culature, the digestion, of the apparatus for breathing, and for locomotion, and for speech and the control of speech, and for sleep. Sleep! Did any of us appreciate sleep until we were deprived of it? The miraculous meshing of heart rate, brain waves, all the involuntary processes. We took everything for granted until it was too goddamned late.

I let her talk on. I figured that was my function for now, to be the ear, the receptacle. I asked if she wanted me to be there for the surgery and she said no, she had enough people to help her out. Maybe I could come later. She said it would really make her feel like a goner, if all the old crew started showing up.

I thought of that when she was actually dying, and all we could do was send chocolates and flowers. Did she wonder where we were? Did it make any difference, as the cancer burned her alive, inch by inch?

I went to New York four months later. She said not to come until she was done with the chemo, that she was as bald as a light-bulb and besides, she felt like shit. I took a cab from the airport to the Manhattan address she'd given me. The landscape of the city was familiar only because of my inability to make sense of it, its parkways and throughways and frantic traffic and unimaginable density.

Janey's building depressed me, even with what I knew by then of rents in New York and how people had to arrange their lives. I rode a creepy, rattletrap elevator up to Janey's floor. She'd buzzed me in, and waved at me from the other end of the hallway. "It's OK," she said as I stooped to hug her. "I know what I look like."

The apartment was small, either two rooms or one and a half, depending on how you counted. She had it fixed up nicely, with good pictures on the walls and a good rug underfoot. She made us a pot of tea, something herbal and medicinal, and we sat at the kitchen table, looking out on the ordinary city street. It was autumn but there was nothing of nature in the view, only a low sky spitting rain. The radiator sent out its mating call, clanking and gurgling.

Janey said, "I'm glad you're here. It makes sense, you always see me at my worst."

I said that wasn't true, I'd seen her at her best as well. We both smiled and maybe we were thinking of the same thing. Janey when she was fearless and outrageous and eager, and just how long ago that had been. "Besides, it's not your worst. It's just illness."

Janey shrugged. "You can get used to anything. I've learned that. It's only hair. It grows back . . ." Her small skull was covered with pinkish bristles. When she smiled, her gums were pale. She looked damaged but fierce, like a prisoner doing hard time. I was in awe of her.

She said she was tired these days. "Tired right down to my radiated bones. But the doctors are happy with me. My lab work is coming back clean. It looks like what's left of me is going to live a little while longer."

She said, "Getting sober is pretty good preparation for getting cancer. No, really. They're both about giving things up. I can do that now like a champ."

It wasn't the last time I ever saw her. You start to think that way once somebody's gone, you start counting backward. Janey had another three good years, and we managed to meet one place or another. A group of us chipped in to get her a home computer and Internet service and we all sent e-mails chattering back and forth. I try not to think of things in final milestones, because then I'd have to count that scattered, morphine-flattened phone call, and all the other sad lasts.

So let me end with that day instead. We drank our tea, and ate pieces of candied ginger from a tin Janey brought out. How many times had we sat together at one or another table. Each of us alone, except for the other. "I didn't look down on you," I said. "I never did. You were the brave one, always."

"Ah, but you were the one I wanted to impress," she said, smiling her pale smile. "All those times I went too far into one or another crazy thing."

And now, she said, she would go ahead of me into dying. No, I didn't have to bother acting all shocked, it was simple fact, statistical probability. And I was not to be afraid, because she would have gone there before me, shown me how it was done. The last voyage of the Starship Enterprise.

She lifted her shirt to show me the bite the cancer had taken out of her, the dark ridged scar, the angry absence. Wouldn't it be something, she said, if they could cut out only the parts you didn't want. Everything that was timid, doubtful, self-hating, sad. Did I know what they had her doing for rehab, to train the remaining shocked, stripped muscles? She was to take a ball, an ordinary rubber ball with some give to it, and practice squeezing it. There were specific repetitions, a few more each day. And then you advanced to involving the whole shoulder, drawing it back and the aching arm along with it, back and back, then extension and release. Wasn't it funny, she said, and she knew I'd get the joke, that after all this time she was finally learning how to throw like a girl?

THROW LIKE A GIRL

DISCUSSION POINTS

1. In *The Brat,* we read Iris's tale of teenage angst and violence. As she gazes down at her tormentor, she muses "if she shot him nobody would ever have to look at him again. That would definitely be something real. Or she could take the gun home and shoot her mother or Kyle." (p. 20) Do you think her actions are primarily motivated by her desire for something exciting to happen? Considering recent school shootings and violence, did this story hold more relevance? Did it resonate more or less? What about the ending—was it what you expected?

2. *The Five Senses* is probably the most sinister and eerie of the stories in this collection. In it, we follow Jessie as she goes on the run with R.B., her boyfriend. In a flashback, Jessie tells a counselor her parents' real problem with her relationship: "They're afraid people will see the two of us together, me and him, and I won't look like anyone they'd want to be their daughter. I'll look like I belong to him." (p. 36) What does Jessie mean by this? What do you think happened to her parents? Do you think R.B. is a sociopath? Discuss the significance of the title.

3. Why do you think the majority of the violence in *The Five Senses* is alluded to and not shown? Do you think it's more effective this way? Discuss the flashbacks. How do they help to further the story?

4. Kelly Ann, the listless Army wife and mother in *It Would Not Make Me Tremble to See Ten Thousand Fall,* decides to enlist herself, much to her family's chagrin. Why do you think she does this? What is the significance of the title? Do you think her marriage will survive her radical decision?

5. *The Family Barcus* is about a suburban family during the 1950s and 1960s and how they are affected when their father leaves his job to start his own risky venture. The narrator, Cindy, reflects back on this difficult time in her family's life and remembers that once, years later, she went to one of those rotating restaurants. How is this a metaphor for her family's ultimate collapse? Were you surprised that the father left for good after telling his daughter that "family is everything. It's our sword and shield against the world"?

6. There is an undercurrent of sadness, almost melancholy, running through most of these stories. Did you find this realistic or disheartening? Why is it that the characters are nameless in *Lost*?

7. In *The Inside Passage,* Mike tells our narrator, "Everybody gets married. Everybody's gotta bite the bullet." (p. 131) In *The Woman Taken in Adultery,* the wife remarks "you start out being married together and you end up being married apart." (p. 219) What do you think of these views of marriage?

8. Many of these stories deal with restless characters trying to change their lives. Chad, the husband trying to make a success of his start-up radio station in *A Normal Life* muses on his radio show "I wonder if any of us can ever really make decisions without second-guessing and regrets." (p. 171) What do you think of this notion? Why was Melanie upset with him after this comment? After Melanie returns from Thailand, she hears Chad on his show saying "the Dalai Lama says that the purpose of life is happiness." (p. 192) Do you agree?

9. Thompson's stories have much subtext within them. What do you think the fire symbolizes at the end of *Hunger*? What does the title refer to? How are all the characters "hungry" in some way? Discuss the painting in *The Woman Taken in Adultery,* from which the story gets its name. How does Thompson use humor in the scene where the narrator is confronted by her paramour and her husband at the museum?

10. *Pie of the Month* starts out as this sweet story of two older women running a pie-making business and ends up with a more subversive agenda, addressing war, violence, immigration, and the economy. Do you think the shift in tone is effective in this story? How has the current political climate affected the town where you live?

11. The title story, *Throw Like a Girl,* describes a friendship over the course of twenty-plus years. Did knowing early on in the story that Janey would die intensify the drama? Her character and the narrator discuss the somewhat competitive nature between them. Do you think that competition is natural in women's friendships? Does this exist in male friendships? Why do you think that the collection is named for this story? Why does it come last?

12. Which story left the strongest impression on you? Which one left the least? Do you find the struggles of the characters relatable? Are you interested in reading more of Jean Thompson?

Q&A WITH JEAN THOMPSON

You've written both short stories and novels. Do you have a favorite format? When do you make the decision about whether an idea will become a story or a novel? Do you utilize outlines in your writing process? You go back and forth seamlessly from first-person narrative to third-person. How do you decide what voice to write in?

I suppose that short stories are my first love, and therefore my sentimental preference. I'm not sure that a particular idea needs sorting into story or novel. The idea is in a sense wedded to form, and the decision process has more to do with whether or not I feel ready, psychologically and practically, for the longer, sustained effort of the novel. First person is more intimate, more confidential, therefore I probably use it for characters with whom I feel a greater comfort level, and whose skin fits me better.

You have worked on the faculty of the University of Illinois, Urbana campus in their English Department since 1973. How do you reconcile teaching fledging writers and finding time to write yourself?

I no longer teach full-time, so that era is behind me. At its best, the teaching of writing and the process of writing are symbiotic, and issues in one's own work get examined and articulated in teaching. I'm not sure that teaching is any harder, in terms of finding writing time, than any other vocation. In fact one's time is often more flexible. The downside is when you have to read a spell of truly careless or outrageously bad writing, and begin to despair of the whole enterprise.

Your story, "Applause, Applause," was featured in **Children Playing Before a Statue of Hercules,** *a short story compilation edited by David Sedaris. How did you come to be included in this collection? Who are your favorite short-story writers?*

David Sedaris came across "Applause, Applause" in an anthology edited by Tobias Wolff, *Matters of Life and Death*. The story obviously struck a chord with him, and he has very often and very generously singled it out. I'm delighted to be included in *Children Playing Before a Statue of Hercules*, alongside many of my favorite short story writers such as Flannery O'Connor, Lorrie Moore, Alice Munro, Charles Baxter, Joyce Carol Oates, and, to come full circle, Tobias Wolff.

You write about characters who sometimes make poor decisions and do horrible things yet it never seems like you are judging them. How do you keep your own feelings out of the picture?

Well, my own feelings are the picture. But like God, one strives to be present everywhere yet always unseen. Withholding judgment is mostly a matter of authorial control, of allowing the reader to arrive at their own judgments.

The Family Barcus *describes a typical suburban family of their time. Do you agree with Tolstoy that "happy families are all alike; every unhappy family is unhappy in its own way"?*

For the most part I do agree, although so many unhappy families seem to have depressingly similar syndromes, such as alcoholism and addiction.

Why did you make **Throw Like a Girl** *the title story of this collection? It reads like such a personal, heartfelt story. Was this based on something you experienced?*

In fact I had recently lost a friend to cancer, although my friend was male, not female. I suppose I combined that experience with my notion of women's friendships, and how charged and difficult they can be. I wanted the title story to be a strong one, to anchor the collection, and I hope that this one is and does.

During the writing process, how helpful is it to read your work out loud? Is it helpful or harmful to read other writers while you are working on a new novel or story? Can you walk us through a typical day when you're at work on something?

The only time I read work out loud is when I'm practicing for an actual public event, a fiction reading, and want to see how something will come across. I think that reading can be helpful while you're writing, as long as you resist the temptation to become too stylistically enamored of your reading material, and therefore imitative. Typical working day: walk dogs, drink coffee, try not to get too involved with newspaper. Sit down and read previous day's new work, edit, brood, read the entirety of chapter/story, see if I feel like the new pages are heading in the right direction, retype, refine, then, once the new work has been incorporated into the whole and I'm pretty sure all that has gone before is good enough to serve as a foundation, launch into that day's new composition. Rinse, repeat.

With a story like Pie of the Month, it starts out seemingly so simple, but there are complex issues afoot, especially with the divorced Mrs. Pulliam, who begins to share her son's feelings about war. Did you set out to write something with an anti-war sentiment or did this just naturally evolve during the writing?

Believe it or not, I mostly wanted to write about pie. But pie in and of itself does not a story make. "Pie of the Month" was written just before the invasion of Iraq, and so that story line was grafted on. The war is played out as a kind of parable of small-town life, and the tone is, for the most part, simple, even naïve. That masks, or translates, the outrage and helplessness I was feeling at the time. The story itself becomes an anti-war pie.

What would you like readers to take away from your stories?

I would hope that readers come away with an appreciation of the transforming power of literature, how it can remove us from the everyday world and let us see with new eyes. I would hope that they would go on to seek out other writing, my own and that of others. There are so many wonderful authors out there who should be read and celebrated.

ENHANCE YOUR BOOK CLUB EXPERIENCE

Keep track of author Jean Thompson through her publisher's website and you can find out if she's appearing in your area: *http://www.simon says.com/content/destination.cfm?tab=3&pid=358973*

If you enjoyed reading this short story collection, your group might want to check out others at this site, which recommends classic short stories for you to enjoy: *http://www.bnl.com/shorts/*

For the more information on school violence, go to *www.uhgfiles.org* and *www.crf-usa.org*.